Moonlight
over
Denmark

Moonlight
over
Denmark

J. H. SCHRYER

Cover illustration: German Submarine in the Atlantic, 1942/3
© akg-images / Alamy

First published 2010

The History Press
The Mill, Brimscombe Port
Stroud, Gloucestershire, GL5 2QG
www.thehistorypress.co.uk

© J.H. Schryer, 2010

The right of J.H. Schryer to be identified as the Author
of this work has been asserted in accordance with the
Copyrights, Designs and Patents Act 1988.

British Library Cataloguing in Publication Data.
A catalogue record for this book is available from the British Library.

ISBN 978 0 7524 4919 7

Typesetting and origination by The History Press
Printed in Great Britain

With thanks to Jenny Hamilton and Martin Fry
for providing time and space for this book to be written

Grateful thanks to the following who have provided specialist knowledge during the writing of this book: to Kevin Slade of the U-boat Society for his exceptional support in giving detailed material on U-boats during WWII; to Mary Curry whose brilliant mind ensures that nothing is left unturned; to Jock and Herbie for their expertise on SOE and military operational information in WWII, and Olaf Krarup for material on Denmark from his firsthand experience in the war.

Prologue

August 1943

'Green light on. Go! Go!'

Hanns felt the short, sharp shove in his back. No deck below, air tearing at his body, his eyes streamed and throat tightened as he fell through the dark, wet clouds. He tried not to hold his breath. Adrenalin pumped, the wind pulled at his mouth as the Halifax veered away to the right. One tug and his 'chute opened, the sudden jolt shot through his torso jarring him upright. He floated down, rocking to and fro like a baby in a cradle. He relaxed as he saw the moon-light shining meekly through the fragmented clouds.

Denmark lay bare beneath him, the lights of Copenhagen in the far distance to the east. No enforced blackout here. It was probably the only country in Europe still lit at night. The war was entering its fifth year with no end yet in sight. It was rumoured that food was plentiful in Denmark. Why else, in 1940, would the Nazis have taken over a country that comprised so many tiny islands?

Hanns orientated himself. At the last minute he hadn't much confidence in the Polish pilot who had circled twice whilst looking for the drop zone. The fifteenth-century Gjorslev Herregarden had been chosen because of its cross-shaped ground plan, which should have been easily identifiable from the air. The anti-aircraft fire remained silent, only the wind now disturbed his dark thoughts. He hoped his radio operator had jumped after him. As if second-guessing his concern, Adam's voice crossed the wind, 'Relax you bastard! Enjoy the ride! You'll get to kill soon enough.' Hanns trusted him. There was no alternative.

Below he saw silhouetted the turrets of Vallø Castle and realised they were about 12km south-west of their drop-zone. They had been dropped from the wrong height and the strong wind had blown them way off course. The forest below gave no real opening. With a bit of luck he would fall between the trees. He swung his body slightly to steer his way through the canopy; his fate now in the hands of the gods. Branches snagged his clothing as he came down. The last ten metres were always a shock. Twenty-two jumps in training didn't make it any easier. The air spilled out of his 'chute as the ground rose up abruptly before him. He landed with a thud midway between two trees; a section of his parachute torn as it caught a branch during descent. Slightly winded, he sat up and crossed himself in thanks to the Almighty. Fortunately, he had only suffered superficial scratches. He struggled out of his kit and glanced around. The hushed dead of night obscured his colleague's progress. There was no sight or sound of Adam. But he *had* been close behind him. Hanns walked a couple of paces, then glanced up. There hung Adam's lifeless body darkly silhouetted between the branches, the cord of his 'chute his noose. A life cut short at nineteen. Hanns suppressed a momentary pang of jealousy. How he craved eternal rest. He had seen too much in Dachau to want to live; horrific things which continued to haunt him even in freedom. But live he would. He had a strong sense of destiny. And a thirst for revenge.

'No more worries for you mate,' he whispered. 'Your war is over.' There was no time to grieve. That would come later. They both understood the risks. Hanns scanned the woods for signs of life, his eyes now fully adjusted to the darkness. Their training had taught them one crucial lesson: to make the night one's friend. He pulled out his pocket torch and a small map of Denmark imprinted on a silk handkerchief. He crouched in the undergrowth to obscure the light and began to take stock. Studying the map, he pinpointed the direction of his target. Damn! It would take hours to get to the designated drop zone. Sudden footsteps close by alerted him to impending danger. Gathering his kit, he removed his boots silently to evade his stalker.

'Over here!' The deep male voice speaking Danish to his companion was too near for comfort. A stocky man in rough clothing came into view, a single rifle slung over his left shoulder. It must be a gamekeeper, thought Hanns, holding his breath, eyeing the man's every movement.

'There were two dropped in the vicinity. Definitely,' Josephy the gamekeeper continued to his companion. 'We were told there were two of them off course.'

Anders came alongside him. Josephy turned his head and continued, 'Mind you, it's lucky we had the special phone, otherwise we'd have been in completely the wrong place.' He pointed to the tread marks at his feet. 'Only one set of footprints. That's a bit worrying.' He bent down with the torch, scratching the earth with his fingernails for clues.

'We must find them,' replied Anders, stepping forward, now fully visible to Hanns. His tall, thin stature gave him a commanding presence, his accent more educated than the gamekeeper's. 'They are going to be in danger. We don't have much time.'

Instinctively, Josephy looked up and pointed to the tree. 'There's one of them. Quick! Cut him down! But I think it's too late for him. He looks like a goner.' He moved forward and leant against the tree to enable Anders to climb onto his shoulders. Once steady, Anders heaved himself onto the thick bough and leant across to cut the cord entangled around the parachutist. 'Just as I thought. There's no pulse. And he's stiff.'

'Hurry! Cut him down, Anders! We must get rid of the body.'

Crouched amongst the bushes, Hanns lined up his sights, cocked the gun and curled his finger on the trigger. Anders realised the imminent danger as if he had a sixth sense and called out the code. 'It's a good day today, better than yesterday.'

Hanns' finger twitched and tightened a fraction around the trigger. He watched the two men for but a second, then stood up to respond: 'It's not so good as yesterday but should be better tomorrow.' Two heads swung around, their eyes locked on him. Hanns could see the tension on their faces. It was Anders who spoke first, 'Come quick! We need to move you somewhere safer my friend!' Hanns felt uncomfortable. He had no friends, only targets that craved death.

'We're sorry about your mate,' Anders added.

'What about him?' Hanns gestured with a flick of the head in the direction of his dead companion.

'I'll move him,' replied Josephy. 'Don't worry. He'll be buried before dawn.'

'Come!' interrupted Anders. 'We must go Hanns.'

Falling in behind Anders, Hanns followed him through the woods. He remained silent as the boots of his escort crunched on the broken, twisted twigs underfoot. They marched for about half an hour, finally coming to a small white-washed farmhouse with several outbuildings. Dawn was just beginning to break. Anders led him towards the end barn. 'In here! Lie low. Josephy or I will bring you food and supplies. Here's some to keep you going. We'll have to move you every couple of days. It's too dangerous to attempt Gjorslev Herregarden. Word's got out. Nazis are scouting the area already.'

Hanns shone his torch around the lofty barn, instinctively searching out a defensible position. The smell of dry hay filled his nostrils, reminding him of childhood holidays spent on his uncle's farm in Shropshire.

'I have to get back to Vallø,' said Anders. 'I'll see you in a couple of days, Hanns. Bye.' Anders shook his hand and promptly left.

Hanns walked over to an old wooden ladder propped in the corner and climbed up to the loft space. Bales of hay stacked to the rafters signalled an ideal hiding place. He knelt down, brushing aside the loose straw. A tiny gap between the bare wooden planks afforded a snapshot view of the barn below. He suddenly felt weary, more from emotional fatigue than physical strain. He settled down, leaning back between two bales. Sleep came easily but it was light and broken.

Chapter 1

Copenhagen, 29 August 1943

Lilian Sørensen hurried out of the Danish Foreign Office just as the clock in the nearby square struck 1 p.m. She walked briskly through the side streets, then turned into Radhauspladsen. It was unusually crowded with SS officers and stormtroopers. Patrols in the city had unexpectedly increased over the last two hours, their vehicles passing regularly outside her office window.

In reality, daily life hadn't changed much under the Nazis. Denmark was permitted self-government, but under the constant watch of the occupying power. Lilian had heard rumours of terrible atrocities elsewhere in Europe but no such things had happened in Denmark. In the distance she could hear the faint sound of military band music, the regular beat of drums. Something wasn't right. The Danish people were becoming increasingly resentful of Nazi-occupation like a dam waiting to burst. Glancing back, it was then that she noticed for the first time the swastika flag flying from the mast on the roof of the Radhaus. She could have sworn it wasn't there earlier that morning. She crossed the square into Frederiksberg.

'Lilian!' she recognised the voice behind and turned.

'Tom.' The tall stocky lad, a year older than her at nineteen, was coming towards her. His square-set jaw, unruly blonde hair and blue eyes made him somewhat attractive in a manly kind of way. His rugged features and tanned skin attested to a life lived outdoors. She already gathered that he worked on his father's farm just outside Copenhagen, but twice a week he came into the capital to study.

'I thought we were having lunch yesterday.' He frowned. 'Where were you, Lily?'

She knew he was sweet on her but had given no indication of returning any affection. He looked at her intently. Her soft, auburn, Shirley Temple curls fell in twists to her shoulders; her hazel eyes had a depth that swallowed his heart. He fantasised about sweeping her up in his arms like his hero Clark Gable in *Gone with the Wind*. He wanted to kiss her pouted lips. He didn't. Too shy to make the first intimate move without being sure whether or not she would reject him. And here, he thought, glancing around, they would have a very public audience.

'I'm really sorry about yesterday, Tom. I had some urgent work at the office. I am sorry, really I am, for letting you down.'

'How about today then? Come out with me today … please.'

'I planned to take my sandwiches back to the office. I'd love to have lunch with you Tom, but …' She lowered her eyes; her long lashes curled at the end giving her face softness. She couldn't disappoint him again. She relented: 'Alright then, but only for half an hour. I can't take the full hour.' She slipped her arm through his and they walked in the direction of Frederiksholms Canal. They came to a tiny café overlooking the canal. Tom held the door open for her and motioned to the corner table in an alcove. Inside was deserted except for a woman and her child sitting at the window table.

'Let me get it today Lily.'

'Thank you, Tom. That's very sweet of you but not necessary.'

'I insist. What will you have?'

'An open cheese sandwich please.'

Tom ordered their food then continued: 'I'm glad we've got this time together.' She watched him quizzically, unsure of his change of mood. He seemed deeply serious as he placed his hand on her arm. He moved his head closer to hers, breathing in her faint lilac fragrance. How intoxicating and sensual he found her. He tried to concentrate. 'Things are getting dangerous in Denmark. It's not safe for you. You should leave.' All the time his eyes scanned the café to ensure no one else had come in or could overhear them.

'Leave? Good heavens, Tom, whatever do you mean?' She flicked her curls from her face in a gesture of nervousness.

'You must have heard the news this morning? The Nazis have declared a state of emergency. The government has resigned and the country is under complete Nazi control.'

'Yeah, I heard it. We were briefed in the office. From eight tonight a curfew will be enforced on the streets.'

'There'll be more than that in due course. There's bad news, Lily. Rumour has it the Nazis are going to round up the Jews.'

'No, Tom. Surely not? They've been left alone all these years.'

At that moment he didn't feel confident to tell her that he knew she was Jewish. It might drive a wedge between them and shatter her openness towards him. Even worse, he might lose her. But he would give his life for her. The Nazis wouldn't lay a finger on her, not whilst he had breath in him. Neither could he tell her that his call-up papers for the Danish military police had arrived that morning.

Numbers were being doubled on the orders of General Werner Best, Hitler's main confidant in Denmark. Lilian sat silently opposite him. She had barely touched her sandwich. They chatted some more, then Lilian glanced at her watch.

'I must be going, Tom.'

'Yes, sure. Let me escort you back.'

'Thank you, Tom. That's very sweet of you.' She stood up.

'And please don't worry,' he muttered, not wanting to spoil their time together. 'I may be totally wrong about the Nazis.'

They walked back into Radhauspladsen. Neither needed reminding of the serious turn of events. Two platoons of stormtroopers goose-stepped across the main square. Behind them a motorbike patrol with sidecar followed. Its engine revved periodically; Nazi flag with black swastika in a white circle on crimson red draped across the spare wheel at the back. Propaganda posters with images of Hitler and the swastika now appeared on billboards and in café windows. Tom and Lilian walked on in silence. On the steps outside the Foreign Office, Tom momentarily caught her hand. 'Take care Lily.'

'I will see you again soon, won't I Tom? You worry me with your seriousness.'

'Yes. Yes, of course. I'll be in touch. I promise.' He waited for her to disappear inside, watching her through the glass doors as she dashed down the corridor towards her office. Deflated at having to part from her, he turned and walked back to college for his afternoon lectures.

Later that same evening Hanns woke to the sound of movement below. This was his fifth location in as many days. Now he was back in the same barn where he had been hidden on his first night. In the three weeks since he had been dropped into Denmark he had remained in hiding. Frustration took its toll, only just staved off by promises from Anders that his time was coming soon. Straining to peer through the thin slit between the floorboards of the loft space, Hanns' eyes adjusted in seconds to make out the silhouette of a single German officer in a heavy overcoat. From the courtyard outside came short, quick footsteps and scuffles. The clip of boots echoed. They were back on his trail. In the semi-darkness inside the barn, Hanns moved silently behind the tallest stack of bales, stood upright, flattening his body tight against the wall. His heart thumped in his chest. Bloody hell, Anders shouldn't have brought him back to the same place. It was obvious they would look here. The farmhouse and barn were only a few miles from Gjorslev Herregarden.

'*Alle reinkommen!*' the brisk order came in a clipped Prussian accent. 'Find them!'

It was close, damn close. The next few minutes felt like hours as Hanns waited, hand on pistol in his right pocket. He had two shots. If it came to it, it wouldn't be enough. There were at least half a dozen stormtroopers below. He was desperate to kill. Repay their violence. There was no middle ground, no compromise. They were all Nazis – tarred with the same brutal brush. From the few exchanges he had had with Anders, he gathered the Danes were growing resentful of Nazi occupation, their autonomy eroded bit by bit. There was a tension under the surface of this polite co-operative nation.

Suddenly a single beam of light shone across, up and down the far wall of the barn, scanning over his position.

He had taken the precaution of removing the ladder from the loft space. Frozen still against the cold stone wall, he concealed his breath. Bastards. They wouldn't get him. The sound of a vehicle drawing up outside was accompanied by shouts. The beam of the torch hesitated, slowly searching back over his space.

'Up there, sir.' The voice of a young SA officer echoed around the barn.

'Here, take that Müller!' The Commander pointed to a discarded ladder at the far side of the barn. Hanns cursed himself that he'd failed to spot the second ladder. 'If they're up there, they can't go far.'

'It's a bit rickety, sir. Doesn't look as if it could hold anyone's weight.'

'Is that a contravention of orders, Müller? You've grown fat and lazy. Perhaps a stint on the Russian front?' The young officer clicked his heels in obedience, fetched the ladder and propped it against the floor of the loft. Halfway up it creaked under his weight, causing him to stop momentarily.

'Carry on! Get on with it! We don't have time to mess about!' The commanding officer stood right below. Climbing to the penultimate rung of the ladder, Müller scanned everything in his line of vision, then prodded a couple of bales with his bayonet. 'Nothing, sir. No one can hide up here. It's thick bales to the wall, sir.' Hanns was grateful to the incompetent fool.

'Let's go. We've wasted enough time here,' the Commander snapped. 'Next stop!'

The men below saluted and in unison chorused '*Heil Hitler*', then retreated. The soldiers and single vehicle moved out of the farmyard, leaving Hanns in total silence. He could breathe again, but for how long?

In London's Grand Central Hotel in Marylebone Road, nineteen-year-old Günter Herz eyed the sergeant major bristling in his crisp uniform, hair Brylcreemed to a sharp centred parting. With moustache protruding like two propeller blades, he sat stock still behind his desk, his huge chest heaving with each intake of breath. The sergeant major began shuffling the papers in front of him. This drab office in a back bedroom wasn't quite what Günter was expecting for his interview. Standing in front of him, Günter couldn't help thinking the sergeant major had probably seen more action in one week than Günter had in his entire life. He certainly looked old enough to have served in the Great War.

What the hell did he know about the frustrations of life in an army labour unit? Günter was in 87 Company of the British army's Royal Pioneer Corps digging day-in, day-out, endless trenches 4ft by 4ft then filling them with concrete. He was sick of the smell of the stuff. It was now August 1943 and he hadn't seen a single gun in three years, let alone trained in how to use one. The pick and shovel on his cap badge was not something Günter was proud of. He had wanted to join the RAF and had sent off application after application, but to no avail. It was the same story each time – German and Austrian refugees, all enemy aliens, could not be accepted as pilots in the very traditional Royal Air Force. There was only one exception that he knew about – his best friend Rudi Steinberg was caught flirting with the commanding officer's daughter on Ilfracombe seafront when he should have been doing drill with the others. His transfer application was accepted immediately and now he was serving as the only German fighter pilot in the RAF. There were times when Günter missed him, still stuck in the Pioneer Corps.

There was some consolation in the fact that his company was made up of Germany and Austria's finest brains. It made life outside army training more interesting. A mini-university had been formed by the Continentals on their own initiative. His contemporaries were all intellectuals: scientists, doctors, engineers, philosophers, dentists, lawyers and artists. Over a third of the Vienna Philharmonic Orchestra was serving in various Pioneer companies of the British army, including his. All great minds with talent. What a waste. They worked like Trojans, determined to thank the country that had given them refuge from Nazi tyranny. But what Günter really wanted to do was fight back. This was *his* war.

'Stand smart, boy,' the sergeant major's voice cut through his thoughts. 'So you want to leave the Pioneer Corps?' Günter noticed how his heavy hands were now folded on the file in front of him, his pen redundant at the side.

'Yes, sir.'

'Do you know why you are here today?'

'Yes, sir. The gentleman that arrived at our barracks spoke to some of us. He hinted at the possibility of doing something special in the forces.'

'And are you prepared to serve in civilian clothes, somewhere in enemy territory?'

'Would I receive protection if I did?'

The sergeant major raised a monocle to his right eye and peered at him, 'I'm the one asking the questions Private Herz, but – no, you wouldn't.'

'In that case sir, the answer is no.'

'Are you proud of the King's uniform?'

'Yes sir, but …' Günter felt it was all going wrong. He was desperate to get out of the Pioneer Corps. Mixing concrete for two years was not his idea of a real war.

'It's always "yes sir but" with you Continentals.' He paused, eyed him much as an owl might watch its prey. 'I thought you wanted to do something proper for this war, Private Herz.'

'Yes sir, I do, but I will only serve in uniform.'

'Why would you want to do that? And what if it means unorthodox training?'

Günter tried to salvage the situation, 'Revenge, sir. I want to kill the bastards that took away my birthright and home. My family's left behind in Vienna. There is nothing more damaging to one's mind, sir, than losing your country.'

The sergeant major's expressionless face made it difficult to tell if that was the answer he was looking for. 'So you're a bit of a philosopher. There's no room for that in the army, Private Herz, not if you want to be a good soldier. You have your freedom. That should be enough.' He muttered something which Günter didn't hear, then waved his hand in dismissal. 'Thank you Private Herz. That's all.' Günter didn't move.

'But sir …' Günter felt he had nothing to lose by adding to his case.

'No, Private Herz. There is nothing more to say. Back to your unit. Dismissed.'

In the corridor outside Günter felt devastated. He had blown the one opportunity to do something different in the war. He shrugged his shoulders and walked down the labyrinth of corridors to the reception area to retrieve his haversack.

≈❧

Arriving back at Pembroke Dock in South Wales, Günter flashed his pass at the guard standing at the iron gate to the

Defensible Barracks. The guard smirked, 'Friend or foe?' His glistening steel bayonet fixed to his rifle pointed at Günter's stomach. Günter glared down the black barrel. Like all his mates, he was used to the question. The guard asked all of them the same question every time they returned to the barracks. It was his idea of a joke but now it was wearing thin.

'Enemy alien,' he replied. At the outbreak of war, all refugees like him had been classified as 'enemy aliens' by the British government. In reality it hadn't meant much – except a few restrictions on travel, but the most drastic measure was their internment on the Isle of Man or Australia for several months in 1940. But that was the past.

Ahead of him, the massive grey Victorian fortification, which had been Günter's base for nearly three months, assured the Welsh coastline a century of protection against invasion. Ironically, Günter and the other Continentals were now patrolling its walls – German refugees in British army uniform on sentry duty protecting Britain, on the look out for Nazi invaders in the bay below.

His friend Ignaz was already rushing towards him, panting. 'Bad news, chap. There's been an accident in the demo room.' Like him, Ignaz was originally from Vienna. His father, a professor of law, had lost his job when the Nazis annexed the country.

'Accident? What sort of accident? What do you mean?'

'Where've you been? You missed it all. But it's lucky for you, it could have been your body blown into the moat.'

'Ignaz, you're not making sense. Slow down.'

'That Major Garratt from the Royal Engineers,' his voice became excited again, garbling the next words as if he couldn't get them out quick enough. 'He was doing explosives training today; only he used live ammo. It went off; one of the grenades went off. Seventeen of them are dead, including two of our lot. We've been scraping bits of blood and guts off the walls all day. It's terrible – there were parts all over the place, we didn't know what belonged to who. It's typical – the first time we get anywhere near weapons and this happens.'

Günter suddenly looked pale. The shock was beginning to sink in. 'Do we know who?'

'Yeah, poor old Abraham Schwartze and Fritz Rosenthal. We've all been summoned to HQ block at 5 o'clock this evening after roll-call. I suppose we'll be given the official version of events from that one-armed major. You know – the one who insists on saluting as he drives past us and zigzags across the road.'

Günter didn't appear to be listening, focusing his gaze across the estuary. 'I can't wait to get out of this dump. I didn't join up for this. I volunteered to fight.'

'Didn't we all, but what choice do we have?' Ignaz was an optimist when he wasn't playing devil's advocate. He always seemed to be around just when Günter needed a boost in morale. 'It's all very well for you to have grand ideas of combat, Günter, but we aren't given a ruddy chance. Come on, let's go back to barracks and get a good old cup of English tea and a Woodbine. It'll make you an Englisher yet.'

'I won't ever be an Englisher. British maybe, but never an Englishman.'

As they crossed the parade ground, Ignaz continued talking whilst Günter walked in silence. 'I'm hoping after this accident they'll give us time off to go into the town. We all need it after the stress of today. Besides, I haven't seen a girl in months. Missing *die Titte!*'

Günter couldn't resist a tease, 'I bet the only woman you've ever kissed is your mother.' He clapped him on the back. 'Do you really think the locals will let a bloody

Austrian or German anywhere near their daughters? They fought our fathers in the last war and don't want to see another German that close unless they can shoot the whites of their eyes.'

Back at their barracks with the other mates, the mood changed. No one felt like talking, all subdued, lost in silence to the memory of their two comrades. They were forced to examine their own mortality, thrown up so unexpectedly by the accident that day.

Hanns was biding his time, becoming increasingly restless for action. It was now the last day of August and he was back in the grounds of the Vallø Castle estate, where he had been first dropped. The beautiful red brick Renaissance castle was apparently one of the finest in Denmark, or so he had been told. Hanns kept his distance from the residents. His first early morning task was to sweep the grates of the fireplaces in all communal rooms downstairs in the castle itself, then make the fires. The rest of the day was spent on forestry work and general estate duties. Anders, as estate manager, had secured Hanns' false papers to work as a gardener and general factotum. Hanns had learnt that Anders himself came from a long line of prominent Danish judges and legal advisers.

It was 11.30 already. At the lodge, Hanns was making a morning cup of coffee before starting his other estate duties. He had already cleaned the fireplaces in the main castle for that day. Anders peered through the latticed window, then disappeared momentarily from view. He knocked before pushing open the thick oak door of the lodge. 'Morning Hanns,' he said, as he strode over to the log-burning stove, his boots echoed across the stone floor of the kitchen. Bending over to warm his hands, he continued, 'It's today, Hanns. We're on the move. We've finally established contact with your counterpart. Josephy is waiting for you at the east boundary of the estate.'

Hanns grunted, 'So the kit has arrived?'

'Yes, it was parachuted in two days ago. We left a gap between the drop and your move so no obvious link could be made. We're hoping to go through Dragør, crossing the bay by sea, but the place is swarming with SS. The U-boat is now in for repairs at Frederikshavn for a few days. It's been decided you should board it there.'

Hanns walked into the larder, dragged a large box out of the way and rummaged behind discarded bags and more boxes to find the secret hatch. He opened it and pulled out his haversack. The contents were already prepared: dried food supplies and chocolate, a transceiver, explosives and ammunition. From a side pocket he took out a .30mm American carbine, a wonderfully light and accurate rifle, the best of its kind; then the .22mm Belgian automatic Browning which looked like a toy. Tiny, its real use lay in being easily hidden in one's clothing. He placed both in a pocket secreted in the lining of his jacket and followed Anders out. The two exchanged few words.

The trek from Vallø was uneventful. Hanns' mission was simple: to cause mayhem, over time, wherever possible, and recruit, train and direct as many resistance fighters as he could muster. The Danish had had a relatively easier time under the Nazis than most occupied countries. British Prime Minister Winston Churchill had nicknamed Denmark 'Hitler's pet canary', for singing a sweet tune to Nazi compliance, failing to fight the regime. But the canary was biding her time. Her tune would change. The British and Americans wanted the gateway to the Baltic to be under their control. For now that meant working with compliant Danes in an underground resistance. Liberation would come – it was not a question of *if* but *when*. Hanns didn't care much for the Danes per se; his loyalty lay with Britain.

At the east boundary, Anders and Hanns were met by Josephy. Hanns followed the two through the countryside. He observed how dead flat it was compared to England's rolling hills. They walked for several hours. Hanns found himself irritated by his companions' irrelevant questions and lack of operational experience. 'Why don't you wear shoes, Hanns? Why do you cover your rifle, Hanns? Why do you walk sideways sometimes like a crab, Hanns?' What did they know of his torments? Frustrated at not being able to vent his anger on the enemy, he oiled his hatred constantly, biding his time. Two years of incarceration in Dachau had disturbed his sleep pattern. Even now that he was free he was constantly fearful of assault or surprise attack. Death of his camp inmates had come swiftly with no warning. Sleep was no succour of safety. His Nazi-instilled instincts forced him to move on, but the Nazis had made him what he was – and they would pay.

Anders broke his thoughts, 'I'm going to have to leave you here. Josephy will continue with you. Good luck. We'll rendezvous once you've made radio contact with Sweden after it's all done.' Anders pulled his gascape closer around his shoulders and left.

Shifting between the hedgerows, Hanns and Josephy moved on, their bodies so close they almost touched. They trekked through the night, stopping periodically for twenty minutes' rest. At the slightest sound Hanns bent to the ground, grabbing Josephy with him. At first light they reached the outskirts of Søvang. The villagers slumbered on; the only sound the muffled bark of a dog in a distant field. A little further ahead two SS guards manned a road block, complacently leaning against their truck with rifles slung over their backs. They wouldn't be expecting any callers at this hour. Then Hanns noticed a third man taking a nap inside their truck. He signalled for Josephy to drop to the ground. *This was his catch.*

In his head he spoke to them: 'Come, my little darlings. Look my way. That's right, my sweets. Just a bit more. Today we make dreams.' The hated uniform burned in his mind. He crouched down, the tip of his barrel, with its integral silencer, hidden in the bushes. His finger slipped naturally around the metal trigger. It couldn't be planned better. The driver, head nodding, startled suddenly, glanced at his watch and started up the engine. After an exchange of words, the other two jumped in behind. The truck moved at a snail's pace towards them. Hanns lined up the driver within his sights. Take him first. The rest die after. His hatred bucked. The bullet cut through the air, ripping the driver's shoulder. His involuntary reaction turned the wheel, jarring the open truck sharply across the road. It hit a large pot hole and turned over. Before the other two had time to react, Hanns rushed forward, pistol in hand. There was no time to make them suffer as he had. '*Guten Morgen*, my friends.' Two swift bullets and they slumped over the side of the vehicle, both dead. Blood stained their thick, pristine uniforms. Hanns tore the Nazi flag from its pole at the back of the truck, soaking the swastika in their blood. Symbols of death, they had their demise.

Josephy gasped, 'What the hell do you think you're doing? This is total madness.'

Hanns ignored his protests, pulling out one of the spare jerrycans that had fallen under the truck as it turned over.

He poured the liquid liberally over their bodies and the canvas-covered sides of the truck. Within seconds he had the truck ablaze.

'You're insane,' hissed Josephy. 'What the hell …? We're freedom-fighters, not barbarians.'

Hanns stared at him, his eyes devoid of any compassion. 'You've not seen what I've seen … Don't worry, my pal, all evidence will be gone before anyone gets here. Like it or not, I've been ordered to make these skirmishes look like accidents. That way there'll be no reprisals on the locals.' He lied of course. He grabbed Josephy's arm, 'Run!'

They took off for Frederikshavn, their final destination.

A few days later, at headquarters block of the Pioneer Corps in Pembroke Dock, Günter was trying to hide his frustration. The major pacing the room was a kind-hearted man, but without an ounce of education. His mate Ignaz was doing the major's daily paperwork after morning drill, for which he earned an extra 6*d* a week in his army pay. How the major passed officer training was beyond him, but then any fool could slope arms and stand to attention on parade. Günter waited until spoken to, army protocol demanded it.

'Private Herz, a telegram arrived from London today. You're to be moved.'

Günter relaxed his shoulders. This was not what he was expecting. He thought he was going to be put on a charge for staying out the previous night. It had been Ignaz's idea. He was the one who'd missed the girls. They hadn't picked up any. Instead they were too late to get back into barracks and had to sleep in an empty bomb-damaged house on the edge of the town. Fortunately there had been no air raid warnings that night.

'Stand to attention properly, Private Herz. Sloppy, very sloppy. This is the army and we have standards to maintain.'

'Yes, sir,' he lifted his head, pulling his shoulders back. To impress the major, Günter had spent an extra half hour polishing his boots that morning.

'You are being sent to special forces for training, Private Herz. To Anderson Manor.'

Günter raised his eyebrows. 'Where's that, sir?'

'You lot. You're never satisfied; always asking questions. Chain of command, Private Herz – speak only when you are spoken to by a senior rank. Remember that.' It wasn't the first time Günter noticed the major's habit of twitching his left eye when harassed. The Continentals had perfected a mimic of him to a tee. Most nights the barracks descended into a frolicking jolly of impersonations until the officer on patrol bellowed, 'Lights out! Enough singing you damn lot.'

'Dorset,' he replied, surveying Günter with his good eye. His discarded monocle bobbed on its cord. 'Take the train to Cardiff, then from Bristol to Salisbury Plain, etc., etc.' He waved his hand impatiently. 'It's all on your ticket. On arrival you'll be issued with a new army pay book and number. It is normal procedure. But first you've got seven days leave starting tomorrow. Make the most of it. It could be your last for some time. Dismissed!'

Günter saluted. 'Thank you, sir.'

As he left, he tried to contain his excitement at the turn of events. So he had been accepted for something. He didn't know what, but at least he would be fighting a real war. He would show them. He would show the lot of them.

Chapter 2

Günter took the early morning train for the five-hour journey down to North Devon. He had decided to make the
most of his leave and head for the village of Knowle, a few
miles inland from the coast, to stay with Katharine, who had
once been married to his uncle Jonathan back in 1938. It
was a strange affair. Jonathan's final fate was still shrouded
in mystery; he was thought to have been incarcerated in
Dachau concentration camp. Katharine was a musician of
note who, he was led to understand, had a dramatic escape
from Vienna after Kristallnacht. A death certificate had
been issued for Jonathan and she had moved on with her
life, marrying a Captain Henderson. Günter hadn't seen
her since before he had left Vienna, when he had faced her
across her desk in the British Embassy. It was she who had
secured his visa and papers to Britain. To get out he had
undergone a phoney Christian baptism under the auspices
of Rev. Grimes, head of the Anglican Church in Vienna.

Günter's life had been in danger for being part of an
underground student movement. The Nazis had mercilessly repressed any resistance to the regime and its sacred
ideology. Then there was the night he had dared to throw
a copy of *Mein Kampf* into the funeral pyre of burning
Jewish books. It hadn't gone down too well and he had
been arrested immediately. Someone had to stand up for

democracy and freedom of ideas, but then he always was an idealist. His mother had often complained that he'd got his head in the clouds. Now he felt it was she who had been naïve, left behind in Vienna with Pa. He worried about their fate. Hitler had swept across Europe with an unparalleled war machine and the whole of Europe was totally unprepared. The lone voice of Churchill's warnings had fallen on deaf ears in Britain. *He*, Winston Churchill, was a realist if ever there was one. Through his thoughts, Günter became aware of the train slowing speed into Barnstaple station. He was to alight a couple stops on at Braunton, exactly fifteen minutes away.

Günter glanced down. His watch said 3.58 p.m. The train was on time. Looking out of the window, he noticed an armoured train manned by Poles, taking on water in her tanks. A double blow of the whistle from the stationmaster signalled that Günter's train was leaving. It was still crammed with RAF personnel and army soldiers, just as it had been all the way down. He had been lucky to get a seat. At 4.08 p.m. the train slowed into Braunton station. The last time he had passed through Braunton was three years earlier on his way to Ilfracombe for six-weeks' training in the Pioneer Corps. That was where No 3 Training Centre of the Pioneer Corps had been based. He hadn't had a chance to see Katharine then.

Günter stepped out of the train and adjusted his army cap. He was exceptionally proud to be wearing the King's uniform. His eyes scanned the platform. The station sign had been taken down, an indication that if the Germans invaded they wouldn't know where they were. The passengers who had alighted quickly dispersed, leaving just two groups of soldiers and WAAF women chatting together and smoking cigarettes. A tall, silvery, grey-haired gentleman in full Naval uniform came towards him. Günter presumed it to be Captain Henderson.

Captain Henderson was already extending his hand. 'Welcome, lad.'

Did he deliberately not use Günter's name? Günter and his colleagues had been warned about not speaking German in public and now he supposed it extended to not using their names too. People were still nervous of an invasion, even though Hitler's attention was focused elsewhere and the Battle of Britain pilots had won the fight in the skies nearly three years earlier.

'How was the journey?' he asked. Now that Captain Henderson was so close to him, Günter could see a kindness through his stark facial features. 'Pleasant, sir, but over-crowded.'

Captain Henderson glanced up and down Günter's uniform. 'So they've made a soldier out of you I see.' He smiled, dispelling any seriousness from his face.

'Yes sir. The army suits me very well, or at least it would if I could fight this war properly.'

'Your chance will come sooner than you think.' What did Henderson know? Günter could hardly ask him. He got the instant feeling that everything was superficial and all politeness with him and that he wouldn't tell him anyway.

'Come, let's get you and that suitcase of yours in the car. Knowle is just down the road. Katharine is waiting for us. She is very excited about you coming to stay.' He coughed then asked: 'How long are you on leave?'

'One week, sir.'

'And then?'

'I have been posted to Dorset for training.'

Driving through the quiet country lanes, it seemed difficult to imagine there was a war on. Captain Henderson remained deep in thought for the two miles to Knowle. Günter found him a little intimidating. They barely spoke during the remainder of the short journey. In the silence between them, Günter reflected how different the English countryside was from his Austria. But it was no longer *his* Austria. The emigration papers were for permanent exile. He wouldn't be going back. He tried not to let it bother him but the scars remained deep. Once the war was over he envisaged a Utopia. Wasn't that what the Youth Movement in Austria had worked for? What he had strived for?

The car took a sudden sharp right turn off the main road and drove up a steep, narrow, hedged lane. At the top, it drew up outside a cottage surrounded by a large, quintessentially English garden. Flowerbeds lined the traditional stone wall which had been built to a height of about 3ft. Around the borders, wilting roses half drooped in the intense summer sun. No one appeared to have had time to tend them. Katharine already stood waiting in the white painted doorway of the cottage, the bottom of her pale blue dress fluttering gently in the wind. Its colour almost matched the cloudless sky. For the first time, Günter noticed that the war was evident even in this sleepy village. The lawn had been dug up for spuds and rows of cabbages. In the centre, a bird table remained with a few dried crumbs that the birds had scornfully rejected. Günter glanced sideways at Captain Henderson. He couldn't imagine him doing any of this. The motto 'Dig for Victory' had been promoted every-where in Britain at the start of the war. Every household was doing its bit to survive the rationing.

'Günter!' Katharine's soft, familiar voice floated across to them. She was already coming down the path towards the gate. She seemed much more relaxed than when he had seen her in Vienna. Since those Vienna days she'd had her long blonde hair cropped to shoulder-length, giving her maturity. 'Welcome to Knowle. It's so lovely to see you again.' Günter grinned, getting his lanky self out of the car.

'Finally out of trouble are we!' Her laughter carried across on the light breeze, penetrating the afternoon's tranquility.

He loved her wry sense of humour. 'Katharine, you always were such a rag. It's really good to see you too,' he said, ruffling his fingers through his mop of hair. They hugged. Captain Henderson cleared his throat behind them, 'Shall I ask Fraser to put the kettle on?'

'Yes, thank you. What a good idea, George,' she replied.

Captain Henderson disappeared. Katharine took Günter's arm and led him into the cottage. The hallway seemed quite dark. He glanced down the corridor to the kitchen at the far end. A revolver lay on the table. How careless, he thought. Or certainly odd. Why would anyone need such a thing in the heart of the countryside? Even if the Germans did ever land, he felt sure they would never find their way to this remote village. What he could not know was Knowle was anything but quiet. He followed Katharine into the sitting room, where she busied herself straightening the cushions of the armchairs.

'Have a seat,' she gestured. Günter sank into the nearest armchair. The soft pastel furnishings made it a comfortable setting, feeling homely and warm.

'How's the army then, Günter?' She turned, flicking loose strands of hair from her face. He could see exactly what men found attractive in her. She wasn't beautiful in the classic sense, but she was energetic, her face alive with a zest for life. In the few exchanges between her and Captain Henderson, he could see that there was something special between them that hadn't been there when she was married to his uncle Jonathan. Neither could Günter forget how, in Vienna, she hadn't been impressed with his foolhardy idealism.

'So, so,' he replied, studying her carefully. 'I've spent two years digging in some God-forsaken army camp. Now I intend to fight.'

'Risk your life for this country? Why?'

'This is my war as much as yours.' His eyes fired up and she caught sight of the same blazing passion that had nearly cost him his life under the Nazis.

She changed the conversation. 'Have you heard from your parents?'

'Just once by letter through the Red Cross. Ma didn't say very much. She couldn't. Life's got tougher for them. She said Papa was well, but I worry for his safety. There are rumours of death camps in Germany and Poland. No Jew is safe.'

'Naturally.' She paused as Fraser came in with a tray of tea, 'Is George joining us?' she asked him.

'No madam, Captain Henderson wishes to finish some business before supper.'

Fraser had served them for just over a year; his loyalty unquestioning. Impeccably dressed and polite, he was punctual, yet always discreet in making himself scarce when required. Before his retirement, he had worked for a number of years for the Duke of Devonshire. It wasn't the money that enticed him back to work, but the war. Everyone had to do their bit, however small, or at least that's what Captain Henderson had told Katharine in the beginning. What she didn't know was that Fraser was bound in service to her husband. It was all part of Fraser's understanding of duty to his country.

'Supper smells good,' piped up Günter.

Katharine smiled. 'You always did enjoy your food. Fraser does his best with what's available. Isn't that so Fraser?'

'Yes, madam.'

'It's fish today. Always fish on Fridays if we can. Fraser gets it from the local fishermen in Ilfracombe harbour. Come Günter, let me show you to your bedroom. It's one of two rooms in the attic. The dormer window has wonderful views across the valley.' Katharine slipped her arm through his again. 'I'm not sure what you'll do here all weekend,' she jested, 'but you may not find it quite as quiet as you first imagine. But it's best not to ask questions.'

Later that night Günter lay awake. The countryside was far too quiet for his liking. He much preferred the background hum of the city. He glanced at his watch: five past midnight. He decided to steal downstairs to make a warm drink of Ovaltine or whatever he could find in the larder. Careful not to wake anyone, he crept out of his room. Peering over the banisters, the only light came from the library door slightly ajar. He strained to glimpse the occupant. All he could see were rows of bookshelves. The click, click of dials was unmistakable. He held his breath, descending two more steps. He paused, wondering if he could make it down the passageway without being detected. The midnight snack might have to be given a miss. Then he hit on the idea of moving when the rapid clicks were occurring. Below him, the grandfather clock ticked away.

Click, click, beep, beep, click.

Günter tiptoed closer to the kitchen. Three more steps and he was there, pushing the kitchen door gently shut behind him. In the larder he helped himself to something easy – a glass of milk and a slice of bread pudding. He munched away on the deliciously moist cake, containing a desire to cut another piece. The dials could no longer be heard. Only the rhythmic tick of the kitchen clock broke the silence. Katharine had said about 'goings on'. Now Günter's imagination began to run riot. The clock struck the half hour. He stood up to leave. On his way back along the hall, the angle of the library door afforded him a glimpse of the person inside. It was Katharine sat bent over radio equipment. The same revolver lay on the desk beside her. Why did she need protection? Günter knew ignorance was bliss. Knowledge, however limited, was dangerous.

The click, click of dials began again. Günter crept back upstairs to his room. He wouldn't say a word, not to her, not to anyone.

The following morning, after a breakfast of porridge, Captain Henderson strolled into the library. Katharine was seated at the polished oak desk by the tall French windows, head bent over studying the latest thick manuals for the new radio equipment. It was her favourite spot, with a view looking straight down the back garden, pond in the centre, and rockery. Runner beans and peas now climbed the arch over the trickling stream, encroaching onto the secluded bench at the far end against the stone wall. Along the flowerbeds, onion sets, sprouts, turnips and carrots had been sown. Down the left side of the garden, fruit bushes of red/white redcurrants and raspberries had been planted. A pear tree bent over against a sheltered south wall. It was idyllic. Perhaps that was why Katharine liked it so much; a complete contrast to city life, away from the Blitz.

'Günter not up yet?' he asked, bending over to kiss the top of her head.

She looked up. 'No. It seems the army hasn't changed him that much.'

'Katharine,' he put his arm tenderly around her shoulder. 'You should rest today, darling. You've been getting over-tired recently.'

'I'm fine, George. Really I am. Did you notice? The new radio equipment arrived from Arkley while you were out for your walk. Fraser has put it in the corner. I was just about to unpack it.'

Through the window, Captain Henderson focused on the figure of Fraser as he plunged the pitch fork into the earth, digging a new patch on the righthand side. Later in the evening, after his duties with them, he would be taking his turn to do a stint as air raid warden around the village, enforcing the blackout.

'Good chap, Fraser,' said Captain Henderson, almost to himself. Henderson had gone to great lengths to detail one of his men as a guard for Katharine. If she ever found out his true undertaking she would reject such protection. Her strong, determined character led her to believe she could care for herself. She had the training. Sir Charles had seen to that, but Henderson still wanted to protect her. Losing her would destroy his very soul. In the two years since their marriage, she had transformed his life. The depth of passion he felt for her still burned through his body as strongly as the first time they had made love in his private quarters in Vienna.

'By the way,' he continued, coming to the purpose of his chat with her. 'There's talk that Sir Charles is being brought out of retirement.'

'What? That overbearing man! You can't be serious, George?'

'I haven't seen him myself, but I've been told the Admiralty wants him for something. Not sure what. I'm not in on this one. Hugo is back at the Admiralty and was good enough to inform me of the scarce details yesterday.'

'As long as he doesn't cross my path again I'll be happy.' She sighed. 'Anyway, I've more important matters to think about. Getting that new radio equipment up and running is a high priority, and I've got to find time later this morning to practice those violin pieces. I've neglected it for too long. There's another concert in the village hall next week to raise funds for the war effort.' She sensed his disquiet, even nervousness, and suddenly looked up into his eyes. 'George, what is it?' She didn't need to ask. She already knew what he was going to say.

'Darling, I have to go away for a few days but I'll be back by the end of the week.'

She dreaded this news. 'It's nothing to do with Sir Charles is it?'

'No, of course not. Don't fret so.'

'I can't bear it George. You being away so often, especially now.'

'I know, but this time Günter's here. He'll keep you company.'

Henderson couldn't subdue her anxiety. 'I will try to phone you. And you know you can always get word to me through Hugo.' He moved closer, tilting her head in his strong hands, bringing his firm lips onto hers. It felt as good and sweet as the day he first kissed her. His commitment to her was absolute. 'Darling, you know I love you.'

She returned the passion, kissing him hard on the lips. 'Yes, my sweet,' she murmured.

His fingers gently stroked her hair. 'I will come back to you. I promise. I always do.' Not for once, she believed him. He walked back into the hall, picked up his case and left the cottage. Alone in the library, Katharine tried not to feel miserable.

Over the next few days she spent much of the time with Günter discussing politics. She listened, rarely offering her own opinion. Occasionally she played her violin to him, slow melancholic music which reminded him of his Vienna. He wondered how his dear mother would be coping with the situation and whether his father was still alive. Katharine had told him that efforts had been made to get them both out of Austria, but the war had intervened before the paperwork could be completed. At the end of the weekend, Günter's leave expired. He left Knowle and took a train en route for Dorset to start the first stage of his training for special duties. In those first few months, no mention was ever made of Special Operations Executive. That came much later.

≈❧

Günter tried to steady himself as the train wobbled at high speed through the countryside. It was standing room only. The soldiers were packed in like sardines, hot and sweaty in their thick uniforms, their shoulders touching for the duration of the several hours' journey to Dorset.

'Günter!' The familiar voice shouted over the heads of the other men. Ignaz was already trying to push his way through.

'You didn't tell me you'd be on the train!' Günter laughed with some indignation, but was pleased to see him.

'Why should I?' said Ignaz, bemused. 'I thought it would be a surprise.'

'I take it we're both off to the same place?'

'Yes. I believe we are. The sergeant major …' He winked at Günter. It wouldn't do to discuss their destination in public. 'We're in for hard training. I hope you're up to it.'

'Keep your voice down, Ignaz,' he hissed. 'Besides, you've been reading too many dare-do books.'

'Let's wait and see shall we? Don't be naïve.'

The train slowed into Wareham station, the nearest to Anderson Manor. Günter and Ignaz stepped out onto the platform. At the far end they saw their new group forming up with a colonel.

'Over there!' nodded Günter. Ignaz followed. They slung their kit bags over their backs, fell into line and quick-marched behind the skipper, Colonel Bennett. The colonel would prove to be an extremely fair and likeable man.

'Keep up, men,' Bennett shouted back down the line. 'What are you made of, eh? Lef' right, lef' right … We want to get there before lunchtime.'

Günter kept apace. Finally, half an hour later, they arrived at the gates of the manor, tired but not as breathless as on previous army marches. The skipper set quite a pace, but nothing like the slim bastard Spike whom they'd had in the Pioneer Corps for the previous two months. In the grounds of the manor, Colonel Bennett turned to face his men, 'Once inside the main hall, I want you to file in front of the desk. You'll be given your army pay books and new cap badges. And you'll be required to sign the Official Secrets Act. Any questions?' He looked from man to man. Ignaz raised his hand.

'Yes, Private Abrahamsohn.'

'Why new pay books, sir?' Günter nudged him, not believing his audacity. He wouldn't have asked the same question of Spike without being given a clip around the ear.

'New names Pte Abrahamsohn. You all need to think of your new English names. Security – your original German backgrounds must be disguised. We can't have you being treated as traitors if captured by the Germans. Oh, and gentlemen … there's been a circular from headquarters. No one may use the surname Churchill, Montgomery or Roosevelt. Is that understood?'

'Yes, sir,' they replied in unison.

'Very good. Ahead! Quick march into the hall!'

Marching down the last part of the main drive, Ignaz turned to Günter. 'What name will you choose?'

Günter grinned, 'I already got a sniff that we might be changing our names and thumbed through the telephone directory last night.'

'Did you now? That was smart of you. You could have told me.'

Günter laughed, 'And you wouldn't have believed me! Anyway we should keep our original initials. It's safer. I'm going for Geoffrey.'

'What about surname? Montgomery and Churchill are out so why not something aristocratic, even double-barrelled?'

'You're so pretentious, Ignaz.'

'Ian to you. My new name is Ian.'

Günter raised his eyebrows and smirked. 'So you did know something! Pleased to be your friend, Ian. I'm Geoffrey Hart. Come on. We'd better keep up with the others.'

The new recruits filed into the oak-panelled hall. Coats of arms and paintings of the aristocratic families lined the walls. Behind a desk sat Colonel Bennett next to a dark, burly, tanned man who was to be their main instructor.

'Here, look at the guy next to Bennett. He looks like the Gauleiter,' whispered Ignaz to Günter. 'From now on that's what we'll call him.'

'Ssh, you'll have us thrown out on a charge. I haven't come this far to be kicked out.'

Colonel Bennett stood up to address the men again: 'Gentlemen, you will be billeted in pairs in rooms in the house, not barracks. You are different from the regular army and will have a number of privileges. There's no one here to hold your hand. You are expected to operate at times under your own initiative. Make sure you appear for parade duties punctually and all correct. These are your final months of training. You will be among the best His Majesty's Forces can turn out. You will not fail. Failure lands you back in the Pioneer Corps. You face several weeks of hard training in the use of all kinds of explosives and weaponry, as well as physical aptitude tests, map reading, orienteering and fieldcraft.' He cleared his throat and continued, 'One at a time, collect your pay books from Major Wetherell seated here and have your new names and signatures ready.'

Günter stepped forward. Wetherell had his pen poised to fill in the personal details. 'Name?'

'Geoffrey Hart, sir.'

'No middle name? It is customary.'

'Er, Oliver, sir.'

'Very good, Geoffrey Oliver Hart, here's your new pay book and army number. Next!'

Günter waited for Ian before heading to their room upstairs.

Katharine placed her headphones down on the desk. Having finished scribbling down the latest set of codes, she marked that day's date in the top left hand corner of the page: 18 September 1943. Her tiny library had effectively become the centre of radio operations in North Devon. Twelve-hour shifts were now the pattern for her on a daily basis, sometimes longer. Fraser placed a tray of tea and a biscuit beside her.

'Anything else, madam?' he asked as he checked the blackout blinds ahead of that evening's enforcement.

'Yes, Fraser. When is Captain Henderson due back?'

'Anytime soon, madam. His telegram said about 4 o'clock.'

'Very good, Fraser, thank you.' She smiled, giving him his cue to leave.

Katharine folded the sheet of codes into three, slipped it in the brown envelope and then into another. Double-sealed envelopes were standard government procedure which had been adopted even when she had been in Vienna. On the outside she scribbled the postal address: 'PO Box 25, London'.

She didn't ask questions about where or what. It would be ready for her husband to take to the post office that evening. She replaced the headphones over her ears and continued taking down the coded messages. She gathered enough from them to realise that they were coming from U-boats located in the Atlantic.

Less than a quarter of an hour later, she heard Captain Henderson's distinctive footsteps on the stone floor in the hallway. There had been a lull in the German command signals for the last ten minutes. She rushed out to him. He was looking tired.

'Darling!' He was pleased to see her and hugged her tightly.

'I've missed you, George.'

'But I've only been gone a few days.'

'Yes I know, but …'

He hushed her with a finger pressed to her soft lips. 'Come, let's go into the sitting room. I want to discuss something with you.' He closed the door behind them. She sat down, eagerly scanning his face for clues.

'There's news from Denmark,' he suddenly said. The gravity of his expression unnerved her. 'I have just come from a meeting with M in London. Intelligence suggests that the Jews are about to be rounded up – looks like either the end of this month or during the first night of October.'

Katharine leant back in the chair and crossed her legs. Both had seen what had happened to the Jews in Vienna. 'What can be done, George? Am I needed for a while at the Embassy to issue visas?'

'No, my dear. The Swedes are taking care of everything. There are also rumours that German ships are heading for Copenhagen. That's how the Danish Jews will be transported to unknown destinations – camps of course. We are trying to get news to our Danish contact in the countryside who will warn the whole network. The question is whether we are too late.' He suddenly leapt to his feet, 'Katharine, could you send a message on your new radio set? I've not yet been brought up to scratch with the latest technology. But you my dear … I can always rely on you. We can't sit back and live on false hope. You know me – I like to get things done.'

She looked at him with tenderness. The intimacy of their marriage had not totally broken his reserve. He still held so much in. They moved from the sitting room into the library, where Katharine set to work on sending the message.

Inside the office in Copenhagen harbour, Tom waited patiently for the harbourmaster Korvetten-kapitän Richard Canmen. Glancing down at his highly polished boots, he stood proud in his uniform. He had been with the military police for nearly a month and found it much more rewarding than he'd expected. He quickly realised that the Danish police were all secretly collaborating with the

Resistance Movement. It came as something of a relief for him. His regular daily patrols took him past the harbour at least once a day, but this time he had been sent on an urgent mission. The harbourmaster was one of the few Nazis that the Resistance Movement could trust to co-operate in safeguarding the Jews. Once rumours of the proposed round-up had circulated the echelons of Nazi power, some voiced their objections. Canmen was one of them. Tom had grown to like him. He often made a point of coming out of his office when Tom passed by, exchanging a few brief words, always asking after his family. It might only be a comment on the weather, but he was a thoughtful man.

Through the slatted window, Tom stared at the fishing vessels anchored in the harbour bobbing gently on the light breeze. Two large ships of the Kriegsmarine were being steered towards the dry dock.

'Good day, young Tom.'

Tom turned at the sound of the Korvetten-kapitän's voice. 'Hello, sir.'

Canmen closed the wooden white-painted door behind him. In his mid-fifties, Canmen was a short balding man whose deep lined face and sallow skin betrayed a heavy smoker. 'So, I understand you've come directly from Georg Duckwitz at the German Foreign Ministry.'

'Yes sir.'

'Go on.'

'I have been instructed to give you this, sir.' Tom passed the telegram and continued, 'Duckwitz is asking for the German Navy's co-operation on a matter of urgent business. It concerns the Jewish population. This was apparently sent by SS General Werner Best to Berlin on 8 September.' Canmen scanned the lengthy telegram typed in bold capital letters:

IT IS NOW MY OPINION THAT MEASURES SHOULD BE TAKEN TOWARD A SOLUTION OF THE PROBLEMS OF THE JEWS. IN ORDER TO ARREST AND DEPORT SOME 6,000 JEWS (INCLUDING WOMEN AND CHILDREN) AT ONE SWEEP IT IS NECESSARY TO HAVE THE POLICE FORCES I REQUESTED. ALMOST ALL OF THEM SHOULD BE PUT TO WORK IN GREATER COPENHAGEN WHERE THE MAJORITY OF THE LOCAL JEWS LIVE. SUPPLEMENTARY FORCES SHOULD BE PROVIDED BY THE GERMAN MILITARY COMMANDER IN DENMARK.

'Well, well. I already suspected as much and took my own precautions. But thank you, lad, for bringing confirmation. You can tell dear old Duckwitz that the German Navy has already been recalled for urgent maintenance and repairs. They won't be available to support the transport of Jews out of Denmark.'

Tom beamed. 'Very good, sir.'

'You can also tell him it is muted the Germans are carrying out numerous important experiments on U-boats on our island of Bornholm. Er, Tom … before you leave, here's something for your family.' He lifted one of the boxes from a pile stacked in the corner of the office. 'This came off the trawler early this morning. Enjoy.'

'Thank you so much, sir. We love fish.'

'Goodbye Tom, see you again tomorrow.'

Before heading back to Military Police headquarters Tom made his way to the German Foreign Ministry to deliver the Korvetten-kapitän's reply. He made his way to the first floor, past Duckwitz's secretary, whose desk was installed in a recess next to Duckwitz's office door. She looked up. 'Duckwitz wants a brief word with you in his office.'

'Thank you,' he replied. The bold letters of Duckwitz's name were inscribed in gold lettering on a wooden plaque across the door behind the secretary. Tom knocked and waited.

'Come in,' came the gruff retort.

Tom opened the door. He approached Duckwitz who was seated behind his desk scribbling in a leather-bound book. The sight of the imposing man, militarily reserved although he wore no uniform, suddenly unnerved him. Duckwitz was not as approachable as Canmen. Tom tried to hide his anxiety.

'Hello, young man.'

'Good day, sir. I have come on an errand.'

Duckwitz seemed distracted, waved his hand in the air. 'Go on.'

'Here, sir. I am required to deliver this letter to you from Korvetten-kapitän Canmen.' Duckwitz took it and placed it on the desk. 'Thank you, lad.' He surveyed Tom for a moment then added, 'Before you go, there's something I would like you to do for me.'

'Yes, sir.'

'Things are moving at quite a pace. I need you to contact this man for me. Here his details are on the top of the memo. It is vital you get to him quickly, without delay.'

Duckwitz moved to the window. He stared out, his back to Tom. Tom glanced down. The envelope was addressed to Anders Olsen, c/o the Vallø Castle estate. Tom knew Anders, but felt it wise not to reveal that to Duckwitz. There was no way of knowing for certain who was trustworthy in the network.

Duckwitz continued speaking. 'Denmark has not suffered as the rest of Europe, but our hour of danger is imminent. If we are to ...' His words became distant as Tom was distracted by the leather bound book open on the desk at today's date. He shot a glance down. It was

Duckwitz's diary. Even though it was upside down, Tom got the gist of the scrawl: '*no power in the world can absolve General Best from his heavy burden of guilt and the unforeseeable consequences of his actions.*'

Tom gathered that the deportation must be fast approaching. Now he knew what he must do. Duckwitz swung around to face him: '... don't you agree?'

Tom knew not what Duckwitz had just uttered. 'Er, yes, sir.'

'Very well, lad. Thank you. Now off you go and deliver that note. It will take a few hours each way. I want you to deliver it personally. Understand? Someone else can cover for you whilst you're out.'

'Yes, sir.' Tom made for the door. Outside the office he bolted down the corridor. His heart raced. Denmark faced its darkest hour. How would ordinary Danes react?

That night, in a shack in the woods on the Vallø Castle estate, Anders gathered the main leaders of the local resistance movement. The movement was still haphazard, unprofessional and relatively unco-ordinated. Ammunition and supplies for them were periodically being dropped into the country by British agents working out of neutral Sweden. Anders had been co-ordinating Hanns' regular missions to intercept the supplies. Now Hanns was required to move north to Faergehaven and finally cross to Frederikshavn to intercept a German U-boat of the 9th Flotilla. Thus far it hadn't been possible to board because the U-boat was still in a base on the Norwegian coast.

Anders sat perched on an old crate, leaning his elbow on a rickety coffee table with a map spread out before him. By candlelight he looked at each of the men in turn, their faces partly illuminated by its light, their shadows cast across the wall behind them. He addressed the men: 'You have all been asked to come here this evening because the situation is rapidly deteriorating. Our country is about to be ravaged. Young Tom here has an update. Tell them, Tom.'

Tom peered at the men gathered around the table. All of them of differing ages put their lives at risk by being in the Resistance. 'This morning I delivered a telegram to Korvetten-kapitän Canmen. The deportation of Danish Jews is imminent. The Captain in England has been informed. He is co-ordinating extra agents from Sweden.'

Anders cleared his throat to speak. 'I also had contact with the Captain. I received a single transmission today, sent from England, not Sweden. Two German ships have been reported en route to Copenhagen. Their estimated date of arrival is the 28th or 29th of September, depending on the weather and conditions. The Jews of this country are their target. The round-up is due to be enforced by 1 October. We don't have much time. We've got twenty-four hours' grace, forty-eight at most. We need to start the chain. Mobilise the population, get every vehicle we can and drive to as many Jewish homes as possible and tell them. Fishing vessels will leave at regular intervals from various locations around the coast to take them to Sweden. Duckwitz has recalled the Kriegsmarine for vital repairs, so the fishing boats won't be intercepted by naval patrols. But first we must get the Jews into hiding. When the Germans raid their houses, they will not find many victims.'

Josephy, who'd remained silent thus far, piped up: 'I'll co-ordinate the movement of Jews south of Copenhagen. We can bring some to Vallø. But it will take cash to do it. We need to secure money for the fishermen's wages. I have managed to negotiate their fee down from 1,500 kroner per person to 500.'

Anders patted him on the back, 'Well done. Thank you, Josephy.'

Tom chipped in: 'What we don't know yet is the status of the U-boats and whether they are heading for patrols of the Sound. They could be our greatest threat, not the naval patrols.'

'Don't worry,' replied Anders. 'Some of them have been recalled for repairs. But anyway, Hanns is staying here and keeping regular radio contact with England. They have a radio operator on the job, tracking the movement of U-boats in the Channel and around our coast. She's the best they've got, so we'll be guided by her intelligence.' He leant across the table, blew out all but two of the candles and signalled for them to leave. 'Now it's time for us to disperse. Good luck. And remember – we are upholding Danish moral values for the sake of humanity. We will not falter.' The men saluted Anders, the leader they respected above all others. They left, one by one, into the dark woods around Vallø Castle.

Lilian Sørensen followed her mother into the ladies' gallery in Copenhagen's Grand Synagogue. It was the eve of Rosh Hashanah, the Jewish New Year, one of the most important festivals of the Jewish religion. It was the only time Lilian and her family attended synagogue – then and on Yom Kippur and sometimes during Passover. Today the pews were half-empty. Her mother gave a cursory nod to the women already seated in the gallery, their heads covered in varying degrees of elaborate headwear and hats. Felt and feathers seemed to be the fashion this year, in spite of the war. The final chants of the introductory prayers in Hebrew floated upwards to the gallery. The young Rabbi Melchior was already moving to stand in front of the Ark on the east wall, about to deliver his sermon. Lilian tried to count the number of men below. There must have been around eighty of them, only a fraction of the whole Jewish community. Melchior's words echoed around the synagogue, causing even the slightest shuffle of feet in the pews to fall to a deathly silence:

'Last night I received word that the Germans plan to raid Jewish homes throughout Copenhagen to arrest all the Danish Jews for shipment to concentration camps. They know that tomorrow is Rosh Hashanah and our families will be at home. We must take action immediately. You must leave the synagogue now and contact all relatives, friends and neighbours you know are Jewish and tell them what I have told you. You must tell them to pass the word on to everyone they know is Jewish. You must also speak to all your Christian friends and tell them to warn the Jews. You must do this immediately, within the next few minutes, so that within two or three hours from now everyone will know what is happening. By nightfall we must all be in hiding. May Hashem bless you all.'

He raised his hand to signal the congregation's dismissal and moved immediately to the lobby. At the foot of the stairs of the ladies' gallery, Rabbi Melchior waited to shake each person's hand. As they filed passed, he gave them each a train ticket. Lilian glanced down at hers. She was to take the late evening train from Copenhagen to Valløby, near the Valløbby Castle estate. There was no time to gather belongings; it might not be safe to return home. She slipped on her soft, brown leather gloves, pulled up the collar of her coat and turned to kiss her mother. Her mother tried to hold back the tears. 'Lilian, darling, don't worry about me and Pa. We're going out via Dragør, but will be at the same meeting point in Sweden. Take care, darling. And remember, I always love you.'

Lilian hugged her tightly. Then, with a mixture of fear and excitement, she rushed out, down the steps of the synagogue to an unknown future.

Chapter 3

Vallø Castle, Denmark, 1 October 1943

Lilian shivered, huddled against the stone wall of the ice house. The cold, damp air irritated her nostrils. She sniffed. Anders bent down, coming through the low arched doorway and started handing out a single blanket to each of the nine people waiting for the all-clear to move. Most of Denmark's Jews were now safely in hiding. Anders began to go over the plan. 'We have one chance,' he said. 'There's no moon tonight. We have to get you out before the raids begin.'

Lilian stared ahead. She had grown up with virtually no religious instruction at all, but that counted for nothing with the Nazis. She shuddered, thinking of uncle Klaus trapped in Berlin. She had no idea if he was safe. Aunt Claudia had died in the flu epidemic of 1918 and poor Klaus had never got over it. Lilian dismissed him from her mind. There was nothing she could do for him until she reached England.

'Josephy,' hissed Anders. The gamekeeper turned. 'The patrols on the estate have moved on. We need to make a run for it now. And remember, not a sound!'

Everyone stood up. The muscles in Lilian's back and legs ached from being crouched down so long. She stepped out of the ice house into the cold night air.

'Quickly! Over there!' Josephy gently nudged her forward, pointing to the dark silhouettes of two men leaning against a tree. 'Quietly, ssh. They'll take you to the next rendezvous. Where are the others?'

'Coming,' she whispered, hearing their shuffles behind her. She beckoned for them to hurry. Anders involuntarily looked up and shuddered. This was the tree where he and Josephy had found the dead British parachutist. How could he forget?

Lilian drew her shawl over her head and around her face, the soft wool felt comforting against her cheek. She ran towards the two men, a single line of people following her. Between the trees, the jagged shape of the castle stood foreboding against the night sky. Her eyes focused ahead, her heart racing. The two men said little, but as soon as they had all gathered, one pulled Lilian aside. 'When we get to the vessel, I want you to take care of a young boy. His name is Dieter.' On hearing his name the small child, no older than four, came out from behind a tree. Lilian nodded and took the boy's tiny cold hand, warming it in hers. 'I promise. I'll take care of him.' She bent down to his level: 'Hello Dieter. I'm Lilian,' she whispered. He stared up at her, clutching her hand tightly. They were led eastwards, carving their way through thick, grasping undergrowth either side of the narrow path. The line of people followed Josephy, hunched over partly in fear, partly against the cold. They heard the sound of water long before they reached the shore. The gentle lapping of ripples against the side of the jetty was easily audible above the light chill breeze. They came to a clearing to see the Sound stretched ahead of them. It was this that they were to cross to Sweden. The cloudy night sky afforded no light from the moon or stars. Two fishing boats were tied to the wooden post of the jetty. As the line of huddled people approached, the fishermen stood waiting to help them into the vessels. One by one they climbed in. The young boy still clutched Lilian's hand for dear life. She glanced back, stifling an involuntary gasp, pulling the young boy closer to her. Searchlights skimmed the dense woodland, casting powerful shafts of light, cutting the darkness like a knife.

'Nazis!' called Anders. This was Anders' second operation that week to get Jews out. Each time was riskier. 'They've reached the castle. When they find nothing, they'll be down here like a shot. We have but ten minutes at most.' He held out his hand for Lilian to climb into the fishing boat. First she bent down to lift up Dieter. 'Ssh, danger,' she whispered to him. His big soft eyes fixed on her. His baby hands clutched the tassels of her shawl as he buried his frightened face into her neck. The two fishing boats bobbed to one side under the weight of the people unevenly distributed in them.

'Thank you, Anders. Thank you, Josephy,' she said in a low voice, trying to contain tears of gratitude. 'I will never forget. I can never repay your kindness.'

'Hush,' whispered Josephy, as he heaved himself back out of the boat. Casting off, he pushed the boat away. 'Off you go now. You'll all be safe soon, keep your head down until you're well out in the open sea. The farther away from these shores the better.' His eyes took in each of the others as he gave them his parting shot, 'Good luck, all of you.' Across the twelve-mile stretch of the Sound, Lilian could see the dotted lights of Sweden. She settled onto the bench and lifted Dieter onto her lap. By now he was shivering. She wrapped her shawl around him, held him close to her body. 'It will be alright,' she whispered, 'we're going on a little adventure.' She felt his body relax against hers, and soon he was asleep.

Out in the open sea the fishing boat carved a path defiantly through the waters. Every inch brought them closer to freedom. Back on the Danish shore, a line of torches lit the coastland, their beams crisscrossing the water. There was nothing the Nazi patrols could do. From that distance it wouldn't be possible for them to tell how many people were crouched in the boat, the canvas around their shoulders masking them as cargo. These Jews, at least, were safe.

ह

Three days later, having spent two nights with other refugees in Stockholm, Lilian was travelling to England alone aboard a ship under Royal Navy protection. Leaning over the railings of the ship, she watched the trail it had left through the waters. The English coast was in full view, only ten miles to go before the ship steered into the port of Hull. Seagulls hovered overhead at the stern of the ship, occasionally screeching. Lilian thought of Tom back in Copenhagen and wondered how he was getting on. All contact with him had to be broken for the time being. Sweden had offered temporary shelter to hundreds of Jews but, like other refugees, Lilian was required to seek long-term sanctuary in another country. She hadn't met up with her parents as was supposed to happen. News had got through to her that they were safe, but their location remained secret. At Stockholm's railway station she had handed over young Dieter to the care of the Jewish Youth Organisation. Now she was quite excited by the prospect of a life in England. Through her thoughts, Lilian felt a presence close behind her. She turned. The grey-suited gentleman smiled, an unlit cigarette clenched between his fingers. She surreptitiously assessed him, reckoning he must be in his early twenties, his jet black hair indistinguishable from his black trilby hat. His brown eyes seemed naïve.

'Enjoying the journey?' he asked, tipping his hat.

'Yes.' She scanned the deck. They were alone, the other passengers all below deck.

'It isn't always as calm as this,' he said. 'We're lucky today. The sea can be quite choppy. It's mild for early October, don't you find?'

He seemed pleasant enough, although Lilian was in no mood for polite talk with strangers. What did he want of her? 'Indeed,' she replied, not wishing to appear rude. 'It's good to get some fresh air. It's so stuffy below deck.'

'I couldn't agree more. And a little overcrowded. Can I offer you a cigarette?'

'No. Thank you.'

'You are from Denmark, aren't you?'

'What makes you ask that, sir?' Her face gave nothing away. He had chosen his moment carefully. Unknown to her, he had followed her every movement from afar since she had boarded ship. She wasn't expecting the next question.

'The accent. I have done some travelling myself.' After a short pause, he asked: 'You're not quite sure where you're staying in England are you?'

She kept a straight face, trying to think of an appropriate response. He surveyed her. In the silence she was beginning to feel a little unnerved, but didn't show it. He had a mysterious air about him. He seemed to know something about her.

'Look,' he lowered his voice, glancing over his shoulder to check they were still alone. 'The British government is interested in whether you would be prepared to do something special for the country that's giving you sanctuary.'

'Go on,' she hinted.

At least it wasn't a no; her response initially more positive than he'd expected. It usually took two attempts and then he didn't always succeed. 'We'd like to offer you a room in an old English manor house. It is suggested that you be assigned to domestic duties until your full posting. Then we have some duties in mind for you.' He paused, allowing her time to take in what he had said.

'Carry on,' she said, turning to look back out to sea, the light breeze tantalizingly blowing her hair in wisps around her face. He still had her full attention.

He took a step closer; their shoulders almost touching. 'Your fluency in Danish … naturally, and your knowledge of German and French could be put to good use. For intelligence reasons you're not to ask questions of those around you, of course.'

'I understand.' In that moment she reflected that he had done his homework. He knew exactly who she was. All refugees coming into Britain were vetted. But somehow this was different. 'Alright. I'll give it a go,' she flicked her hair from her face, 'but as long as it doesn't mean leaving Britain.'

'I'll make sure that point is registered with the powers that be.' He reached into his jacket pocket and pulled out a train ticket. Still they were alone on deck. 'With your limited knowledge of English, you will be discreetly escorted from the ship to the station by one of the ship's crew. He will knock on your cabin door at eleven fifteen. Once at the station, please make your way to the clock in the centre. Wait there and a suited gentleman will join you. He will shadow you to your final destination. Here's your ticket to the south of England. As you can see, it's valid any day of the week, but you are to board today if possible to avoid complications.'

'I understand.' She glanced down. The destination was Anderson Manor, in Dorset. It didn't mean anything to her, but then, why should it? 'Am I to know your name?' she spluttered. 'What if I am asked to …'

He said nothing, smiled as he tilted his hat, then turned and walked down the deck. She never saw him again.

A few days later Geoffrey Hart collapsed onto his bed. Getting used to his new name hadn't taken as long as he had expected. Günter Herz was a person of the past, a shadow left behind in Vienna. He was now Geoffrey Hart. His room mate Ian felt the same. The change of name and the army uniform went a long way towards beginning to feel British, although they were still not British nationals. Training had moved up a notch week on week. That morning they had completed a ten-mile jog before breakfast, carrying full kit. Inside a freezing makeshift tent at the top of the final hill, they had had an hour's lecture. It always varied, but this morning's was on the operational use of enemy small arms. The men returned exhausted.

'I don't know if I can take much more of this, Ian. Every muscle in my body hurts,' said Geoffrey. 'Are they trying to kill us? Whoever designed that assault course we did yesterday needs their head tested. Not a single safety net and they were live bullets the instructor was firing at us.'

Ian stretched out on his bed, arms folded behind his head. He laughed. 'What kind of wimp are you? They're testing us to the limit. Granted, we may never need half the training, but when we do it for real, at least we know we can do it. It prepares us physically and psychologically for tasks we never knew we could do when we first started here.'

'I might have expected that kind of response from you. You're always so philosophical.'

Ian didn't open his eyes, just grinned slyly. 'You could always fail the assault course.'

'And land back in the Pioneer Corps – No way.'

Ian grunted in response, too tired to reply, his chest heaving air into his exhausted lungs.

Geoffrey glanced at the large round clock hanging over the door of their room. He didn't give up moaning. 'We've got less than an hour before the next exercise across that raging river.' He reached into the bedside locker. 'Fancy some chocolate?'

Ian opened his eyes momentarily. 'Army-issued chocolate, no thanks. Women – Yes.'

'Haven't got any of them. We've about as much chance of meeting girls here as pigs growing wings and learning to fly.' Geoffrey munched through a strip of chocolate before placing the packet back.

'There's a pretty new lass in the kitchen,' Ian said casually. 'She arrived two days ago, I believe.'

Geoffrey sat bolt upright. 'Really?'

'She's not for you,' Ian replied, his hands still firmly behind his head. 'The officers will have her first – she's got breeding. It's in her face. Don't think for one minute she'll look at us refugees.'

'Speak for yourself. I'll give it a go.'

Ian winked. 'I bet you a packet of Woodbines you don't even get near her.'

'Deal.' Geoffrey suddenly had a new lease of life. 'Come on. Let's get back outside for that exercise. It sounds a doddle. Race you there.'

'You've certainly changed your tune,' said Ian getting up.

Half an hour later the men were in the cold water, explosives thrashing around them, the noise deafening. The river was swollen by recent rain torrents and threatened to destabilise them or drown the unwary. The instructors split them into pairs, one assumed to be wounded, whilst the other dragged him to the bank. From the far bank the instructors covered their path in rounds of live ammunition. Ian tried to hold Geoffrey's head above the water, finding his body a heavy weight. At that moment a stiff, dead dog infested with flies floated past. Geoffrey tried to contain a retch at the stink. It was all designed to surprise them and catch them off guard, given to their instructors courtesy of the local vet.

'That's all we need,' he spluttered to Ian through gritted teeth.

'Shut up,' Ian hissed, 'Unless you want to drown us both. This is hard enough without your twitter.'

The sergeant major bellowed from the river bank: 'Move it, move it gentlemen. No slacking – not today, not ever. This isn't a game. Your lives depend on it. You've got to cross that river in two minutes or you're a goner.'

Geoffrey, through chattering teeth, managed: 'Next time you can be the non-swimmer. I think you've drowned me at least twice.'

'Relax!' Ian finally reached the bank, dragged Geoffrey over it as Geoffrey clung to clumps of grass. Ian checked the pulse of his supposed injured companion.

'Well done, gentlemen.' The sergeant major towered over them. 'Tonight you get the night off.'

Later that evening Geoffrey and Ian headed for the local village pub. Seated across from the bar Ian leant closer to Geoffrey: 'See that lass in the corner talking with the young spotty officer? She's the one I was telling you about. The new one that's started in the kitchens.'

Geoffrey peered over his mate's shoulder and lifted his glass of beer to his lips. Between sips he replied, 'Hey, she's alright.' Across the room her eyes suddenly caught his. He smiled. She looked away quickly.

'Don't look now, Ian, but she's just smiled at me,' mused Geoffrey.

'Oh yeah. Pull the other one.'

'She has. I'm telling the truth. I reckon it won't be long before you owe me that packet of cigarettes. Just watch me. The officer's standing up. He's leaving. Now's my chance. Oh, she's being joined by two other girls.'

'Brilliant – the more the merrier. Let's introduce ourselves.'

As they approached the table, the two girls puffed on cigarettes through thick, red lips. Both bleached blonde, their hair was piled high above their heads in a complicated style. The third sat quietly – she was the one Geoffrey had his eye on.

'Good evening, ladies. May we join you?' It was Ian who ventured to speak.

'It looks like you already have.' The two blondes giggled, eyeing them both up and down as if weighing up a tasty morsel in a baker's shop. They looked at each other again and collapsed into giggles. They were a bit silly, but still, girls were girls.

Geoffrey ignored them and focused on the third girl. His eye caught hers again. Her thick, auburn hair was tied with a velvet bow at the back. Just a hint of lipstick dressed her lips. Geoffrey caught the fragrance of lilac on her clothes. Standing so close to her he could see the softness of her slightly flushed skin. With barely any make-up on at all, she was by far the most attractive girl in the room. He tried not to stare too intently. For once in his life he was speechless – he who had no qualms about voicing his objections to the Nazi regime in Vienna and had put his life at risk. He found himself without the words for even the simplest of greetings. She had bewitched him.

'You're welcome to join us but at your own risk,' she added. She caught his gaze again, holding him for several heartbeats too long. Ian nudged Geoffrey to sit down. The two blondes chatted away, flashing their long eyelashes at Ian.

Minutes later silence descended on the pub. Geoffrey and Ian became acutely aware of a policeman stood at their side. In unison they looked up.

'Gentlemen, you're both under arrest,' said the police constable.

'What?' Geoffrey shuffled in his seat looking for an escape route.

'I repeat. You're under arrest. You have the right to remain silent.' From nowhere another policeman stepped forward with handcuffs. He turned to the other officer, 'Bloody Germans, all right. I knew it as soon as I clapped eyes on them. They don't speak the lingo.'

The blonde seated on Ian's left piped up, 'What have they done, officer?'

'Never you mind, miss. They're coming with us.'

Geoffrey and Ian stood up to be led out of the pub to the waiting police car. They walked, dejected, towards the exit. Geoffrey glanced over his shoulder to catch the eye of the auburn-haired lass. What she must think of me, thought Geoffrey. He had blown his chances.

Inside the black Maria, Geoffrey protested again: 'What have we done? Here.' He fumbled in his jacket. 'My identity card.'

'I don't want to see any fake papers. You can speak with the inspector at the station. Until then I suggest you remain silent.'

It wasn't far to the police station. The minute they arrived they were taken into separate interview rooms for questioning. They were forced to empty the contents of their pockets onto the table in front of them.

'Name and occupation?' The police inspector, a slim middle-aged man with impeccably polished shoes, stood gripping his hands on the back of a wooden chair. As he faced Geoffrey he thought about the catch – this was the scoop of the century. He'd get promotion for this on his patch.

'Name and occupation?' he asked again.

'Geoffrey Hart. One of His Majesty's soldiers.' Instinctively Geoffrey suspected the inspector wasn't going to buy his answer.

'Geoffrey Hart you say.' He began to pace the confines of the room. 'Are you aware, Mr Hart, that this country is on a high state of alert?'

'Yes, sir.'

'There's a war on. And as such we're on the lookout for people like you. Fifth columnists, Nazi spies. We know all about your lot. An English country pub, eh? British army uniform? Think us country boys stupid? An ideal place to gather information? Or so you thought? We aren't easily fooled. Pulling our innocent local girls into your web, we know your dirty tricks.'

In the pause Geoffrey ventured: 'I don't understand the problem, sir. I'm a British soldier.'

'British soldier, my arse. The thick accent gives you away. You're German.'

'Not exactly German, sir. Austrian – but not. I'm a British soldier. We're based at the manor.'

'A likely story. Don't think I buy it for one minute.' He turned to the young police officer standing in the doorway. 'Take him to the cells PC Manners.'

'Yes, sir,' replied Manners. 'The blighters must have parachuted in during the night.'

'Thank you, PC Manners. I can do without your comments. Cuff him and to the cells.' PC Manners took Geoffrey by the arm, handcuffed him and led him out.

'No! You don't understand.' Geoffrey shouted in a last attempt to salvage the situation. 'Colonel Bennett will be fuming when he hears of this.'

'Will he now? Take him away, PC Manners.'

Geoffrey was taken along the corridor, down several stone steps to the cold basement. Ian was already in one of the two cells. PC Manners prodded Geoffrey into the empty one and slammed the door. Geoffrey's heart sank to his boots. How would he get out of this one?

Back upstairs the police inspector turned to PC Manners. 'Ask the operator to get a Colonel Bennett on the phone, please.'

'Yes, sir.'

'I am going to get on with a report for the Chief Constable. It's Wormwood Scrubs for them in the morning.'

Early the following morning saw Geoffrey and Ian's release from the police cells. Back at the manor an angry Colonel Bennett cautioned them. 'You could have jeopardised the whole operation here. You were overheard speaking German as you entered the pub.'

Geoffrey and Ian stood silently next to each other, facing Colonel Bennett.

'Security cannot be breached but I am a fair man. Considering your past record and after some deliberation I have decided to grant you a second chance. One more slip up, gentlemen, and you are RTU – returned to unit. That means Pioneer Corps. Understood?'

'Yes, sir.'

'Very well. It's back to training. You need to complete this morning's assignment. See these?' Bennett bent down to pick up the explosives at his feet. 'Your task is to hide these bloody explosives in something believable. It's got to past muster, gentlemen.'

'Yes, sir.'

'Dismiss!'

Geoffrey and Ian left the office. Outside they parted company. Geoffrey walked towards the kitchens. As he approached the building the smell of freshly baked bread filled his nostrils. He often stole down here foraging for extra rations after a gruelling night exercise, sometimes on his own, sometimes with the lads. The Colonel's instructions at the daily briefing that morning still rang in his ears.

Geoffrey half expected, half hoped, that *she* would be there. He didn't even know her name. From the kitchen doorway he saw her; her elegant hands not fit for domestic work. Bent over the massive iron cooking range, she rhythmically stirred a giant black pot of steaming liquid. Geoffrey surmised it was the lunchtime soup. He took in every detail, even noticing her jacket carefully draped over the back of a chair. The sleeves of her blouse rolled up, he didn't fail to take in her sensuous feminine shape as the fabric of her army skirt stretched tight against her thighs. His eye noted her slender legs in stockings down to her sensible army-issued shoes. She was suddenly aware of his presence and swung round. Her hair swept up into a bun revealed her slender neck, forming an ethereal necklace of unimaginable beauty.

'Good morning,' he ventured. He moved a few steps closer, his new rubber-soled boots lightly squished on the cleanly-swept stone floor. His stomach turned somersaults, his mouth ran dry. He took a few steps closer.

'Hello. You got out then,' she said, a slight smile parting her lips.

'Yes. It was all a big mistake and rather embarrassing.' He surveyed her for a second or two. 'Inexperienced country police officers.'

'I'll always remember the look on your face.' She failed to suppress a giggle.

'The police officers certainly won't forget. They nearly had a fit when the Colonel marched in with half a dozen senior military officers to claim us.'

She laughed, 'I did begin to wonder if you were a German spy.' His face fell.

'I'm teasing you Private … erm?' She wanted to be polite, but knew she was a little forward in her comments. She would never have spoken to a man like that in Denmark, but then here she was alone, no family or friends to answer to.

'It's Private Geoffrey Hart,' he said. 'But you can call me Geoffrey. I'm one of the fairly new ones here.'

'I've seen your lot across the parade ground.' It was a good start, better than the previous evening. At least she had noticed him.

'You don't have any spare bread by any chance do you?' he ventured.

'It's rationed but ...' She smiled again. Her eyes seemed mischievous, which he took as a cue of encouragement.

'It's for the latest exercise, please. We have to hide explosives in something.'

Without another word she turned, walked towards the larder and reached for a loaf from the row of bread along the shelf. 'Here. Take this. Is it big enough?' Her soft lilt betrayed an accent he couldn't place.

He nodded. 'Thank you.' His hand briefly brushed hers. She blushed. 'You're not from around these parts are you?' he risked.

'No.'

At that moment he imagined she was in his arms. She moved a step closer. His stomach knotted even tighter. The delicate scent of garlic from her breath now sweetened his senses.

'So, where are you from?' He fixed his gaze on the long, dark eyelashes framing her hazel eyes flecked with shards of green. He surmised she must be about eighteen or nineteen. That was irrelevant. He was lost to her.

'Denmark.' She whispered in a soft husky voice, her crimson lips pouting again. Unexpectedly, she touched his shoulder, picking off some fluff. 'It was a bit silly of your friend to speak German in the pub last night.'

'You looked beautiful last night.' He had to say it.

She blushed. 'You'd best get going. Take the loaf before they miss you out there.'

He, who didn't like taking orders from anyone, obeyed without hesitation. He turned and scurried out. Instinctively feeling her eyes piercing his back, he dared not turn. Her essence would haunt his dreams. Feelings of impatient infatuation welled inside. He would have to find an excuse to come here again, ask her out on a date. It had to be her. In that moment he knew he couldn't love anyone else, not ever.

He could have kicked himself. Still he didn't know her name.

By the end of the following week, Geoffrey's impatience was at breaking point. He hadn't told Ian about his encounter with the Danish girl in the kitchen. Ian would tease him mercilessly for not asking her out. Winning the wager of a packet of cigarettes was far from his mind. All he wanted was her. Even when he tried consciously to forget her, she penetrated his dreams. Ian was beginning to notice his restlessness but put it down to the pressure of intense training. That morning before breakfast, Geoffrey strode, almost ran, towards the kitchens. What if the other staff were there? Would he get even a moment to speak with her?

Lilian turned at the sound of footsteps on the kitchen floor. 'Oh, it's you again. Come for more bread?' This time, as he suspected, she wasn't alone.

'No, I've come to see you,' he hissed, beckoning her outside. She walked towards him and then leant against the doorframe of the outside buttery, waiting for him to speak. 'It's a week since I've been able to see you.'

'Is it?' She pretended to forget the time span.

He looked at her teasingly. 'You're really pretty, you know.'

'Oh, just pretty? Last week I was beautiful.' She patted down her apron as she moved confidently back inside to the long oak table, its edges worn and rough from eons of work. He glanced at the two piles of vegetables waiting to be prepared. He had to ask her or miss his chance forever. 'Er, would you like to, er, go out sometime soon? Saturday? It's my day off.'

'Well, that depends.'

'On what?' He raised his dark bushy eyebrows in concern. This wasn't going the way he had rehearsed for the last forty-eight hours.

'Whether I'm just pretty or beautiful.' She flicked her hair from her face and carried on peeling the carrots.

'You are, without doubt, the most beautiful woman I have ever met, with the prettiest of smiles.'

'And you are the smoothest of charmers. But ...' she held him in suspense for a few seconds longer. 'Yes then. You have a date.'

'I'll meet you on Saturday morning at eleven by the gates.'

She hesitated, momentarily thinking of Tom back in Denmark. He wouldn't approve of her going on a date with any man, let alone an Austrian, even if he was a refugee from Nazi oppression. But she was alone in England, and besides, she and Tom were not an item. She added: 'The future does depend on whether you want me only for my looks.'

'No, of course not. I want to get to know you better,' he replied seriously. Beneath her easy-going manners and relaxed pose she was a tough one with a free-spirit and an independent mind.

'Saturday it is then,' she confirmed. 'Shouldn't you be on some assault course or something at this time of day?' She looked down as her right hand scraped the blade of the knife along the next carrot. Then, slicing into it with practised skill, the blade thudded rapidly on the table.

He wanted to be in her presence longer and tried to distract her: 'I can't discuss my movements – even the training – you know that.'

'I guess if you tell me what you're doing you'll have to silence me forever, and there's only two ways to do that.' Still she didn't look up. Geoffrey knew he shouldn't ask but couldn't help himself. 'Really? And what's that?'

'The first is to slit my throat; the other is to kiss me.'

His face reddened, stood before her like a naïve schoolboy. All the while his stomach churned. He could barely feel his legs. He laughed nervously, 'This place is probably crawling with hidden devices recording our conversation. I bet they even know that I'm sweet on you.'

It was her turn to blush. 'You had better leave. They'll be missing you.' She put the knife down on the table and waited. Was she really expecting him to kiss her? He glanced around. They were momentarily alone. Trusting his instinct, he grabbed her and planted a kiss on her moist lips. His heart missed a beat, his being lost in a moment beyond the present. She gently pulled away. 'Now you'd better go,' she muttered, 'before we both get caught.'

'See you on Saturday,' he said as his parting shot. He found himself almost skipping outside. As he glanced back to catch one final glimpse of her she had moved on to the potatoes. Outside everything took on a clarity that hadn't existed before: the sky seemed bluer than blue, the air fresher. His eyes followed the individual lines of dark green ivy trailing down the building. Each twisted and turned through myriad others, one dependent on the other, neither able to pull apart without damage to themselves or the others. How like life they were, he thought. A wave of elation shot up his spine. He had a date with her – and a kiss to boot. Wow! But what a fool – he still hadn't asked her name.

❧

Sir Charles shuffled through the stack of papers on the floor in his temporary office in the Admiralty. Captain Henderson waited for him to finish moving bundles of them to alternative piles spread out in haphazard fashion across his desk. Henderson couldn't fathom how he could work in such chaos. Nothing much had changed over the years. Sir Charles' paunch was larger than ever and his braces were much more strained than when he had last seen him. This Captain Henderson put down to the life of a retired gentleman in Suffolk.

'Ah, this is what I was looking for,' declared Sir Charles, looking up and twiddling his moustache. The war was far from won and Sir Charles had been easily persuaded to come back into the circuit on a temporary basis. The Americans had entered the war and plans were being drawn up for the eventual invasion of Europe. In the meantime, there was much to be done on the intelligence front. As long as Sir Charles kept his other failings in check he would survive in the business. In reality, Captain Henderson wasn't sure it was a good idea to have him back but this time it wasn't his decision. Hugo as M had secured enough support and Henderson had reluctantly given way because of Sir Charles' sharp mind on matters of espionage.

'We can get down to business then,' stated Henderson.

'Yes, you now have my undivided attention. How's that stubborn young wife of yours?'

'Katharine's very well. Thank you. She knows I am in London, but not that I'm seeing you.' There was no need to distress her unduly.

'I understand. She's still on the old radio business?'

'Yes.'

'We are expanding the Radio Security Service, George. We are planning more Y stations up and down the coast and we'd like Katharine to co-ordinate bringing in the amateur radio hams. They will be the new recruits. There're a ready source and one which we used at the outbreak of war, if you remember.'

'I know. It has been decided that they'll need a week's training at Arkley.'

'I saw the memo from Hugo this morning when I arrived.'

'He and I would like Katharine to come up. Then the new recruits will work on the radio sets from home. They'll do the usual twelve-hour shifts, then send any noted transmissions via courier to Box 25. From there it's passed to Bletchley. That way the chain and network are both covered. We'd like her to start at the end of the month. She'll be given accommodation on site of course.'

'Very well. I'll prepare her.'

'Can you manage without her for a week?'

Captain Henderson shot him a look. He didn't appreciate Sir Charles' feeble attempt at humour. 'What do you take me for?'

Sir Charles chuckled, 'I still can't get used to the idea you're finally married.' He paused, then continued, 'There's some more news from Denmark, George. The situation is grave now that the Nazis have attempted to round up the Jews. Intelligence suggests that about 600 didn't get out. We're trying to establish where they've been taken. Most are thought to be in Theresienstadt. Do you have anyone who speaks fluent Danish?'

Captain Henderson paused, seated himself in the nearest chair, and leant forward. 'I do. There's a young girl working in the kitchens at Anderson Manor. She came over from Sweden, escaped Denmark on a fishing boat. She's also fluent in German. We've earmarked her for intelligence work at Wilton Park. Hugo saw to it – got her hooked on the ship over here. She hasn't started yet.'

'Good, if you get me her file I'll make sure she's detailed for you within three weeks.'

'I will ensure Hugo attends to it right away.'

'That's not all; there's more news from Denmark.' There was no easy way to break it to George. 'Jonathan's still alive.'

Captain Henderson's face froze, his body paralysed, except his heart which pounded like a piston. He tried not to show a reaction, his right hand thrust deep into his jacket pocket, fist clenched. 'Does Katharine know?'

'No.' Sir Charles moved to the drinks cabinet to pour them each a large brandy. 'Here. Take this. I know it was the last thing you were expecting to hear.' He passed him the tumbler. Captain Henderson flung his head back allowing the liquid to hit the back of his throat. It burned like the anger within him.

'We need to pull him out. Shortly after you returned from your last trip to Vienna, Hugo discovered his whereabouts in a forced labour camp near the Polish border. He arranged for him to be broken out. It was a devil of a job and he was in a terrible state, largely from his time in Dachau.'

'And Denmark? What on earth is he doing in Denmark?'

'To cut a long story short, Churchill's policy of setting Europe ablaze hasn't exactly been a success.'

'Indeed.' Henderson coughed.

'Hugo has been chewed out several times. He brought Jonathan back to England and after an assessment it was felt his previous extensive undercover experience could get things back on track to good effect. It took nearly a year of intensive rehabilitation from our clinic, but Jonathan showed signs of promise so we brushed up his training.'

'Brushed up his training? Wasn't that rather dangerous given his physical state, not to mention his psychological scars?'

In a rare gesture Sir Charles admitted failure. 'Unfortunately, we underestimated his mental scarring. But let me finish. Jonathan was in the earliest SOE group. We needed him in Denmark to provide us with a link to the Resistance. What harm could he do with that simple task? So two of them were parachuted in earlier this year, but only he survived the jump. He couldn't use his old identity so he's there as Hanns Faltitschek.'

'She mustn't know.' Henderson's fist tightened further in his pocket, his nails dug hard into the palm of his hand. What if deep down Katharine still loved Jonathan? He couldn't risk losing her to him. He wouldn't take that chance. 'She mustn't know,' he repeated, lips set and drained of colour. 'Katharine might ...' His voice trailed off.

'Of course, George. You have my word on it. I would not want to jeopardise my place in the "family". M needs me.'

Henderson knew that didn't always count for anything. Staring across the desk, he thought how subdued Sir Charles seemed in comparison to his old bombastic self. Maybe time had taught him a lesson in patience and civility. But could he be trusted on personal matters? Captain Henderson didn't really have any choice. 'Yes, you're accountable to M, but you forget yourself Sir Charles. I am head of foreign operations. You are ultimately answerable to me. Don't forget it. You need to pull him, Jonathan – and pretty damn quick. He is so unstable, he's a grave liability.'

'I agree, George. He's causing mayhem and the Resistance leaders have expressed deep concern. The sight of a Nazi uniform seems to send him crazy.'

'Who do you have to go in and pull him out?'

'I've already earmarked one of the new SOE recruits. A group of twenty-five of them is being trained at Anderson Manor, all originally refugees and fluent German-speakers. One of them happens to be Jonathan's nephew Günter, now Geoffrey Hart. We've decided he's the one for the job.'

'I will travel via Anderson Manor on my way back to Devon.'

'Leave it a couple of weeks, George, if you wouldn't mind please. He's about to go on special exercise at Portland Bill.

We need him dropped sometime early New Year. I'm finalising arrangements.'

'I think that's too late.'

'We can't do it sooner for logistical reasons. The Resistance is keeping Jonathan out of action for the time being.'

'Very well. I'll pay Geoffrey Hart a visit later in December to finalise. Is that all?' Captain Henderson stood up impatiently.

'Yes, George. Except – what do we do with him when he comes back?'

'That is my concern.' Henderson turned and walked towards the door. He reflected how events had not turned out as expected. If it was left to him, Jonathan wouldn't have been trained up – he wouldn't have made that misjudgment. What he had to do now was make sure Katharine never found out.

❧

That Saturday morning Geoffrey met Lilian by the gates of Anderson Manor as arranged. The grey November sky could do nothing to dampen his spirits. Having asked Ian about her, of course he had known her name all along. Ian had reluctantly conceded defeat and given him the packet of cigarettes from their wager.

'This is a romantic walk through the woods, Geoffrey,' said Lilian as she slipped her petite hand into his. They walked on, their feet rustling through fallen leaves. Overhead the trees had shed all but a few of their last remaining leaves; the ground below them a splash of autumnal colours.

'Aren't you a little cold, Lilian? Here, you can borrow my overcoat.' Geoffrey wasn't used to being romantic but knew it was what all girls dreamed of – a knight in shining armour. In his case it was more a refugee in uniform.

'No, I'm fine. Thank you.'

'There's an abandoned huntsman's hut in the woods. We can have our lunch there.'

He glanced at her; her eyes had a mischievous look: 'What? To have your wicked way with me?'

It wasn't what he was expecting. 'Oh no, certainly not. I wouldn't dream of it. Being with you is enough for me.' They continued along the path, following its bends and curves through the woods.

'Over there.' Geoffrey pointed to a tumbled down wooden shack slightly obscured by overgrown stinging nettles. He grabbed a stick. As they approached the door he beat back the worst of the dead nettles and brambles. Then he reached for Lilian's hand to help her. He pushed open the creaking door. Inside the hut, the air smelt damp and musty, a few cobwebs around the rafters. In the corner there was a stove with a rusty saucepan, under the window a table and two chairs; behind them, a sofa and single armchair. Geoffrey sank into the sofa and beckoned to Lilian. He reached into his rucksack for the food. They munched their way through the Spam sandwiches and sipped ginger beer.

'This is a rather splendid picnic Geoffrey. It must have cost a fortune.' She nestled a little closer to him.

Geoffrey grinned. 'I traded it for two packets of cigarettes.' Then added nervously: 'You're worth it. I could have got more but we can't expect venison on our first date!' He put his arm around her shoulder as they continued eating and chatting.

'If I didn't know better, I might think you were trying to seduce me,' she said.

'Don't you want me to?'

She stared him straight in the face. How he wanted to kiss her with passion. He wanted it more than anything else. Hadn't he dreamt about it every night back in the barracks? Her face moved within inches of his. He took the plunge, brought his lips to hers. She responded, her tongue exploring through his parted lips. Her mouth tasted sweet. The heat of his body pressed against hers sent a shiver of ecstasy through her. They rolled to the floor, entwined in a passionate embrace. Then he moved on top of her. Her soft breasts pressed through her blouse against his firm chest. With her thighs against his, her lustful heat drove him crazy. She disentangled herself, planted a kiss on his cheek and whispered, 'I want you but we ought to be getting back.' With a feeling of elation and yet regret that it hadn't gone further, Geoffrey took her hand and they walked back to Anderson Manor.

'Will you be my girlfriend?' he asked somewhat naïvely.

'You're a bit late on that score.' She felt his grip tense. 'I think you'll find, Private Geoffrey Hart, that I lost my heart weeks ago to ... a chap by the name of Günter Herz.'

'How did you know my original name?' He looked straight at her and knew he could love no one else.

'Now that would be telling,' she mused. He shot her a look. 'Alright then – I saw it on one of the labels of your pack. You must get that changed.' The fact that she had taken an interest in him was enough for him. He ventured to suppose that now he could be sure that she had same feelings for him. At the gates of the manor, he pecked her on the cheek and said goodbye.

'Till next week,' he called out as she dashed towards the auxiliary buildings.

Chapter 4

After two weeks of rough living and trekking north-west in Denmark, Hanns and Josephy finally reached the tiny inlet of Frederikshavn on the northern coast, some 300km from Vallø. The deceptively deep waters at points along this secluded stretch provided an ideal surfacing point for U-boats.

They had successfully linked up with the local coastguard who had offered them his bath for cleaning up and handed Hanns a Kriegsmarine uniform to try on for fit. Hanns was to board the U-boat as an ordinary seaman but carrying special documents. Waiting for the all-clear, he sat in the coastguard's kitchen scribbling on a scrap of paper. Josephy glanced over his shoulder. 'What are you drawing Hanns?'

Hanns slid his hand over it to cover it. He put his pencil down and smirked, 'the Smiling Shark.' Then muttered under his breath: 'Smile no more my little beauty. Your days are numbered.' Then he crumpled the drawing and stuffed it into his trouser pocket.

'What's that, Hanns? What did you say?'

'Nothing, Josephy. Just going over the plan in my head.'

'You have everything you need, yeah? Are you sure you're up to this?'

'Sure I am.' His head was swimming with thoughts of revenge. The mutilated corpses of his fellow agents murdered in the field and emaciated bodies of his inmates in Dachau haunted him day and night. His head pounded with it all. The bastards were going to pay. However long it took, they would get what was deserved.

'It's time to go.' Josephy placed his hand on Hanns' shoulder. 'But, my friend, I'm afraid I won't be coming with you. Not on this one.'

'What?' Hanns swung around.

'It's too risky, Hanns.'

'For who? You or your network? You're just like the others – no spine when the chips are down.'

Josephy wisely remained level-headed. 'You'll see it's all for the best. Besides, we trust you implicitly to do the job single-handedly and well.' He smiled. 'Come, off we go down to the harbour. They're waiting for you.'

Stepping out into the night, the eerie stillness added to Hanns' sad, pain-filled thoughts. Soon he heard the voices of the crew. Their shapes came into view, bent over loading the U-boat with basic supplies. He chuckled inside. You won't be needing all that, he thought. This little sucker isn't going far.

As he approached the scene the U-boat captain turned: '*Guten Abend*. Come!'

As Hanns neared him, the Captain spoke again: 'Herr Faltitschek … *Ja?*'

'Hanns Faltitschek, sir. Reporting for duty.'

'Good. I'm expecting you,' nodded the Captain. With Hanns' identity confirmed he looked over his shoulder to check they couldn't be overheard. 'Do you have the papers?'

'Yes, captain.'

'Very well, you are responsible for them until we are on the high seas.' He slipped a tiny bronze key into Hanns' hand: 'It's the only safe in the strong room at the back of the little beauty, near the engine room. You're sharing a bunk with Fritz. Now off and help the men. We depart in twenty minutes. Oh … one moment.' Hanns turned, his hand wrapped around the knife held in his pocket. 'Hanns, I was impressed with the reference from your former Commander. I look forward to having you on my vessel.'

'Thank you, Herr captain. It's an honour for me to serve under you.' Hanns' politeness hid a world of inner turmoil, slowly relaxing his grip on the knife. Revenge receded to the depths of his unconsciousness. Ahead of him the long, slim, grey-bellied whale-shape of the U-boat lay peacefully in the water. As Hanns climbed the ladder at its side the shark emblem appeared to be smiling directly at him, its dancing eyes beckoning him, challenging him. The tall skinny figure of Fritz ran along the narrow deck towards them. Stubble on his face attested to at least a day without shaving. A stale stench came from his unwashed body. 'Come, follow me,' he said to Hanns.

Inside the stuffy U-boat the air stank of the same terrible odour as Fritz's clothing. Hanns had smelt worse. He followed Fritz to their bunk: 'You'll be hot-bedding with me and Georg. We work in shifts. While Georg and I work, you sleep, then you and I work whilst Georg sleeps and so on. You get the picture.'

Hanns looked at the sleeping quarters. The beds ran almost the entire length of the aft compartment of the U-boat, interspersed with machinery. Stacked three high with barely 2ft between them, the narrow beds were no more than a wooden bench with a primitive curtain for privacy. The whole interior felt claustrophobic and damp. As he waited for Fritz to issue the next move, he focused his mind on the mission in hand. Instructions from the Admiralty in London had made it clear that documents relating to German weapons developments were on board. His task – to intercept and replace them with false papers. Looking down the narrow confines of the corridor, he momentarily pitied the other men. What a hell of a life banged up in this hole for weeks on end. How was he supposed to survive all the way to Ireland? But then he had other plans; this tub wouldn't last that long.

Hanns followed Fritz and two other seaman as they passed through the connecting bulkheads towards their post. Leaning against the cold iron hull of the U-boat, feeling the hum of the generators, he listened to the other seamen chatting. Then the deafening sound of the engines heightened as it plunged down, down, down. His stomach leapt to his throat. He tried to contain the urge to vomit. Bloody hell, he'd experienced nothing like this before.

'You alright, mate?' Fritz noticed Hanns turn as white as a sheet. 'I thought you were used to this.' He eyed Hanns suspiciously.

'Hungover. Eggs and bacon for breakfast. I think the eggs were a little off.' Fritz seemed reassured by his response. Hanns waited for the U-boat to finally level. He turned to Fritz: 'The Captain needs me. I'll be back shortly.'

'Sure. But don't forget lunch soon. It's gruel today. You wouldn't want to miss that!'

Hanns made his way through the U-boat to the sound of constant tap on metal. Banging himself a number of times, his head narrowly missed the ceiling. A living coffin, he thought; and a slow death trap. Reaching the engine compartment, he looked to the left. This was the door he needed, marked with a sign *Authorised Personnel only*. He twisted the large, round metal wheel to unlock it. Inside was complete darkness. Fumbling for the light switch, he finally illuminated the small cupboard. Sealed boxes lined the walls on the left. The writing was in Polish or some eastern European language he couldn't translate. But he needed no translator. The symbols on each indicated to him small arms. He didn't bother to open one to confirm. Besides, it might give the game away. He pulled out the crumpled drawing of the shark from earlier and took a few moments to scribble down the code. Then, looking up, he saw a safe right at the end. Just as he was about to open it, he turned, sure of footsteps behind him.

Nothing.

He tried to relax, took some deep breaths, but all he could breathe in was stale putrid air. He opened the small, square safe mounted half way up the wall. It was empty except for a packet of cigarettes and ball of string. This was not the U-boat with the documents on it that he was looking for. He deemed the mission a failure, shrugged his shoulders – that's life. He had to get off as soon as it surfaced again. Bending down again he slipped his wedge of papers in, locked the safe and turned to leave. Taking a piece of plasticine from his other pocket, he pressed the key to form a perfect mould. In a few hours it would harden leaving a permanent print that could be copied again. The U-boat Captain may have the master key but Hanns had a copy. He smiled to himself and made his way back to the other seamen in time for the lunchtime gruel.

That night at Portland Bill near Weymouth on the south coast of England, Geoffrey and his comrades were completing their final major mission in training before their assignments behind enemy lines. Crouched in the bushes opposite the fortress his mate Ian looked at him and their third companion Walter with indignation.

'How the hell do they expect us to scale that bloody wall?' moaned Ian. 'There's not a notch to grip.'

'Thanks for stating the obvious, Ian,' said Geoffrey. 'We've just got to work it out.'

'Yeah, but be rational Geoffrey. How can we break into the fortress and leave again without being detected? It's an impossible task. I'd like to see that major have a go. They're having a laugh on us.'

Geoffrey stared at the solid structure. 'And don't forget, even if we manage to get in, there's two battalions of infantry who haven't a clue we're coming in.'

'It shouldn't be too difficult,' declared Walter. 'A bit of lateral thinking and we're in.' Geoffrey and Ian had warmed to Walter Freud as soon as they had first met him. A grandson of the famous Sigmund Freud, he had a brilliant mathematical brain. He had also been in 87 Company of the Pioneer Corps, but enlisted straight from a year behind barbed wire in internment in Australia. He too had been head-hunted for special duties. Somewhat reserved at times, he was inclined to be sullen if he disagreed with the instructors. The instructors thought him a little insolent, prone to question orders and cut corners during exercises. Walter eyed the scene ahead. 'I reckon we can do it. We've got no choice but to navigate that wall.'

'Be my guest,' replied Geoffrey. 'I'm staying here. How will they know if we've done it or not anyway?'

'Because we'll leave a message inside. Are you up for it Ian? Geoffrey?'

'I tend to agree with Geoffrey. It's a bugger of a challenge. You're on your own Walter.'

'Alright chaps, you stay here and keep watch. Give a single owl hoot if there's danger, but don't for heavens sake give us away.'

'As if we would,' hissed Ian. In completely dark clothing, Walter moved out of the bushes and crept forward. Soon his shadow was out of sight. Ian passed Geoffrey his flask of whisky, 'Here have a swig of this to keep warm. Either he'll be back in ten minutes having failed miserably or we're in for a long night.'

Two hours later there was no sign of Walter. Geoffrey presumed he had abandoned them. 'Let's give up, Ian, and go back to base,' he said. 'I don't know what's happened to him, but he's probably been captured and we're wasting our time out here. It's an impossible challenge anyhow. Our instructors are having a laugh.' Ian took no persuasion as they began their amble back to billets.

Colonel Bennett was seated inside the dimly-lit main hall waiting for the groups to return. He looked up as Geoffrey and Ian approached.

'Well, well gentlemen. What's kept you?' They glanced at each other puzzled, feeling like naughty schoolboys standing in front of him. 'Walter's been back long ago. I've sent him off for a shower. Where've you been?'

Geoffrey was quick-thinking, 'We got lost around the back of the fortress, sir. We worked out that no one could possibly enter it from any angle.'

Colonel Bennett cleared his throat, raised his monocle, bluntly declaring, 'What the hell are you made of? By God, Walter managed it. The only one who did. Out of twenty-five men, he was the only one who succeeded. He has what it takes, gentlemen.'

'Yes, sir,' Geoffrey and Ian replied in unison.

'He penetrated the control room at the centre, right

under the noses of the guards, then filled the anti-aircraft guns with plasticine "explosives". Brilliant! Absolutely brilliant,' he chuckled. 'He left completely undetected. God knows how he did it, but he did. That takes initiative. Dismiss, gentlemen and get some sleep. Up at 5.30 as usual tomorrow morning.'

Geoffrey had to hand it to Walter. A fellow Austrian but, for all his brains, Walter had more guts and charisma than him.

❧

On his return from Portland Bill, Geoffrey found Anderson Manor more or less deserted apart from his small group of Continentals. He assumed most of the other recruits were already on special missions or waiting in a temporary holding camp. Tension was rising amongst Geoffrey's group. It couldn't be long for them now. His first call was to the kitchens, but Lilian was long gone. He rushed straight to the porter's lodge. Two letters awaited his return. One was from the Red Cross, only the second letter he had received via them during the war. He knew this would have to do with his parents. The other he didn't recognise the handwriting but had the stamp of the military censor. He opened the first. It was from Switzerland, the content brief:

'We are sorry to inform you that your father's whereabouts are unknown. As soon as we have any further information we will contact you again.'

It was dated a week ago. He picked up the second. The scent reminded him of Lilian. He was desperate to see her again, couldn't stop thinking of her, and he could barely concentrate on day-to-day training. He knew they would be separated for quite some time once he was sent abroad but they didn't have to be apart now. Geoffrey hurriedly slid his finger through the envelope. It was from her:

Dearest Geoffrey, please accept my apologies for this brief letter. I can't tell you any details, you understand. I think of you always and can't wait to see you again. You fill my life with joy and now I miss you terribly. As soon as I have some leave I will let you know. Love and kisses, your sweet Lilian xx.

His heart sank. Was there any way he could find out where she was? He sat on the edge of his bed, pen and paper to hand to reply to her. He scribbled furiously to catch that morning's postal collection:

My dearest beautiful Lilian, it pains me to be separated from you. You mean so much to me. Please be careful with the risks of the war and all that. I am desperate to see you again. Most here have all gone off and I expect it will soon be my turn. The place is not the same without you. I miss you and want to see you soon. Write to me often. I long for your letters and you even more. All my love G.

He folded the letter and slipped it into an envelope, marking it c/o British army censor. Ian entered the room, slinging his rucksack on the bed. He began emptying the contents into the bedside cabinet. 'You seem in low spirits, Geoffrey. What's wrong, mate? You can tell me.'

Geoffrey glanced up. 'It's Lilian. She's been posted somewhere and I've no idea where. I miss her terribly. I can't live without her.'

'Steady on – don't be so dramatic. It's your first real love. One girl's pretty much the same as another.'

'You don't understand. This is different. I feel it in my soul.'

Ian suppressed a laugh. 'You feel it all right, but not in your soul. I ought to be more understanding but here … have this.' He passed him another envelope. 'It came for you this morning. It looks like a female hand. Maybe it's from her.'

Geoffrey tore it open.

'Well what does it say? Tell me Geoffrey.'

'Wait a minute please.' Geoffrey raised his hand. His eyes scanned the page quicker than a dart hitting a board. 'She's got a day's leave at the end of the week. Yippee!' He flung the letter in the air and with it all cares to the wind. 'I've got to meet her. We're supposed to be on that death ride exercise, the one designed by the Gauleiter. Damn it! Cover for me, Ian.'

'Calm down. Of course I will. We've plenty of time to think of an excuse. But remember, Geoffrey – this time make sure it's a memorable one for both of you. Something that Lilian will remember for the rest of her life.' Geoffrey didn't miss the twinkle in his eyes.

'If you're saying what I think you're saying, I'll thank you to mind your own business sometimes, Ian.'

'Are you up for another wager?' he asked, 'I bet you another packet of Woodbines that you sleep with her.'

'No Ian! I won't wager on her again. I love her and won't be disrespectful to her name or person. I shouldn't have done it the first time.'

'Gosh! Things have changed,' he replied.

The sudden barking orders of the sergeant major outside stopped them in their tracks. 'Gentlemen! Parade ground!'

Geoffrey and Ian rushed out, adjusting their caps just in time to join the back of the parade.

Later that day, at Wilton Park near Beaconsfield in Buckinghamshire, Lilian shuffled her chair nearer the equipment and slipped on her earphones. The cell on the other side of the wall held two German POWs. Bugging devices had been fitted to the light fittings in each of the prisoners' cells. Intelligence was vital. Her job was to listen to their conversations, tape anything that sounded relevant and pass it back to Colonel Brown, head of Intelligence Section. There were a dozen, maybe more, German-speaking refugees in the complex working as listeners. Their fluency in German and knowledge of the dialect were proving invaluable to the British government. Lilian had started out in the main office, typing up POW reports. Earlier that week she had been moved to the listening post when one of the other refugees had been moved off site elsewhere. From the conversations thus far she had gathered that the two men in the cell she was tracking were high-ranking Germans: a U-boat commander and Luftwaffe pilot. It was the practice of British military intelligence to keep one of each service in a cell to glean better information. Thus far they had only exchanged mere niceties, both respecting the other's authority. At lunchtime that day they had been interrogated again by British officials. Lilian's shift began at two o'clock, immediately after they had been returned to their cell. Through the hidden microphone she heard one of them clear his throat. She pressed the button to start the tape recording.

'How was it?' he said in German.

'I didn't give them a clue,' came the reply. 'I pretended I didn't understand.'

'Good.'

'How about you?'

'Of course not.'

'Did they ask you about the documents?'

'No, they don't appear to know that their safe-keeping has been given to 9th Flotilla. Their intelligence seems flawed. No one will ever suspect the Kreigsmarine are involved in this one.' There was a lengthy silence. Then the same man cleared his throat again and continued in German. 'They'll follow the Danish coast. Enemy shipping can't get even close. Three will be leaving within this month, but the documents are on only one of them.'

'Doenitz is a genius to involve the fleet. No one knows which is the one.' There was another silence. 'I could do with a bloody cigarette.'

'Yeah. Me too. At least the British are decent enough to give us one at breakfast and before bed. It's better than nothing. How long do you think they are going to keep us banged up in here?'

'Don't know, but fancy a game of cards?'

'Sure.'

German U-boats are being used, thought Lilian. She held her breath. Denmark! That was all she gathered in that session. It was enough. She stopped the tape, rewound it, took it off its speel and placed it in a large brown packet. Now she understood why she had been earmarked for this post. Strategically, her country was important to the Reich.

Leaving the building, she crossed in the front of the White House, walked along the paths around the expanse of green lawn towards the commanding officer's wing. Three days to go and she would see Geoffrey again. Her heart raced with excitement at the thought. How could she possibly wait? In her mind she counted the hours and minutes before she would be him again.

෨෯

It was Katharine's final day at Arkley. The house had been requisitioned by the Special Intelligence Service for matters relating to secret radio interception and transmissions. She had completed a week of training up new amateur radio hams to run Y-stations up and down the coast. Intercepting enemy radio transmissions and U-boat messages was a high priority. Some of the codes were sent back to Arkley to be dealt with by the central bureau of the Radio Security Service; others were sent elsewhere, but Katharine was not privy to that information. That morning, whilst relaxing over a cup of tea at breakfast, she was handed a telegram from Sir Charles. Her eyes rapidly scanned the black typed words:

'Coming to see you. Arkley. 10 o'clock. C.'

Whatever it was of importance, it couldn't be dealt with by letter or phone. Now her train journey back to North Devon might be delayed. How she detested the way he had master-minded her marriage to Jonathan! It had seemed like a real whirlwind romance straight out of a novel, but in the end the relationship had caused her much pain. Sipping a second cup of tea, she decided to turn the situation around and ensure the meeting went her way. Maybe Sir Charles could help her after all. There was a delicate issue which had been bugging her for a couple of weeks and it was something she couldn't possibly discuss with Captain Henderson. Sir Charles was her only chance. Maybe fate was about to deal her a fair hand. She relaxed and continued reading *The Times*. Half an hour later she heard his voice down the corridor long before he came into the room. Nothing's changed, she smiled to herself.

'Ah, my dear Katharine!' Sir Charles bumbled towards her, wearing the same blue suit as the day she first met him. He had dispensed with his usual colourful braces. Katharine stood up, extending her hand. 'Good morning, Sir Charles. How lovely to see you.' She lied, gritted her teeth through a charming smile.

'Long time no see, Katharine. You are looking very well, my dear. And how's that husband of yours?'

'George is keeping well, thank you. How's retirement and life in the country?'

'Dreadful. I'm bored out of my mind for hours on end. Rationing has put a stop to the endless rounds of aimless social chit-chat and tea parties. Aimless as they were, at least I mixed with my own. And now I've been stuffed on some committee full of dithering idiots. It's not my idea of retirement. Bit of part-time work I was told. As if I need it. I've even had to take up pig-keeping for the war effort! Come, let's go into the billiard room. I've been assured we won't be disturbed there.' Following him down the corridor, they passed a number of rooms with operators, hearing the click of dials, various radio equipment stacked on desks and against the walls. In the heart of the countryside, it was an ideal place for clandestine operations.

'Here,' Sir Charles pushed open the door to the billiard room, allowing her the courtesy of passing through first. The oak-panelled room was traditional, a few empty glasses of parsnip wine left on the fireplace. The strong pungent smell of tobacco hung in the air. 'Come sit by the fire,' he motioned. 'It's not lit at this time of day, but we might as well be comfortable, ah?' He proceeded to sit his vast bulk in the opposite high-back leather chair facing Katharine. He lost no time in getting to the point.

'You know me, my dear. I never beat about the bush. Let's get to the point.' He coughed before continuing, 'I need a little help. It has to do with radio equipment.'

Katharine raised her eyebrows. 'Can't you do it through normal channels?'

'You always were damn forthright and irritating with your questions.'

She eyed him carefully, noticing the pulse in his neck quickening. 'We understand each other very well by now, Sir Charles. We're not here for niceties.'

'I need an extra set of transmitters and soon. But I can't have them traceable to stores. All I can say is this – it's for the Resistance.'

'Very well,' she replied with apparent obedience, knowing she needed his help in return.

He made as if to get up. 'There is just one thing,' she interrupted him. He relaxed back into the chair, the leather creaking under his weight. 'Go on.'

'I've intercepted some irregular transmissions recently. They're coming from U-boats in the Atlantic, thought to be from the fleet knocking out Allied shipping and supply convoys. By the time they've hit the ships, it's too late to depth-charge them. They scurry off and are virtually undetectable, except … I think I have located a series of submarine pens along the French coast at Brest.'

'Well done, girl. By God, you're as brilliant as ever! Don't worry, I'll see to it you get a medal for this.'

'I'm not interested in medals.' For a second her face looked unexpectedly innocent like a child's. 'The pens at Brest aren't the whole story. There's movement around the Danish coast.'

'You always did have more for me,' he beamed, inclining forward, his shirt buttons straining over his paunch.

'I want to confide something in you which mustn't get back to George,' she said. Sir Charles nodded his agreement. Katharine continued, 'I've been picking up something off the Danish coast. Again, it's U-boats rather than surface shipping. You might think me mad, Sir Charles, but I suspect it could have to do with Jonathan.'

'Jonathan?'

'Yes.'

'But that's absurd, my dear. He's dead. You know that. A death certificate was issued for him.'

She peered at him over the top of her glasses. 'I know it seems irrational. But what if?'

Sir Charles knew better than to dismiss her notion. He would hear her out. 'So why do you think it has to do with him?'

'The captain of this particular U-boat transmitted back to base that a new member of their crew has been behaving rather oddly, shouting disjointed things in his dreams. Each dream is exactly same – he's killing in horrific manner. It appears from the last transmission that they are monitoring him but taking no action.'

'But why Jonathan? I'm not sure how useful this piece of information is to us.'

'Call it intuition.'

'I can't act on intuition Katharine. You know that.'

'But all your agents act on intuition,' she watched him levelly, knowing he couldn't deny some truth in her statement. She had wondered whether it was wise to reveal everything to him, but now she had no choice or risk her sanity. 'They're not taking him seriously, but in his dream he shouts just once about being a doctor, repeats the same words as the very night he was taken from our apartment in Vienna.' The tremor in her voice prompted a rare gesture from Sir Charles. He leant across to her and touched her hand. 'Don't distress yourself. Take your time. Tell me. I am listening.'

Her lip quivered. 'He's said, he's said … "How dare you barge into our apartment. We're both British. You have no jurisdiction over us." Those were his exact words, Sir Charles, *the exact words* when he was taken that night. It isn't a coincidence. And as he was dragged away he promised me he would be back. It's him – I just know it. He is alive, believe me.'

Sir Charles rarely reacted to any situation but a shiver ran up his spine, raising the hairs on the back of his neck. He gave nothing away but asked: 'What do you want me to do?'

Katharine began to breathe more calmly: 'I can't go through the usual channels. I need to know if it really is him. If so, George might … well you know him, he wouldn't let Jonathan come between us a second time. I never did know whether or not George had a hand in Jonny's disappearance. I need to know if he was in any way responsible.'

'That I don't know – honestly. But we do know that it was Susie who betrayed Jonathan and you avenged her yourself. Look, you know as well as I, that things happen in the Secret Service that are for the security of this country. I don't need to tell you that. George is a good man, and one that would put duty before anything. Remember – there was a time when he put duty before the woman he loved.'

'Yes.' She seemed distant, far away in another world or place. An eternity of silence passed between them. It was she who broke it: 'Sir Charles, please. I need your help. I have no access to files. George keeps me out of the frame these days.'

'That makes two of us, my dear,' he smiled. 'Still, from what I understand, unofficially of course, he has a couple of operatives in the region at the moment. However, my sources tell me they have lost proper contact, causing quite a fuss in his department. They're a couple of days overdue with their update.'

'It all fits. Don't you see?'

'Well, no dear, I don't, but let's say I do. What do you want of me?'

'I need your help in getting me out there. According to the last transmission, the U-boat is heading for Norway and then the south coast of Ireland.'

'I can't agree to that. You're needed here for the radio service. You can't possibly disappear and be chasing all over the place. George would be the first to notice. I have another suggestion. I am owed a favour or two. Let me organise an independent excursion with a first-rate agent. I think I have just the person for the job. I have come to see you as family, my family. I may not still hold the title of M, but I have kept a watchful eye as any Mother might. Now, if you'll excuse me my dear, I really have to be going.'

As they left the room together, she reminded herself that she had to be patient. Give him time to get on with the job. She hadn't expected him to be quite so co-operative without a fight. He seemed to have mellowed in his old age.

Friday could not come quickly enough. Geoffrey ran all the way to the railway station, arriving just as the train pulled in. He dashed through the ticket hall and onto the platform, straining above the heads of the crowd. Most were men in army uniform. Passengers hung out of the train windows, furiously waving, scanning the waiting crowd in a vain hope to see the person meeting them. Geoffrey could barely contain his excitement and hoped Lilian had made that train. He wanted his face to be the first she saw when she alighted. Moments later she was stepping out of the carriage, dressed in an emerald green coat and hat.

'Lilian!'

'Geoffrey!' They pushed through the jostling crowd, flinging themselves tightly into each other's arms. The separation hadn't lessened what he felt for her, nor she for him. It seemed a lifetime since he'd last hugged her.

'Come, let's not waste any time,' he said, grabbing her hand. 'I've packed a picnic. Let's head off for the woods.' They walked. Half an hour later they reached the edge of the woodland.

'Lilian, it's so good to be with you again. I haven't stopped thinking about you.'

'Me neither.'

'I suppose you can't tell me where you're stationed?'

'No but don't take it personally. Anyway, it's not a million miles away. We can meet on our days off as long as we coincide our leave times.'

Geoffrey suddenly glanced up at the menacing dark clouds. 'It looks as if it's going to pour at any minute. We'd better run for cover. Let's head for the hut before we get wet.' Without warning a single clap of thunder broke the heavy electrified air. The rain came down with a vengeance. They ran hand in hand through the trees, the rain drenching them in a matter of minutes. They came to the woodman's hut, still as deserted as the last time they had been there. The door creaked as Lilian pushed it open. She shook the rain off her coat. Geoffrey followed.

'My hat and coat are ruined,' she said.

'Here, it will be okay. Let me put them on the chair by the stove. I'll light the fire to dry them out and warm us up.' He rummaged at the bottom of his bag for matches and lit the stove. He sank into the sofa and reached into his kit bag for two blankets and a small towel. 'You'd better take off your wet stuff Lilian and dry your hair with this towel. Then you can put the blanket around you. And … I won't look while you're changing, I promise.'

Lilian removed her soaked clothes, wrapped the blanket around her body, then hung the wet garments over the back of another chair.

'Come and sit with me,' gestured Geoffrey patting the seat beside him. 'As I said – we'll soon warm up.' Lilian obeyed. He passed her a sandwich and poured tea from a flask.

'This is a new situation for me,' she said looking at him with a hint of amusement and tenderness.

He laughed, 'So you don't usually undress in the company of young men and shelter in huts.'

'No.' She shuffled a little closer to him, their thighs almost touching.

'It seems like ages since we were last here, Lilian. I have missed you terribly.'

'And I you. Would you like to … you know what?'

'What?'

'Kiss me.' Her pouted lips cried out for it. Her expectant eyes indicated she might even be ready for more than that.

Geoffrey was out of his depth. 'The lads and I … back at base, we do chat about girls and things. Most say a man should take it slowly, be respectful.'

'So that's a no then?'

'Not exactly.' He could feel the heat of her body through the thin blanket. Resisting her was impossible.

She shifted slightly to turn to him. The blanket dropped a touch off her shoulders to reveal her cleavage. 'It's time you stopped listening to your mates and kiss me,' she mused. Seconds later her lips pressed hard against his. The intense passion of the connection surged through his body and soul. Then he drew back.

'Kiss me again,' she murmured. 'We could be in the field tomorrow and dead within a week. I don't want to die without being kissed properly by you. Touch me.' The blanket slipped further off her body. She stood up, her shapely, youthful body in perfect form before him. He wanted her, and she him. Now there was no holding back. Geoffrey moved both hands over her soft breasts. The nipples became erect under his touch. The delicate round mounds gently rose and fell with each of her breaths. The sight of her breasts sent a mixture of nerves and love coursing through him. He bent down, kissing each breast in turn. Carefully, she unbuttoned his shirt, the one piece of clothing that had remained dry under his thick overcoat. 'You won't need this,' she whispered. She slipped her hands over his chest, caressing him, then down towards his trousers.

'But ...' he protested, desperately wanting her yet trying to hold back.

'Ssh. With the war on we don't know what the future holds. Love me, kiss me.'

His shirt off, the heat of her skin pressed against his sent his mind spinning. Her tongue, gentle and hot, now explored his mouth. 'God, I love you,' he mumbled. She wrapped her legs around him and he thrust deep inside her. Their passionate lovemaking lost all sense of time. Moments later he peaked too soon. Exhausted, he collapsed back on the couch. Lilian stroked his chest as she lay in his arms. That date would be forever etched in his memory.

At Anderson Manor, Geoffrey strolled towards Colonel Bennett's office, sensing that this was the day he would be told about his posting. Why else had been summoned so early that morning? He knocked and waited. With months of training completed and the final exercise successfully behind him, he and his colleagues were at the peak of physical fitness. Maintaining it was a priority and thankfully took away from the hours of boredom whilst he waited for his mission. Adrenalin still ran high; the tension and uncertainty of not knowing when and where was beginning to take its toll. His mate Ian had just been given his assignment, but all Geoffrey was allowed to know was that it was somewhere in the Adriatic. Ian had left the previous day, but no updates on him were permitted for security reasons.

'Come in.'

Geoffrey entered. It wasn't the colonel who faced him across the room but Captain Henderson. 'Hello Geoffrey. Come in. Close the door would you please and have a seat.' He motioned to the chair in front of the desk, then sat down himself. He cleared his throat. 'You must be aware by now from the nature of your training the kind of missions that you may be asked to undertake.'

'Yes sir.'

'Good. I have had instructions from the Admiralty. Your mission has come up. It's a lone drop. Does that bother you?'

'No sir.'

'Good.' He reached into his pocket, pulled out his cigarette case and offered one to Geoffrey.

Geoffrey took one. 'Thank you sir.' Henderson passed him a lighter, then lit a cigarette for himself.

'You are to be dropped into Denmark at the end of the week. It will be a full moon so there should be some light if the skies are clear. The drop zone will be on South Zealand.

We need you to pull out an agent. You're to head for the Vallø Castle estate near the east coast of Köge Bay. Once you've made contact with the Resistance, they will take you to our man. They are expecting you.' He paused. In the momentary silence he thought about how he would break the news carefully. 'Only …' he eyed him levelly. 'This agent is a special case. He's Hanns Faltitschek, but of course that's not his real name.' Henderson took a puff on his cigarette then continued. 'It's actually your uncle, Jonathan.'

In the silence between them Geoffrey's head pounded, his thoughts so loud it was as if they would burst out. 'Uncle Jonny?'

'Yes.' Captain Henderson paused a moment longer to allow the news to sink in. 'We tracked him to a forced labour camp, having spent months in Dachau concentration camp. We broke him out, lost two men in the process, but we did get him out. Naturally he was in a hell of a state. We brought him back to full health and trained him up. He was dropped into Denmark last year. But now it appears that he's not well again and that's where you come in. We haven't been able to pull him out because he boarded a U-boat. But we understand it is heading back to Denmark and we want you to intercept him once he gets off. Here …' Captain Henderson passed a set of maps and codes across the desk. 'But there's one very important thing. Katharine must not know he is still alive, understood?'

'Yes sir.'

'If all else fails, she must never find out.'

Geoffrey watched as Captain Henderson flicked the final bit of grey ash from his cigarette into the ashtray on the desk. 'There's a second part to this assignment.'

Geoffrey raised his eyes, still staring intently at Captain Henderson. 'You are to board one of the U-boats of the

9th Flotilla at Frederikshavn. They are an unmistakable fleet – their emblem is "the Smiling Shark". The U-boat is heading for the coast of Ireland, we think, with important scientific and military documents on board. Your job is to retrieve them.'

'Yes sir.'

'That's it in a nutshell. Any questions?'

'No sir.'

'Very well then, that's all for today Sergeant Hart.'

'Sergeant sir?'

'Yes. You've just been promoted. Good luck.'

'Thank you sir.' Geoffrey stood up and made his way to the door. Inside his feelings were a mixture of excitement and trepidation, but he would do his best for King and adopted country.

Chapter 5

Second week of January 1944

Seated inside the ramshackle hut in the woods not far from Anderson Manor, Geoffrey turned to Lilian. Her youthful face lifted his spirits. He slipped an arm tenderly around her shoulders, his other hand moved to clasp hers. His emotions were mingled with melancholy that this would be their last time together for a while. He couldn't tell her he was being posted the following day. He decided to say nothing and savour the moment of their last time together for a while. Life was fragile, especially in wartime, but deep inside he felt immortal. She appeared relaxed, not suspecting anything. Geoffrey reached into his pocket, 'Lilian, my darling. Here, there's something I want you to have.'

She looked surprised, glancing down to see the silver brooch in his palm. Its dainty cut diamonds, set in the shape of a bow, were quite exquisite. 'Geoffrey!'

'My mother gave it to me just before I left Austria. I want you to have it. I love you Lilian and haven't stopped thinking about you. In the days when we're apart, you can remember me by it.'

'Thank you. I will treasure it beyond belief,' she smiled, touched by his romanticism. 'But why now?' Suddenly she drew back, concerned that he was going away.

'Ssh, don't worry, my love. It's true my course has nearly finished, but we don't have to worry about that yet. Don't panic. Here, come closer.' Hugging up to him gave her reassurance and comfort. She nestled her head into his chest. He began to caress her arm, then moved his hand gently from her shoulder down towards her chest, slipping it into her blouse. She didn't resist. Her breasts felt warm and soft, the nipples becoming erect under his touch. She groaned in pleasure as she became aware from a glance of the excitement swelling in his trousers. He turned her face towards him, kissing her firmly on the lips. She clung to him. Feeling his hardness against her thigh, she began unbuttoning his flies as he slipped off her blouse. Her warm flesh against his chest sent a thrill down his spine. He ran his hands gently down her legs, parted them and climbed on top of her. She relaxed beneath him. Then he was inside her; the excitement like a dam that had been waiting to burst since the first time they made love. This time, for him, the physical connection thrusting deep within her felt more passionate than the first. The warmth of her body melded with his into one union. Groaning as she nibbled his bottom lip, he suddenly felt her quiver. She was crying. He thrust harder and harder. Finally satisfied he withdrew, holding her tight in his arms. With her face against his chest, she suddenly looked up, tears still in her eyes, 'Oh Geoffrey, I want this moment to last forever.'

'Is that why you are crying?'

She nodded.

'One day, it will,' he said.

'Take me with you,' she whimpered.

'You know I can't do that. And we mustn't speak about it. Ssh.' He ran his hand down her naked back, feeling her relax again beneath his touch. Bending forward, he pecked her on the forehead. She noticed that now his eyes had a boyish twinkle, as if he craved danger.

'You scare me sometimes.' She spoke so softly. 'Why do you have to be brave? Why can't you be a conscientious objector?' She felt his body tense.

'I can't sit back and let others fight this war. You of all people should know that.'

'Let's not argue, Geoffrey. I hate it.'

He began to stroke her forehead. 'One day we will be together. You have to trust me on that.' It was hollow reassurance. Neither knew what the future held, least of all him, being assigned to hazardous duties

At 8 a.m. deep under the North Atlantic, the commanding officer's voice resounded through the U-boat. 'Action stations! Action stations!'

All sense of time and place had been lost to the crew. It seemed like they'd been underwater for several days but actually it was thirty-six hours maximum. Hanns scrambled to his feet from the narrow bunk he shared on rotation with two others. Sleep had been fitful during the break off watch. The last part of the journey had been less than smooth. Days without water for washing, Hanns felt the grime engrained in his clothing, the stubble on his face now an unkempt beard. He had become accustomed to the stench, every man on board in the same situation as him. After several days at sea, the sweat of the men had turned to condensation dripping down the iron walls of the monstrous tomb.

'Prepare to surface,' the order echoed through the U-boat. Hanns made his way to the control room where the tall lanky figure of Fritz stood with shoulders hunched, arms wrapped around the observation periscope checking for enemy shipping. The bow of the U-boat began its push upwards towards the surface. The sea around the coast of Ireland could be rough at the best of times. That day was no exception. The U-boat rocked and dipped on the choppy waves as it neared the coastline of Galway Bay. Fritz turned to Hanns. 'You're needed on deck, mate.'

Hanns climbed the ladder. The fresh air instantly hit his lungs, invigorating his spirits and clearing his heavy head. He had missed it cooped up inside the U-boat for so long. The wind blew through his dishevelled hair. The voice of a fellow seaman called across to him: 'Starboard side! Watch on the starboard beam for enemy destroyers.' The U-boat headed for Inishmore, the largest of the Aran Islands off Galway. The high sheer west-facing cliffs of the island loomed above them. Cruising along the length of the island, they steered towards a secluded bay where they could anchor. The men of the island could already be seen standing on the shoreline waiting to ferry them in. All ordinary-seamen scrambled to line the deck, having changed their leather tan deck shoes for pampooties, the soft calf-skin moccasins for going ashore. Then they descended the ladders into the waiting curraghs, the lightweight canvas-covered boats. The special boats were coated in tar and designed to withstand the rough seas of the region. Along the port side of the U-boat, a chain of eight men had begun passing boxes down the line into the curraghs. Momentarily lowering his binoculars, Hanns glanced aft to see the tenth crate being loaded into another curragh. He gritted his teeth. *Bastards!* Trading weapons for fresh water and fish was no justification for their survival, he thought. Hanns suspected the crates were destined for insurgent Republicans in Northern Ireland, but as yet he had no proof. As soon as he did, the crew would pay with their lives. *They would die.* In the meantime, he would observe, take in everything and wait for his moment to strike.

'Hanns!' Fritz's voice cut through his thoughts. 'It's time to go ashore!'

'Ay, ay mate.' Hanns had already slipped on his pampooties, having carefully hidden his own deck shoes by wedging them behind a toilet in the Heads. The hollowed soles of his deck shoes concealed a tiny camera issued by Sir Charles' special outfitters prior to his parachute drop. Initial disappointment that there had been no military documents to photograph on board gave way to optimism that he was about to stumble upon something equally significant.

'We've been given the local harbourmaster's office to clean up and shave,' said Fritz. 'And don't forget – later there's a Hooley! See you in Mad Mick's place. It should be quite a spree.'

'Yes, mate.'

'Oh, and before we leave tomorrow morning there's a special treat in store for us. The local women have knitted us Aran sweaters. It's a custom. We'll damn well need them for the journey back.' He gave a cursory nod towards the conning tower. 'She becomes a freezing tomb in wintertime. See you later.'

'Yeah, Fritz. Till later.' Hanns climbed over the side of the U-boat and into a curragh to join six other crewmen. Pulling up the hood of his grey, oiled jacket against the chill wind, he stared ahead towards their destination.

That evening, Hanns made his way to Mad Mick's. He entered the bar, thick with tobacco smoke and ringing with raucous laughter. In one corner stood an old man playing Irish music on his fiddle. At a tap on the shoulder, Hanns turned. 'Hello Fritz,' he said.

'Got your woman yet?' Fritz smirked through drags on a cigarette.

'No. I've just arrived.'

'Take your pick. If she likes the look of you, you get lucky. There's plenty to choose from.' Fritz's breath was laden with the smell of stout. Hanns wondered what the women got out of the deal. His eye was caught by a slender girl with long ginger curls glancing in his direction. She's the one for me, he thought. 'See you later Fritz,' he murmured.

Hanns pushed his way directly towards her. She smiled all the while as he came up to her.

'Hello there,' she said, her voice surprisingly well-educated. 'How are you today? Are you from the boat?' Hanns nodded. She reached for a glass from the nearest table and passed it to him. Hans threw back his head, gulping the stout down his throat. She seemed impressed.

She took the glass from him. 'Fill this again, please,' she asked the barman, then handed it straight back to Hanns. Her eyes signalled for him to follow. They jostled their way through the drinkers towards the staircase at the back of the pub. As if seeking reassurance, Hanns thrust his right hand into his trouser pocket, feeling the gold cufflinks chink. They were still there. Under his breath he thanked Sir Charles profusely for his foresight. They might come in handy as a bribe or to soften a contact. As he went upstairs he wondered why she offered her services to rough seaman. She opened one of the bedroom doors to reveal a modest room with a low ceiling furnished with a double bed, single wardrobe, cabinet and fringed rug on the floor.

'May I know your name?' he asked.

'Elena.' She leant forward to switch on the lamp beside the bed. Its dim light couldn't penetrate the black-out curtains.

'A beautiful name for a beautiful woman.' Hanns meant it.

'Thank you.' She closed the door. Hanns looked around the room. Above the bed hung a picture of the Cliffs of Moher crudely painted in watercolours. On the window ledge a single bowl of scented lavender provided the only feminine touch to the room. Silently Elena approached him. He stood still as she wrapped her arms around him, moving her hands down his back. At first he flinched at human touch, not used to acts of tenderness. Then she felt the tension ease in his shoulders. Somehow she sensed he needed time to take things slowly. Taking his hand, she led him to the bed and began unbuttoning his shirt. Quietly she stripped him naked, gasping at the red lesions lacerating his flesh. Although healed, the sight filled her with pity. What terrible suffering he had endured. She undressed herself, conscious of his tortured nakedness, desperate to show him human kindness. He watched her, not moving, not signalling his consent, just staring back at her. Then feeling her gentle therapeutic touch, he began to respond to her. Looking at her supple mounds of perfect flesh lying beside him, his mind shot back to the tortured souls of the camp.

Hanging flesh and bone, the pain of hunger, no softness, only death.

His mind screamed out. In a sudden movement he was on top of her, piercing her buttocks viciously, her gasps unheard by him. A few seconds felt like ten minutes to her but she wasn't afraid. Then, his violent lust satisfied but still inside her, he lay clutching her for dear life. She lay beneath his heavy weight waiting for release. Her sobs slowly dispersed. He released his grip on her. She twisted to face him, still slightly shaking from the experience. His eyes tearless, for all the world dead, his face unflinching, she felt another pang of pity. What torment lay in his soul? Now she held him tight, burying his head in her bosom and stroking his hair. They must have lain there for at least half an hour. Sanity returning, he looked into her face. 'I'm sorry, Elena. It's never happened before.'

'It's okay. I understand.' Her comforting words washed away his guilt.

He sat up and reached for his trousers. 'What the hell's a girl like you doing in a place like this?'

Her reply was barely audible. 'It's part of the deal.'

He stared back at her. Somehow she trusted him and explained: 'We women dare not break the chain. When you and your mates unloaded the weapons earlier, someone has to pay the price, be the middle man.'

'But why would you support them?' He feigned knowledge, hoping his hunch was accurate.

'Not by choice.'

There. He had his confirmation. So the weapons were heading to Northern Ireland. She continued, 'We do as we are told. All of us. Our survival depends on it. Without the black market our small community couldn't survive this war.'

Hanns slowly buttoned up his shirt, then reached for his jacket. It stank of stale sweat and oil. He didn't respond directly to her comment. 'Thank you for the evening,' he said.

'Anytime,' she replied. 'And when you come back to our island, come and see me. We're never told when the next lot is due until the day before. But promise to come and see me.'

'I will,' he smiled. 'Come, let's go downstairs and I'll get you a whisky.' Hanns followed her out. That evening had given him all the confirmation he needed. He knew his next course of action.

❧

Katharine picked up the telephone receiver and dialed the operator. 'Sir Charles, please.'

The polite, efficient female voice answered. 'Certainly, madam. Putting you through.' Katharine bit her lip nervously. How would she start off? He wasn't going to be too pleased with her interfering, but she felt she had no choice. As she waited, she saw Fraser passed through the hall with a tray of newly-made jars of jam. She longed for an end to rationing.

'Hello?' It was Sir Charles on the end of the line.

'Sir Charles, hello. It's Katharine.'

'Hello, girl. What a surprise.'

She lowered her tone. 'Sir Charles, I need to talk to you. It's something that can't be sent by the usual means.'

'Just a moment.' He switched to a scramble device. 'Go on. I'm listening.'

'It's about the latest radio transmissions. I intercepted something at 2300 hours off the Irish coast. 53° 1′ N; 10° 4′E. It was a U-boat of the 9th Flotilla.'

Silence at the other end, then: 'Yes. Go on girl.'

'It surfaced a few miles off the Aran Islands and seems to have docked there overnight.'

'Is it the same bloody one that's been knocking out our shipping recently? If so, we'll blow its bloody brains out of the water and the crew with it.'

'That's just it, Sir Charles. We can't.'

'Can't what?'

'Blow it out of the water. I fear that one of your agents is on board.'

'So why are you telling me? If you don't want it targeted, why didn't you keep the information to yourself?'

'Because another transmission Y-station may pick it up and George was standing over my shoulder when it came through. He knows about it. He doesn't know who; just that it's a British agent on board. I'm calling you now because he has just popped out to take some mail to the post office. And he mustn't know.'

'Katharine, I can't sacrifice British shipping and food convoys for an agent, however good he might be. I've got to knock the blasted boat out before it wrecks any more supply lines.'

'It's Jonathan on board,' she stated bluntly.

Deadly silence. Then heavy breathing down the line was all that she could hear.

'Be rational, Katharine.'

'I know it's him,' she said with a tremor in her voice. 'Fortunately George doesn't know that bit. It's the same U-boat that I tracked before. I am certain of that.'

'Very well, leave it to me. I'll give it 24–48 hours protection. If he can't get off in that time, there's nothing further I can do.' It could have been a golden opportunity to liquidate Jonathan. He had become a gross liability, but Sir Charles had reasons for a stay of execution that out-weighed killing him. This he concealed from Katharine. 'Have you managed to track its exact location now?'

'Yeah, it's dived again and is now passing around the west coast of Ireland. Decoded commands indicate that it is heading back to Denmark.'

'Did you pick up any more information about the Aran Islands?'

'No, I didn't.'

'Why there do you think?' He tested her.

'I don't know, but maybe Jonathan is the clue.'

'Keep it to yourself for now. Leave the rest to me. I'll write up a confidential memo for the PM alerting him to the situation. Thank you Katharine. We'll speak again soon.' A click of the receiver and he was gone. Katharine padded back to the library to track the latest movements of the vessel.

❧

Three days later at the Admiralty in London, Sir Charles turned his attention to the morning's meeting with Captain Henderson, who had travelled up from Devon to spend a few days at the War Office and Special Intelligence Service HQ. He stared out the window. Much of London's pavements were still icy and slippery from the overnight frost. The lakes in Hyde Park had frozen. The weak January sun strained to make an impact. Sitting back at his desk, Sir Charles shuffled through the files, counter-initialling the intelligence reports as read for that morning. Captain Henderson was due to arrive at eleven. That moment the telephone rang.

'Hello Sir Charles.' It was one of the secretaries. 'Captain Henderson sends his apologies. He is going to be ten minutes late.'

'Very well. Thank you, Daphne. Oh, could you pop in and collect the newly stamped files from my desk? Hugo can make sure they reach their destination.'

'Very good, sir.'

Sir Charles replaced the receiver. He wasn't sure what Captain Henderson would do with the information he was about to give him that morning. Henderson was a perfectionist who preferred to vet the agents personally. Tracing the route of the weapons from Ireland required a delicate operation. But first they had to get Hanns/Jonathan out of Denmark and debrief him.

True to his word, Captain Henderson was precisely ten minutes late.

'Good morning, Henderson.' Sir Charles lent back in his chair. 'No brandy, I'm afraid. Even my source of supplies has run out. Tea will have to do.'

'No tea. I'm fine, thank you. I have just come from the East End. Terrible carnage and devastation. The V1s are wreaking havoc on Londoners. If we could locate the launch sites … but intelligence on that front isn't what it should be.'

'Everything possible is being done. Hugo is liaising with the RAF. Photographic recce missions haven't yet thrown up anything significant. The devil is the bloody Huns keep moving the launch sites.'

Captain Henderson seized a pause in the conversation to seat himself opposite Sir Charles. 'Our agent is almost ready to go,' he said. 'I've sent him to Savile Row this morning for kitting out. You must ensure that when he comes back he is incommunicado, strict secrecy. No contact with the outside world and no movement off premises between now and his mission.'

'I know the procedure, George.'

'Good. What news is there on the U-boat?'

'Your wife tracked it late last night, docked off the Aran Islands. This morning it was located going around the coast of Ireland and presumed heading back to Denmark, if it doesn't make an unscheduled stop in Norway. Shetland will monitor it, of course, and Katharine doesn't know that you are aware of the exact situation.'

'Good. Please keep it that way. She mustn't learn about Jonathan.'

'Relax George. Leave it to me.' Sir Charles reached for the bottom drawer of his desk, unlocked it and pulled out a single file. 'I have prepared a confidential report for the PM. There is something else that you should know about the Aran Islands.'

Captain Henderson showed no reaction, staring at him across the desk.

'I have another source there,' Sir Charles continued. 'It has been confirmed that Jonathan was indeed amongst the crew that docked yesterday. But that's not all. The U-boat was carrying special cargo.' Swivelling his chair around, he got up and walked to the large map on the wall. Different coloured flags and pins protruded from odd angles, plotting a course across the English Channel, Irish Sea and Atlantic. 'Here,' he traced his finger along the white line of pins. 'This is the little bugger we're tracking. As you can see, at the beginning of the week it left Kiel, skirted the Danish coast, docking briefly at Frederikshavn before making its way around Scotland and Ireland, then down towards the North Cornish coast. Two days later it stopped overnight at Woody Bay just along the North Devon coast from you. We are surmising there must be a fresh water supply there.'

'But the coast is mined along there.'

'Of course, but they managed to dodge them.'

'And the cargo?'

'Arms. German and Polish-made rifles and so forth.'

Captain Henderson reached into his pocket and pulled out his silver cigarette case then nodded towards Sir Charles. 'Any objection if I smoke?'

'Carry on.'

Captain Henderson puffed away, the thin line of smoke rising above his head. 'Where were they loaded? At Kiel?'

'No. That would be too obvious. We reckon in the few hours it stopped at Frederikshavn. That way no one would suspect anything, least of all the Allies.'

'And it's headed for the Republic,' stated Captain Henderson. 'And smuggled on from there to Ulster.'

'Exactly. We suspect the weapons are being traded for fresh water and supplies. The one thing Admiral Doenitz needs to keep his whole fleet going.'

Captain Henderson leant forward as Sir Charles seated himself back down in his chair. 'It doesn't explain everything, Sir Charles.' Sir Charles could rely on Henderson's logical mind to come up with a plausible answer. It was why he had invited him that morning. 'What's really in it for the Huns? They need the weapons for their own war machine. No, there's more to it. Money must be changing hands … and enough for them to make weapons for themselves and their clients.'

'Once we've de-briefed Jonathan, I want to send in a small team to penetrate the network at both ends – Denmark and Ireland. Will you provide me with the necessary authorisation so I can proceed?'

Captain Henderson nodded. 'It makes sense. When Hitler loses the war, as he's bound to do with the Americans on our side, we don't want the gun-running fraternity harbouring Nazi war criminals and building a safe haven with weapons. What kind of fools do they take us for?' He stood up, walked over to the window and stared down. Admiral Hilton was crossing the courtyard below. 'And the military documents?' he asked.

'We don't yet know if the documents were on board or whether Jonathan has managed to retrieve them. We've had no direct communication from him for two weeks.'

'Please tell me when you do.'

'There's one further matter, George. That Danish girl you briefed, she's also going in soon. Near Kiel.'

'Yes, I know. I've already set up the lines of communication between her and Katharine. Each day at 6 a.m. our time Katharine will relay to her the latest Allied news for broadcasting to the German people. They are communicating in German just in case they're intercepted. And … Katharine doesn't know her true identity.'

'Of course,' replied Sir Charles. 'What do you take me for? I'm as careful as you George in such matters of State.'

Henderson glanced at his watch. 'Well, I must be going.' Sir Charles passed him a thin bundle of confidential files across the desk.

'Thank you.' Henderson slipped them into his briefcase and walked out.

❧

Walking along Savile Row, Geoffrey Hart looked along the tops of the buildings for the outfitters Kilgore and French. Pausing outside the shop, he admired the finely hung fabrics with a half-made suit in the window. The pre-war quality of the cloth was like nothing he had seen before, not even in his uncle's tailoring business back in Vienna. He went up the three steps to the door at the top. An elderly man in a grey suit opened the door for him.

'Allow me take your jacket, sir.' His arms were already outstretched in anticipation. Geoffrey removed his jacket, trying to take in the sophisticated room around him. It didn't appear to be the right kind of place for being kitted out with special equipment. But then who was he to judge?

'If you would like to come this way, sir.' Geoffrey followed him to the back of the premises. Two men, equally well-attired, appeared to come from nowhere and fell in behind them. Geoffrey was led into a tiny cupboard of a room, several shelves of boxes lining each wall. The elderly gentleman who went by the name of Jenkins pulled a piece of paper out of his pocket. Unravelling the crumpled page, he muttered, 'He wants what?' He regained his composure and continued calmly: 'That's quite a shopping list. Does he intend to kill the entire German army on his own? Your uncle has already radioed through a list of items to Sir Charles over two weeks ago. I've barely had enough time to develop some of that. And now this! Tut, tut.' Geoffrey tried to peer over the top of the page. Jenkins turned to rummage through one of the boxes at eye-level. Still, neither Geoffrey nor the other two men said a word.

'Churchill wants to set the Continent alight but what he fails to realise is I need time to perfect the equipment. I take it sir that you will be using all the usual array of weaponry?'

'Er yes,' replied Geoffrey.

Jenkins glanced up; his spectacles perched halfway down his aquiline nose. 'I suggest you peruse this at your leisure.' In his hand he held a thick manual on weaponry. 'Tell me if there is anything else you need from here.' Geoffrey flicked through the pages. Some of the items looked odd, others plain fun. Jenkins watched silently then added: 'The lapel thumb knives catalogue no js 188 are excellent. You should most definitely have a pair of those. We have them in stock.'

Geoffrey pointed to catalogue no N254. 'This looks like an essential one.'

'Very good choice, sir. The sleeve gun is a silent single shot pistol. You slip it out of your sleeve, wrapping your fingers around it like so.' Jenkins curled his thumb and two forefingers around his measuring yard-stick in demonstration. 'The trigger is close to the muzzle thus aiding unobtrusive firing. I will make the necessary adjustments to the sleeve in your uniform, sir. I take it you are left-handed.'

'Yes.' Geoffrey raised his eyebrows at his astute sense of observation.

'Do you smoke a pipe?' Jenkins turned and poked around in another brown box.

'No I don't.'

'Well, I suggest you start. You have a choice of two pipes from my little collection. This one contains a storage compartment, rather boring if you ask me, but the other is a single shot gun. A very useful tool.' Geoffrey raised his eyebrows again, not at all convinced that it would work. 'You have to be accurate of course,' added Jenkins.

Geoffrey took the pipe, turned it over and examined it. 'A neat little thing. Thanks.'

'Now finally, I will include a set of pens and pencils that all work on the same principle. They are timing switches, as are these incendiary pellets which you can insert into a cigarette. Place it anywhere along the length of the cigarette. But remember you have only two minutes before it goes off – depending where you place it.'

'What happens then?'

'A red hot flame shoots out of the end. And depending on which way you place the pellet the intense flame will last about 4 to 5 seconds. It will not kill but it makes an awful mess of your opponent's face. In an emergency the pellets can also be an excellent way of starting a fire and, on occasion, they can scupper the odd lock. Now, follow me!'

During all of this Geoffrey had failed to notice that the other two men, both tailors, had been eyeing him up and down, taking visual measurements of his size and noting any quirky movements and habits. One of them motioned for him to stand in front of a long mirror. He snapped his fingers. The other tailor began measuring with a tape.

'On the right hand side or left?' he asked.

'Excuse me?'

'Does it rest on the right or left, sir?' After a further pause he added, 'The budgerigar, sir, is its preferred nesting on the right or left? Please excuse me a moment.' He briefly brushed his hand over Geoffrey's crotch. 'Sorry sir. Necessary to know which side your, erm, male bit hangs, I'm afraid. We need to allow for extra cloth because it is not the only thing that will be hidden down there.'

'I see.' Geoffrey cast his eyes around the room whilst they continued to measure him. The ornate plasterwork of the ceiling hadn't been noticed when he had first entered. Across the length of the shop two chandeliers hung casting quite substantial light.

It was Jenkins who spoke next, 'Your trousers, sir. I intend putting in a couple of pleats at the front to loosen the garment. That way we can attach a Sten gun with silencer.' He picked up the weighty catalogue and turned to page 213. 'There it is no M211. It folds up rather neatly and will hang discreetly unobserved down the inside of your trouser leg, attached to your belt ready for use. Your knife will lie flat in the sleeve of your jacket under your armpit. In a search it is invariably missed and it's very quick to draw out.'

The clock on a desk behind chimed the half hour. Twelve thirty already. Jenkins scurried around and then declared: 'All done. You're all finished sir. This is an urgent job, I understand. All will be ready for you for collection the day after tomorrow.'

'Thank you.' Geoffrey turned to the other two. 'Thanks so much, gentlemen.'

One of them rushed to the door and held it open. He unfurled a long gentleman's umbrella with a flourish that would not go un-applauded in a theatre. 'You may be glad of this, sir. It's raining outside now.'

'Thank you.' Geoffrey took it, descended the steps and out into the drizzle of the London streets.

Submerged at 73 metres, the U-boat had finally reached smoother waters. Inside, the stench of unwashed men living and working in close proximity had built to an unbearable pitch. In the command room the Captain turned to Fritz, shouting above the noise of the engines and clunking of metal. 'Two minutes, we begin taking her up. We aren't far from the Sound. We take this motherfucker through the narrow passage between Denmark and Sweden. Orders to lie just below the surface.'

'*Jawohl Herr Ka-leu.*'

'Make sure the men understand – we go silently through the Sound.'

Further down the U-boat, the men hunched shoulder to shoulder on the iron floor, gulping the lukewarm gruel. Food was now in short supply and they hadn't had a decent morsel to eat for fourteen hours. Tired, grimy and irritable, several fights had broken out during the night. Clutching his bowl of gruel, Hanns surveyed the men around him. There were Georg and Dieter, both boxers who had fought in their respective youth teams before the days of Hitler. To his left sat Jan, Stefan and another Hanns. What did their petty quibbles matter? They were all going down – the whole bloody crew.

He suppressed the hatred; revenge running through the very blood in his veins. He tried to focus on his plan of action, but the constant pounding in his head affected his concentration. Suddenly he flinched at unconscious pain, his left eye twitching, before stuffing another mouthful of gruel down his gullet. His fingernails were caked in black grime; his nostrils seemed permanently etched with the smell of oil. He took a gulp of weak black liquid they called ersatz coffee. Their tin cups were only ever a third full in case the U-boat took a sudden dive.

'Time to go! All men to stations!' ordered Stefan, standing up.

Struggling to get up in the limited space, Hanns ignored the cramp in his legs and followed the others down towards the engine compartment and the Zentrale.

Bells suddenly rang out. 'Dive! Dive! Dive! ... Dive, you motherfuckers! Take her down!'

The U-boat took a sharp turn down, the clattering of bells incessant and rattle of machinery being clanked into position deafening.

'Down, down, down! Good. Now level her! Good. Cut engines and silence!'

After several minutes of total stillness the same voice came over the speaker: 'Keep her still. There's a destroyer up there.'

A few minutes later the Captain released the first torpedo. The U-boat rocked and clunked as they exited. Then total silence. Everything still. Holding their breath, the men clung to the nearest pipe or metal machinery, waiting to absorb the shockwave they knew was coming.

'Take her down again. Slowly, gently!'

There was barely time to obey orders. The torpedo hit its target. The impact and subsequent shockwave caused the iron war machine to rock. Hanns clung to one of the venting levers on the ceiling of the Zentrale. He tried to suppress an urge to vomit, but it was too late. He wasn't the only one. The sound of retching men and smell of vomit now mingled with the stale stench and engine fumes. The lights flickered as the U-boat rocked to and fro.

'All men to emergency positions!'

In the ensuing commotion Hanns smiled to himself. His moment had come. The majority of the men rushed towards the other end of the U-boat. Alone with Stefan, the other Hanns and Georg, Hanns drew from under his armpit the blade that had lain tight against his skin. In one swift thrust he pierced Stefan in the back through his left lung. Stefan's heavy body slumped to the ground. In another quick action Hanns took out seaman Hanns. Aware of a scuffle behind him, above the noise of the engines, Georg turned: 'What the fuck?'

Hanns plunged the warm bloodstained blade into his chest. Knocking him backwards, he then climbed on top of Georg to suppress the screams with his free hand. In seconds the life drained out of him. There was no time to lose. Hanns rapidly scanned the ceiling for the flood valves. He chuckled to himself.

Damn! The flood valves couldn't be seen.

The second plan had to come into action. He reached into his pocket, pulling out the duplicate key from the safe which he had moulded during their outward journey. He left the Zentrale, pulling the heavy iron door behind him, sealing closed the evidence of the murdered crew inside. He hurried to the engine compartment. He unlocked the two large safes, taking the depth charges. Hanns made his way to the torpedo compartment. Placing the charges behind each torpedo, he set them going. There wasn't much time and there was every chance he would go down with the crew. He grabbed a *Tauchenretter*, part of the Dräger breathing apparatus, hanging behind him. The special equipment was his only chance of survival. He pulled it over his head and face and headed for the conning tower.

The first explosion came as a surprise, lifting the entire U-boat upwards at an angle. In the engine compartment, shouts accompanied panic-struck bodies as they were flung around its confines. Then deadly silence. The entire living tomb plunged into darkness. The hull ruptured. Hanns felt and pushed his way through the men towards the conning tower. He fumbled for a torch in his pocket. A sudden rush of seawater immersed the conning tower. Hanns struggled to stay upright, pushing relentlessly on the hatch. It failed to give way. Under the pressure of water it proved virtually impossible to open. The Dräger escape breathing equipment, although primitive, ought to save him. He braced himself for the next hit.

Three, two, one …

The second explosion tossed the U-boat causing a volcanic-like eruption of water above it. He felt a stiff body brush against him. Hanns shone the weak light of his torch at it. The Captain was a goner. Hanns pointed the beam of light upwards and hammered on the hatch. Trying to push it, he winched it with a long metal bar. As he struggled, the third and final explosion struck. The hatch burst open. The last thing he saw was the 'Smiling Shark'. The U-boat sank to the seabed.

❧

Katharine stared blankly into the darkness beyond the window of the library, numbed by what she had just picked up on the radio transmission. She pulled back the blackout blinds slightly, confident no bombers would be going overhead so early in the morning. Dawn had yet to break. During the night snow had fallen. She rubbed her hands to get warm, the fire in the grate not yet giving out sufficient heat to warm the room to a comfortable temperature. Dazed, she replaced her headphones over her ears.

Nothing. Total silence.

She barely heard the grandfather clock chime 5 o'clock in the hallway. Her mind filled with the panicked screams of the men's final moments. She had heard it all over the radio. It wasn't them she worried about – they were the enemy. It was Jonathan. He must have suffered with them. It might even have been one of his screams she'd heard amongst the terror and chaos. Sir Charles had promised her forty-eight hours' protection on this one. He had broken his promise. For the first forty-five minutes of her shift there had been only sporadic transmissions from the U-boat. Then sudden pandemonium had broken out. She had ascertained it had been heading for the strait between Sweden and Denmark.

She stared blankly at nothing in particular. Still nothing came over the radio equipment. Now Jonathan was gone and she still didn't have answers to her questions. Did her husband have any part in Jonathan's original capture in Dachau? Did he have anything to do with Jonathan's death that morning? She dismissed the last notion, trying to rationalise that George was no killer. He probably didn't know Jonathan was alive then, let alone working on a U-boat. As soon as she could, she would phone Sir Charles.

The sound of light footsteps down the passageway entered the library. 'Madam, are you alright?' asked Fraser.

'What, er,' her distracted reply gave him cause for concern. 'What time is it Fraser?'

'Five thirty, madam.'

'You're up early.'

'Yes, madam. I couldn't sleep. Are you all right? You seem distressed.'

'I'm fine.'

'Would you like a cup of tea?'

'Yes. Thank you Fraser. That would be very nice.'

He pattered off down the corridor to the kitchen. Katharine turned back to her scribbled notes of the last moments of the crew. She scanned her writing:

What's going on?

Emergency stations, emergency stations.

This fucker's flooding. Bring her up!

It was no good being melancholic. What was done was done.

A few moments later a voice said behind her: 'Madam, here is your tea.'

She turned and managed a smile. 'Thank you Fraser.'

'Can I get you anything else madam?'

'No thank you. I'd prefer to be alone now.'

'Very good, madam.' He left her to her thoughts.

With Fraser gone, Katharine stared back down the garden at the dark silhouettes and shapes. For her, that day began to dawn as the final closure on the past. She might never find out the truth about Jonathan, Dachau, the U-boat and his death that night.

Chapter 6

15 January 1944 – Wilton Park

Lilian sat waiting for the conversations of the prisoners-of-war to start in the cells behind the wall. She pulled Geoffrey's last letter out of her uniform breast pocket. It was almost three months to the day since she had started at Wilton Park and exactly a month since Geoffrey's last letter. She missed him terribly. The last correspondence was a brief note, the envelope stamped as passed by the military censor. Keeping the letter in a pocket close to her heart was somehow comforting. She didn't really need to read it for she had memorised every word, but somehow seeing his handwriting made it more real. She scanned the brief note:

> Please don't worry about me. Everything will be alright. I am being transferred to another camp. It may be a while before I can get leave. I love you. G

She feared in reality he had already been posted abroad. The door opened behind her. Sergeant White entered. 'The CO wants to see you in his room.'

'Now?'

'Yes.'

She replaced the letter in her breast pocket, unplugged the recording equipment and put on her coat over her khaki uniform. She hurried out across the paths around the neatly cut lawn, shivering in the chill January air. The weak sunlight and blue sky lifted her spirits. She wondered what could be so important that she was taken off her monitoring shift. She entered the White House by a side door, hanging her coat on a peg in the entrance. Along the corridor she knocked on the CO's door and waited.

'Come in,' he called. Lilian entered and found Major Higginbottom standing with his back to the window, lighting his pipe. His grey bushy eyebrows almost masked his tiny eyes peering out of round, rimmed spectacles. Lilian stood to attention and saluted.

'Ah, Lilian. Have a seat.' She obeyed and sat cross-legged in the chair facing him. Major Higginbottom took the first puff from his pipe, surveying her carefully. 'Your mission has come up.'

'Yes sir?'

'Captain Henderson tells me you are fully prepared.' He exhaled again from his pipe.

'Yes sir. I am.'

'Here are your documents. You're going in as Lilian Schwarz.' He passed a small bundle of papers and a passport across the table. 'Pulling out our airmen isn't going to be easy. Some of them may have suffered psychological trauma, but we believe you're the right person. You'll be dropped at night near Kiel. The port is heavily fortified but just outside is fine. The DZ is being prepared as we speak. The rest of your time in the region, whilst you wait for orders about the airmen, you're to set up a Black Propaganda radio station. Working with a local underground resistance fighter, you'll be giving daily news bulletins in German to the German people. Undermining their morale by masking as a genuine German radio station is crucial at this point in the war. You leave the day after tomorrow. Until then I would like you to continue your shifts on the listening bugs. Any questions?'

'Yes sir. Will I be accompanied?'

'No. It's a lone drop.' He placed his pipe on the desk in front of her, looking straight at her. 'I am sorry there wasn't the usual amount of time allocated for training, but your past experience was deemed preparation enough.'

In that moment Lilian realised that Captain Henderson had thoroughly investigated her past. There wasn't much the British Secret Service didn't know about their recruits. He must know her true identity.

Major Higginbottom continued: 'You could be in for as long as six months. We'll get word to you and pull you out sooner if necessary. In the next few months the war is about to enter its most critical stage and we need you in Northern Germany.'

It was widely suspected that a major invasion of Europe was on the cards. Sicily and Italy were already in Allied hands.

'Any more questions?'

'No sir.'

'Fine. Then dismissed.' His pallid, severe face broke into a smile. 'Good luck.'

'Thank you sir.'

Lilian saluted and marched out, back to her shift. As she strode along the path again she knew it would be a long time before she saw Geoffrey again. Her feelings for him couldn't be allowed to interfere with her vital task. She was now under strict secret war status and all correspondence was forbidden until she returned. Separation was inevitable but, in his naïvety, Geoffrey would think she was safe in England. Any thought of love and the future would have to wait.

❧

That same afternoon, the harbourmaster of Frederikshavn paced the confines of his office. The meagre fire in the grate barely warmed the room. Outside it was threatening to snow but nothing had yet fallen. He was expecting Anders, who had travelled from Vallø for the meeting. Word had reached Anders through the network of the Resistance Movement that there was unexpected news about Hanns. Anders was there to establish the truth.

'*Guten tag*, Herr Käpitan. Thank you for seeing me at such short notice,' said Anders as he removed his black trilby hat in a polite gesture. The harbourmaster stopped pacing the room.

'My pleasure. You are very welcome, Herr Olsen. How can I help you?'

Anders formed his next words with caution. 'You remember the British destroyer that was sunk a couple of weeks ago off the coast. I understand there were survivors.'

'Yes. Eleven of them.'

'Do you know what happened to them?'

'After a brief medical check in the First Aid Centre over there ...' he nodded through the window towards the direction of a hut with a corrugated roof. 'They were all taken over the border and handed to the authorities. They'll be in a POW camp somewhere in Germany now.'

'Anyone else?'

'What do you mean?' The harbourmaster feigned ignorance, playing for time. From the look on Anders' face he ascertained the man standing in front of him wasn't a pushover.

'Did anyone else survive that day?'

'Yes, as a matter of fact, they did. A lone crewman from a U-boat of the 9th Flotilla.'

'I'd heard such rumours,' replied Anders. 'They aren't rumours then.'

'No.'

'Do you know the identity of the man?'

'No, but the U-boat sunk shortly after the British destroyer went down. It's not known exactly how the U-boat sank – possibly a technical fault on board after it released the torpedo that hit the destroyer. That's what my superiors are saying. Only one man survived. He was pulled out of the freezing water semi-conscious and taken straight to hospital.'

'And he did survive?'

'Survive, he did. But I have no idea where he is now.'

Anders smiled: 'You pre-empted my next question. Thank you. His name?'

'I don't know.'

'You mean he came into your area and you don't even know his name. How come, Herr Käpitan? Isn't that a bit negligent?' The Käpitan appeared uncomfortable. 'His name please Herr Käpitan.'

'I told you – I don't know.'

'Very well. I must bid you good day, sir.' Anders extended his hand. The harbourmaster responded with a hearty shake. Anders hesitated as their hands still clasped for a few seconds longer than was usual. Anders noticed a flicker of something across the Käpitan's face. He pressed his thumb firmly twice into the Käpitan's hand. The Käpitan returned the gesture. The coded hand squeeze, the Käpitan knew he could trust Anders.

'He was Hanns … Hanns Faltitschek.' Anders didn't say a word. The Käpitan gestured to two wooden chairs by the fire. 'Here, come and sit down. Let me explain.'

Anders sat down, balancing his trilby on his knee. By now the fire was beginning to throw out some heat, the pine logs crackled away. The Käpitan drew his chair closer to the fire and bent over to warm his hands. 'One of our lot brought him in. In the confusion of getting the British seamen out of the water, the Nazi patrols missed him. I spotted him floating on the water. Everywhere around him men were screaming. They were on fire, trying to douse themselves below the water, but all the while freezing in the sea. All efforts were being made to get them out.' He paused, far away in thought. 'As I said, I spotted him. He'd lost his Kriegsmarine jacket, but his shirt had the emblem of the Smiling Shark. I recognised it immediately. He gave a single half-splutter before going unconscious. One of my lads went into the water, dragged him out and resuscitated him behind the wagon near the medical centre. It was too risky to take him inside.'

'Why didn't you let the Nazis deal with him? After all, he was one of them?' Anders' words fell on deaf ears. The Käpitan was back at the event, re-living it.

'The sea was a bloodbath. Men lost limbs. The screaming, the anguish – by God it was grim. Hell on earth. Eleven of them were still alive but in a terrible state.'

'What about Hanns?' prompted Anders gently. 'Why didn't you hand him to the Nazis?'

The Käpitan came out of his reverie. 'I knew who he was.'

Anders sat calmly waiting.

'I'd given him his Kriegsmarine uniform before he left. I knew damn well who he was.'

'What happened next?'

'Bloody hell, I said to my men: Do anything but for God's sake get him off the site. And they did.'

'Where can I find him now? He needs complete protection.'

'He has protection enough.' The Käpitan coughed, then held his hands to the fire again.

Anders had one last card to play. 'Have you heard, Herr Käpitan, that the Protectorate is about to promote you. You have done a good job of guarding this coastline against invasion and your efforts are being rewarded. It means more money for you and your family. I know it's been a struggle for you with the death of your wife. Information could bring its just reward.'

'Is that so?' the tone of his voice indicated disinterest.

Anders gently prompted again. 'Where is Hanns?'

The harbourmaster held his face in his hands. 'May God my maker help me.' He parted his hands to reveal some of his face and spoke. 'He's being looked after by the monks at Gjorslev Herregarden.'

Anders suppressed a smile. So close to home! 'Thank you. Congratulations Herr Käpitan on your promotion. I understand it is effective immediately. You deserve it. You've done the right thing.' He touched him on the back, turned and left. A final unexpected backward glance, Anders noted the saddened figure of a burdened man still bent over the primitive fireplace. Anders didn't hear the Käpitan's final words whispered under his breath: 'Yes, but you are in for a shock.'

17 January 1944

Lilian had boarded the bomber at RAF Manston just after midnight. The heavy snow clouds diffused any light from the stars. Her superiors had informed her that her mission couldn't wait for the weather to improve. One and a half hours later the Halifax flew over the Danish/German border; the drop zone a few kilometres north-west of Kiel. Squashed on a bench against the plane's vibrating fuselage, four of them awaited their destination. Each was heading for a different location in Germany. Lilian noted she was the only woman on board, although it was hard to be certain in the dark, with all wearing heavy gear. The pilot's voice shouted above the noise of the engines, 'Four minutes till the first one to go, six till the next.' Lilian was to be the second. A few minutes later the rear hatch opened. Cold air rushed in. The person at her side jumped into the darkness. The plane arced and circled before straightening up. 'One minute till go.'

Lilian shuffled and stood up. She adjusted the goggles over her eyes. Green light on, she jumped. The plane's altitude over the landscape was lower than she expected. Falling rapidly, she pulled the rip cord. A couple minutes until landing, she was on course for the designated field. She came down with a thump. Her 'chute collapsed behind her. In the complete stillness she unharnessed her 'chute and rolled it up. Eyes now adjusted to the darkness, she ran across the field to the nearest hedge and stuffed the 'chute underneath, covering it with weeds and debris. She crouched along the hedge, moved a few steps, then waited. In the darkness she strained to make out the time on her watch, but it was impossible. A double owl hoot sounded close by. She waited. It sounded again. It couldn't have been more than a few seconds later there was a tap on her shoulder. Lilian knew not to react and stood stock still.

'*Kommen Sie!*' whispered the female voice, reaching to help Lilian with her kit.

'*Nein, ich bin …*'

'Ssh, let me help you.'

Lilian had to trust her, but decided to pass her the kitbag with supplies and clean clothing rather than radio transmitter and accompanying equipment. Skirting the hedges of two further fields and climbing over a gate they came to a lone farmhouse. Lilian's companion opened the front door into a large kitchen with low ceiling. A dim light glowed from its stand on a long wooden table. Placing her bag on the floor, Lilian took in the surroundings. They were alone. On the mantelshelf over the fireplace stood a single silver candlestick next to a photograph of a young man in Nazi uniform.

'My name's Helga. Come, I'll make a warm drink and then show you to your room.'

'I'm Lilian.' In the light of the kitchen it was the first time Lilian could see Helga's features. Her long blonde hair reached to her back, tied in a red ribbon at the end. At about 5ft 5in she was somewhat striking for a farmer's daughter.

Helga surveyed Lilian up and down. 'You're quite a fit little thing. You dropped on time.' She smiled, then noticed Lilian glance at the photograph on the fireplace. 'Ah, that's my younger brother Frederic. God rest his soul. Called up in early 1940. Died at Dunkirk. Do you think he's handsome?'

'Yes.' It would be impolite to say otherwise.

As if feeling the need to explain herself further, Helga stuttered, 'It's not what you think. He had no choice. He was no Nazi. None of our family are.'

'I understand.'

'Do you?' Tears welled in her eyes.

'Yes.' After a pause Lilian added, 'You must miss him.'

'I do. Our family does what it can to resist. There aren't many Germans prepared to go against the State. Most are bystanders to the brutality. There are rumours of death camps, you know. And Jews disappearing.'

'So I've heard.'

'If it's true, it makes what we're doing even more important.' She passed Lilian a hot milk. Lilian savoured the warm
liquid hitting the back of her throat. 'Come Lilian, bring
your drink upstairs with you. You ought to snatch a few
hours' sleep. We have to set up the radio equipment early in
the morning. We'll be using Ma's room.'

'Doesn't she mind?'

'Not at all. She's off visiting my aunt.' Helga headed for
the stairs, continuing to chat. Lilian followed.

'There're only three rooms upstairs, built into the loft
space. I'm afraid the toilet's downstairs out the back.
Here, this is your bedroom.' Helga pushed open the bedroom door. The room was simple. A single bed, already
made up with crisp white sheets and a brown blanket,
was pushed against the far wall. The only other furnishings were a small bedside cabinet, modest dressing table
with chair and a washbasin with mirror. The slope of
the eaves meant there wasn't enough height for a wardrobe. 'I'm next door,' said Helga, suddenly tossing her
blonde head. 'When she comes back, Ma is in the other.'
Nothing was said about her father. Lilian didn't ask. They
bade goodnight and Lilian settled down to a few hours'
sleep.

Next day at noon, Anders arrived at Gjorslev Herregarden.
Striding down the drive towards the manor in a dark suit,
white shirt and tie, he felt his formal dress would be more
appropriate when meeting with the monks. At the large
wooden door, he rapped on the metal knocker. It was
opened by an elderly monk.

'Good day sir. May I see the Abbot, please?' Anders asked.

The monk nodded, pulling the door wide open, then gestured for Anders to follow him. Inside, the panelled hallway and stone-floored corridors felt icy cold in the middle of winter with no heating. It was a sparse life with few comforts but then who was he, Anders, to judge? He followed the monk down the corridors to the Abbot's library. The library was light and airy in spite of the dark bookcases lining floor to ceiling, almost bowing under the weight of old leather-bound tomes. The air smelt of beeswax polish which the brothers made on site and used to buff the furniture. In the centre, a round table with a globe accompanied a writing set and quill pen. The Abbot stood by the long French windows, staring down the avenue of trees at the back. 'Come in,' he said at the sound of footsteps behind him. He turned around. His face revealed a long diagonal duelling scar across his left cheek. His age was difficult to fathom, possibly mid-forties, his cheeks serene and unlined from years of meditation and prayer.

'It's good to see you again Herr Olsen.'

'Thank you Father,' replied Anders.

'I received word yesterday from the Captain in England.' Anders looked a little unsure. As if second-guessing his thoughts, the Abbot smiled, 'It is fine. We can speak freely here.'

Anders got straight to the point. 'I understand Hanns, er, Jonathan, is safe.'

'Yes, but …' the Abbot paused, turning to look back down the gardens. The once neatly mown lawns were laid out in rows of vegetables to be self-sufficient during the war. Fruit trees had been planted against the secluded wall at the end. Beyond, vineyards then open fields and not a sign of human life. 'He's in a really bad way. Physically he's not the man he was.'

'I am not surprised. Where is he now?'

'Here being looked after by our monks.'

'And the Nazis?'

'We haven't had an SS search in months. They appear to have decided we aren't worth bothering with. But still ... we can't afford to be complacent. We have to be vigilant.'

'Captain H wants him back in England. We have to get him out of the country.'

'I'm not sure he is ready to leave.'

'May I see him?'

'Yes sure. Very well, follow me.'

In silence they walked from the library towards the west wing. The occasional sound of chanting could be heard faintly echoed, embedded in the very walls of the manor. They passed several doors until they finally they came to one at the end.

'If you do take him,' said the Abbott. 'I must have assurance that he will be safe and receive full protection.' Anders looked him straight in the face, 'You have my word. The whole network is in place to make certain he is looked after.'

The Abbot knocked twice, then opened the door. Over his shoulder Anders could see the hunched shape of Hanns seated beside the half-closed curtains, rocking back and forth in a chair, rubbing his hands in a continuous motion of obsession. Hanns was a shadow of his former self, dressed in a long brown habit in case of a Nazi raid. Anders took in the gaunt, pale face of the man ahead of him. He waited for the Abbot to speak first.

'Hanns,' whispered the Abbot as he approached. 'I've brought someone to see you. A friend.'

The rocking movement gathered pace, the actions of the hands more frantic. Hanns looked straight at Anders.

'Hello Hanns.' Anders knelt down beside him. 'How are you today?'

'Fine. I'm always fine.' His voice had lost the power it once had. The rhythmic hand washing speeded up.

'I see the rest here has done you good.'

'Fine. I'm always fine.'

The Abbot leant forwards. 'Here Hanns. Your aperitif for today.' He passed Hanns the goblet of schnapps then glanced back at Anders. 'It always perks him up. You'll see the difference.' Hanns tipped it back, gulping down in one mouthful as if it was his last lifeline. He thumped the empty goblet down on the table beside him. It was the first time he broke into a smile but for all the world his eyes had lost their life. The Abbot nodded in Anders' direction. Anders piped up, 'We thought you might be ready to come back to the castle with me.'

Hanns grimaced through gritted teeth. 'I haven't killed enough of the bastards yet. Revenge is not the Lord's. It's *mine!*' Despite this outburst, his eyes seemed distant.

'Don't worry yourself about that now Hanns. We need to make sure you're protected,' answered Anders.

Hanns broke into insane laughter. His voice hoarse, he spluttered. 'I *am* the protection. My mission isn't over. I am not Hanns. I am Jonathan. Jonathan Walters. I save life. I take life. Ha, ha, ha.'

Anders touched his arm. 'You don't need to concern yourself about that at the moment. Come with me. We are ready to go back to the castle.' For a second Hanns hesitated. Anders thought he wasn't going to agree.

Hanns replied, 'Take me back. Ha, ha, ha. I need to prepare.' The rocking to and fro stopped. Slowly, unsteadily he stood up. The Abbot and Anders exchanged glances. Anders took Hanns' arm and they followed the Abbot out through the corridors down to the main entrance. A car already waited outside. The Abbot and Anders exchanged their farewells. Anders helped Hanns into the car. Hanns seemed subdued. The car drove off for Vallø Castle.

☙

A few days later at the farmhouse near Kiel, Lilian had successfully installed the temporary amateur radio station. It had taken two days to fine-tune the equipment in the attic room. Helga was about to deliver the first German propaganda broadcast that morning. Lilian had been in regular morning contact with Katharine back in England, spending the first few days compiling news reports and items from the information passed to her. Having breakfasted, Lilian came into the bedroom and leant over Helga at the desk. 'Here's the first report.'

'Thanks.' Helga had painted her lips with a dark red lipstick, giving them an ugly prominence. Lilian felt it exaggerated her otherwise striking features, but she wouldn't be so unkind as to tell her. Lilian fidgeted in the Nazi uniform loaned to her by Helga. In spite of the cold weather, the uniform was far too heavy and hot. She felt intensely uncomfortable as a Jewess wearing the hated garb of those who would have her dead. Above the desk Helga had hung a picture of Adolf Hitler in the event of an unwelcome search by the SS.

Lilian glanced at her watch. 'Two minutes until you're on air.' Helga placed the headphones on her head. Lilian motioned with her finger, counting down the seconds. The broadcast began.

'*Guten morgan. Heil Hitler!* This station brings the latest news to the people, for the people ...'

As soon as Helga had finished each news item, she cast the sheets to the floor. Lilian gathered them up, shredded them, then went downstairs and threw them onto the kitchen fire. After that morning's broadcast they had a break from air time for three hours. The next broadcast would be down to Lilian. In the interim period she settled into her bedroom, scribbling out the reports for the next broadcast. No word had yet reached her about the airmen. Until it did, she was to continue with the propaganda radio station.

5 February 1944

Nearing its destination over the Danish coastline of South Zealand, the Halifax bomber shook as it passed through some turbulence. Creaking disconcertingly, the noise from its engines was deafening. Alone and with adrenalin running high, Geoffrey crouched in the back in full parachutist kit. Underneath his Denison smock the thick cloth of the Nazi uniform chaffed his neck. He peered out of goggles which screened most of his vision, leather helmet pulled tight over his head and face. Struggling to keep the cold at bay, he rubbed his hands. To keep his mind off the impending jump, he thought back to the last night he had been with *her*. The clearness of Lilian's face was fading in his memory but he could smell her delicate scent as if it was yesterday. Remembering her soft embrace, his dreams were still wrapped in the essence that was her. The love he might never see again touched him momentarily with melancholy. He refused to admit the possibility that danger waited for him in the darkness.

The pilot spoke only once during the whole flight, muffled against the constant hum of the engines: 'You're in luck, sucker. The moon's out.'

A few minutes later the green light was on. Geoffrey jumped out of the back hatch, the rush of freezing wind pinning his headgear tighter against his face. The ripcord pulled him upright as he floated down. The pre-arranged drop zone was the grounds of Gjorslev Herregarden. In the moonlight, Geoffrey could make out its crucifix-shape, the same intended location as Hanns and his colleague eight months earlier. Before Geoffrey had time to think, it was the final rush to earth. He landed with a thud, rolled a few metres, then scrambled to his feet. To all intents and purposes it was a successful landing, except he soon discovered his extra kit had not been dropped behind him. In the still night air he looked around, listening, surveying the landscape. The monastery ahead of him was in complete darkness, not a single light on. He removed his Denison smock and rolled it up, tying it to his kitbag. He reached into his pocket and pulled out the powder Jenkins had given him back in London. Sprinkling it on the ground would throw the dogs off his scent if a search party should scour the landscape.

In the shadows, Anders and Josephy waited cautiously before giving two owl hoots. Geoffrey returned the code. Out of the shrubbery Josephy darted across to him. 'Come!' he hissed. They came up alongside Anders. 'It'll take too long to get to Vallø tonight,' said Anders. 'We'll rest overnight in a farmhouse two kilometres from here. At first light, we move.'

Half an hour later they reached the farm, a large stone building with numerous outhouses and barns. The farmer was expecting them. He motioned for them to come in. Huddled around the kitchen table, Anders spoke first with updated information. 'As I said earlier, at first light we move. Another drop of supplies is expected tomorrow evening. The network is increasing its sabotage against our unwanted guests. We will target trains, rail networks and factories making weapons for the Nazis. Geoffrey, I want you to co-ordinate the distribution of supplies until your next posting. We have yet to find out when you can board at Frederikshavn. Any questions?'

The three other men, including Geoffrey, shook their heads.

'Good. Let's get a nap in the armchairs by the fireplace. Josephy has agreed to keep watch till dawn.'

At first light the following day, Anders shook Geoffrey by the shoulder, 'We move now.' Geoffrey suppressed a yawn and gathered his small amount of kit. The thick, grey Nazi uniform felt heavy over his body; his feet hot from the long black jackboots. Within a few minutes they got into a black Mercedes, made brief farewells to the farmer and his son and headed off towards the Vallø Castle estate. Anders drove, acting as chauffeur to the high-ranking Nazi officer sat in the front next to him. Josephy sat in the rear. Anders smiled at Geoffrey, 'No one will ever suspect anything with you as our escort.' The rest of the journey was spent in relative silence; no one in the mood for conversation. They passed two patrols outside the medieval town of Køge. The SS acknowledged them, saluting *Heil Hitler*.

'I'm taking you to my place in the grounds,' said Anders. 'Its location is discreet and Hanns, your uncle Jonathan, should be there. When did you last see him?'

'Before the war.'

'Be prepared. You may not recognise him.' Anders parked the car at the side of the castle. They crossed the lawns and headed towards the woods. On the edge nestled a beautifully proportioned red brick house with veranda. Inside,

Annie was boiling water for coffee. 'Come and have some lunch,' she smiled at Geoffrey.

'Thank you.' Geoffrey followed her into a dining room, table laid with embroidered cloth and plates of cold meats, cheese and bread. She was a striking woman, gentle in spirit, whose beauty and grace could still be detected in her white-haired years. 'He won't join us for lunch,' she said. 'I've just taken something up to his room. But you can see him directly.'

'Oh,' was all Geoffrey could muster in response. She seemed unperturbed by the Nazi uniform in her house. Anders joined him at the table, helping himself to a hunk of cheese and bread.

'Does he know we're getting him out?' asked Geoffrey.

'Not yet. We've got to get him to the safe-house on the border with Germany. We're flying him back on a bomber, taking him back with two of our pilots that were shot down and rescued. We have someone co-ordinating the operation near Kiel.'

'And my role is to escort him there?'

'Yes,' replied Anders, taking another piece of bread, then sipping the coffee his wife had just brought in. 'You're a Nazi officer taking a prisoner to a POW camp. It's the perfect cover – the only one we can reliably use. When he's safely taken care of, we need to get you on that U-boat. The one we suspect with the documents has been moored in Norway the past three weeks. Intelligence from the Captain tells me its repairs are almost done. It should be perfect timing for you.' Geoffrey looked across the table at Anders. What a man that he should risk his life helping Britain. But then he was fiercely patriotic, loved Denmark, his homeland, and was prepared to help Britain and America bring down Nazism. Denmark *had* to be liberated and Anders was prepared to do his bit. If betrayed, he and his family would pay with their lives. Geoffrey didn't ask but sensed that Anders was quite high up in the Resistance Movement.

Anders pushed his chair back and stood up. 'I see you've finished, so let's go. I'll take you to Jonathan.' A few minutes later he opened ajar the only door in the basement. Josephy rushed forward to check who it was. 'It's me,' said Anders. Josephy relaxed, opening the door fully to let them in. Huddled in the corner sat Jonathan reading the previous day's newspaper, humming to himself. Geoffrey followed Anders into the room.

'I've brought someone to see you Hanns,' declared Anders. Jonathan grunted, but didn't look up. 'It's your nephew from Vienna.'

The newspaper fell to the ground. His head shot up. His eyes were hollow and vacant. The man before them was a shadow of his former self, gaunt, face drawn tight and haggard from years of suffering. Malnutrition evident from his scrawny body, weeks at sea on the U-boat had prematurely aged him. Geoffrey saw in his face a ruthlessness that wasn't there before. He wasn't the brilliant, kind and loving doctor that he remembered. He seemed consumed with hate. Completely calm, Jonathan stood up and walked steadily towards Geoffrey. To Jonathan the man before him wasn't his nephew. The Nazi uniform pierced his consciousness; the hated swastika burnt in his psyche. He couldn't distinguish beyond it. His head began to thump, throbbing hard at his temples. Jonathan screwed up his eyes as if a bright light had penetrated his vision. On the surface he remained composed.

'Hello Jonathan,' said Geoffrey, not sure whether to touch him on the shoulder in some form of greeting.

Anders stepped forward. 'He's come to take you home to England.'

Jonathan didn't say a word, but held his hands up in surrender. Something inside snapped. Anders didn't see the tiny blade hidden flat against Jonathan's hand. Jonathan lurched forward. In one deft sweeping arc motion he plunged towards Geoffrey's neck. Geoffrey saw it coming. Months of training had taught him to observe the unexpected. He grabbed Jonathan's wrist, twisting it behind his back. The blade fell to the floor. Geoffrey held him to the ground. Jonathan's tense body relaxed.

'You're a bloody lunatic, Hanns,' said Josephy through gritted teeth. 'You forget yourself as soon as you see a Nazi uniform.'

Anders motioned for Josephy to keep quiet. 'He's been through enough. Let him be.' Geoffrey gradually helped Jonathan to his feet, now like putty in his hands. Jonathan reflected not an iota of emotion, withdrawing into himself. His eyes cold, he murmured, 'They slaughter men. They slaughter women. They slaughter children. They have no mercy. I have no mercy.'

Geoffrey spoke. 'It's all right. We'll get through this. Tomorrow I'll take you to the border and you'll soon be back in England.' Anders moved over to Jonathan and touched him gently by the arm. 'For your own protection, we need to search you.' Jonathan didn't flinch as Anders checked for further weapons. Then he beckoned to Geoffrey. Geoffrey followed him out of the room and went upstairs to snatch some rest. Anders wanted to meet him later that afternoon to show him something.

At three thirty exactly Anders knocked on Geoffrey's bedroom door. Geoffrey was lounging on his bed reading the latest *Zeitung*. He had removed the heavy Nazi overcoat with red wheat sheaf insignia on the collar and was just resting in shirt, braces and trousers. Anders peered around the door and couldn't help thinking how strangely striking and natural Geoffrey looked in the uniform. 'I'd like to show you something before it gets dark.'

'Damn Nazi propaganda,' he said, discarding the half-read newspaper to the floor.

Anders ignored his comment. 'I'm taking you somewhere,' he said. 'I want you to observe. Nothing more. You might need to radio the contacts after you've delivered Hanns, your Jonathan, to the border if you encounter any difficulties. I suggest you leave your jacket. Here, you can borrow my overcoat to hide the uniform. We don't want to alarm anyone.'

'Understood, Anders.' Geoffrey slipped on the brown wool-made overcoat. They went out into the grounds. Grey clouds signalled dusk was already setting in; the dense woodland behind the house looked dark and foreboding. They wove their way through the thick, closely packed trees. Anders knew the route well. After what seemed like ages, they came to a clearing. In the distance Geoffrey could hear muffled shots. Anders beckoned to follow. Beyond the clearing there was a deep quarry. About a dozen teenagers were lined up doing target practice. The depth of the quarry meant that they couldn't be heard beyond. Anders stepped out of the shadows with Geoffrey close behind. A tall youngster about sixteen with masses of thick, brown, wavy hair ran towards them, extending his hand towards Anders.

'How's it going Olaf?' asked Anders.

'Very well sir. Progress has been slow but we're getting somewhere now.'

'You look half dead, young man. I hope you've been getting enough sleep?'

'Not really sir. Not with having to finish the school work as well as this.'

Anders turned to Geoffrey. 'Geoffrey, I'd like you to meet Olaf. He is your point of contact if you should need it. All coded radio transmissions should go via him.' They shook hands as Geoffrey nodded in acknowledgement. Geoffrey knew not to ask questions, although he suspected the truth. Membership of the Resistance Movement across Denmark was increasing every month. What Anders wouldn't tell him was that Olaf headed the youth resistance movement in South Zealand. Training in the quarry took place daily, except for Sundays, when most of them were in church or Sunday school. The youngsters took extra school lessons on Saturdays as a cover for their operations. Afterwards the Victory Group, as they had called themselves, assembled in the woods for training in various acts of sabotage. Geoffrey couldn't help but notice how young some of them were. Why should they risk their lives? It seemed so incredible to him.

Anders shrugged the rucksack from his shoulders. It was weighed down with explosives for their next act of defiance. He passed it to Olaf. The target: a factory making parts for German tanks in a suburb of Roskilde.

'Thank you sir.'

'The next consignment will be delivered in two days.' With no further exchange of words, Anders motioned for Geoffrey to go with him to depart.

Back at the house, Anders turned to Geoffrey. 'You leave at first light tomorrow. Josephy will be your driver. And don't forget to polish your boots. SS officers are impeccably dressed. Sleep well.'

'Thank you. Goodnight Anders.'

≈❦

Alone in the room in the lodge on Vallø Castle estate, Jonathan peered at the four walls. Every night Josephy left him for a couple of hours and every night he checked to see if Josephy had locked the door. The frustration ate at his soul. He couldn't easily escape, but there was *no way* he was going back to England. In the dim light he glanced at his watch. Two fifteen. Josephy wouldn't be back for another hour. Was it his imagination or had Josephy forgotten to turn the key that evening? He lived in hope, went over to the door and rattled the handle. It opened. He dashed back to pick up his rucksack There was no chance he was going home. His work wasn't done. The bastards hadn't paid nearly enough for his suffering.

The hall was deserted; all members of the household asleep. Quietly, he opened the back door. The sub-zero February night air hit his face. Fortunately for him it hadn't snowed so no tracks or footprints would be left behind. With no money and not wanting to stop to get food from the kitchen in case he was heard, he ran out towards the woods. He would pillage and raid isolated farmhouses wherever possible; live as someone on the run. He skirted the edge of the woods. Banding a stick behind to cover his tracks as he walked, he headed for the boundary wall of the Vallø Castle estate. In the distance there were no lights on at the gate-lodge. At this point he slowed to a walking pace. Although the place was in complete darkness, muffled voices were arguing inside. He crept past. Moments later he was outside the grounds and running down the road. At a fork in the junction, he took the left road. He knew his final destination: the Neolithic burial site on the Knudshoved Odee peninsula. No one would ever think of looking for him in the ancient tomb. From there he would co-ordinate his reprisals. Half an hour later his pace slackened, his lungs tight, his legs feeling like lead. He willed himself to keep going. A search party from Vallø would find him too easily since he hadn't gone nearly far enough.

Half a kilometre later, breathless, he stopped. The land was as flat as far as the eye could see. Dawn was breaking on the horizon. His fingers were frozen in spite of stuffing them in his pockets; the rest of his body sweaty from running.

'Halt!' came the order from the semi-darkness.

In a flash Jonathan dropped flat to the ground. The jack-booted Nazi came over to him, accompanied by two others in the patrol, kicked him and rolled him over with his foot. 'Identity papers.' One held the barrel of a gun at his chest.

Jonathan reached into his pocket for his papers and held them out.

The officer took them, shining his torch over the name. *Hanns Faltitschek.* He grunted, then smirked, 'Ah, *jahwol*. You're one of the network.' Jonathan wasn't going to be intimidated. '*Nein*, I am due on the milking shift on the farm over yonder.' He nodded eastwards. They seemed convinced, but Jonathan was taking no chances. As the officer went to pass the papers back, in a single swift movement Jonathan pulled the gun with silencer out of the position flat against his armpit. With a muffled double bang, two officers fell to the ground dead. The toecap of the third headed straight for Jonathan's face, knocking him backwards, his gun flying across the road. Jonathan tried to scramble up. The SS officer sneered, 'You can do better than that!' Although Jonathan had been kicked, he realised the officer wasn't going to shoot him or he'd have done it immediately. What he didn't know was another patrol had turned the corner and was marching towards them. Suddenly he heard their boots crunching on the road. There would be no way out of this one.

'Shoot me!' he challenged. 'You won't. I'm more valuable to you alive.' *Surrender, he would not. Kill the bastards, he would.* He had one weapon left, now biding a bit of time to pull it out. 'But first a cigar. Want one?' Jonathan asked, reaching into his pocket, pulling out the tin in a flash before they could shoot him.

The officer answered, 'We know that trick.' He turned to the SS patrol behind him. 'Werner and Helmut, take him to HQ! I'll deal with him shortly.'

The two officers stood to attention, *'Jahwol*, sir.' They grabbed Jonathan's wrists, yanking them behind his back, pushing him roughly to the ground. 'Get up,' they yelled, kicking him.

Jonathan stumbled up, the calf of his leg numb. 'Do you know who I am? You'll regret this when the *Abwehr* finds out.'

'Run man!' they sniggered. 'There's nowhere for you to hide.'

Jonathan reached for the thumb blade on the lapel of his jacket, swung around and thrust it towards the man's jugular. He hit his target spot on. The man screamed as blood spurted out of his neck like a fountain. 'You bastard,' snarled Jonathan. Two hands landed on his shoulder and shoved him to the ground struggling. They beat him to near death. Blood oozing from his mouth and chin, two front teeth knocked out, eyes swollen, he was barely conscious. They dragged him to a hand cart, heaved him onto it and headed for HQ. Why didn't they shoot him on the spot? Death would be preferable for him now, except he still had to exact his revenge – total, absolute revenge. Survive he would for that one aim.

By the time they arrived at HQ, he was exhausted and aching from the bruises, in a semi-conscious state. The commanding officer was back at his post. He didn't wait to interrogate Jonathan. 'Take him to the truck!' he ordered.

'Yes, sir.' The young SS escort clicked his heels, grabbing Jonathan roughly by the elbow. The cattle wagon at the siding was being loaded with boxes of food supplies, ready for transportation over the border into Germany. The Nazis had plundered the land and the people's livelihood to support their war machine.

'In the middle carriage! Guard him!' he yelled at another officer.

The scenario familiar, Jonathan smelt the stench of bodies too close to each other before he even saw the huddles of men and women inside. Barely able to move and bruised all over, he was pushed up into the stinking wagon. The door slid closed behind him, only weak daylight seeped through the cracks in the wooden doors. Shouts were accompanied by the locomotive steaming up at the front of the train. He knew he was heading for a concentration camp, the question was – which one? This time he just knew deep down that he wouldn't come out alive.

Chapter 7

Dawn was about to break over Denmark on a Saturday, heavy with clouds threatening rain. It was just after 5 a.m. Anders rushed into Geoffrey's bedroom, shook the slumbering figure facing the wall. 'Wake up! Hanns has gone!'

Geoffrey rolled over and sat bolt upright, trying to focus his bleary eyes. 'Gone?'

'Quick! Get up! I need you to warn Olaf.'

Geoffrey scrambled out, pulled on a pair of trousers over his pyjamas and hastily buttoned up his shirt. Anders passed him a thick, brown jumper, dark overcoat and cap, then Josephy's rifle to sling over his shoulder. 'Good. You look the perfect gamekeeper.' He glanced at his watch. 'Hurry! To the quarry whilst it's still dark. Olaf will be doing the last of the night training. Heaven knows where Hanns is, but he can't have got too far. We have to make sure he doesn't give himself away.'

'Shall I radio the Captain in England?'

'No, there isn't time. I'll do that. Off you go.'

Geoffrey stepped out into the freezing February air. The ground under foot was frozen, the sharp frost stinging his hands. Everything was still and quiet. He pulled on thick gloves, his warm breath cutting the biting cold air. Hurrying through the woods he was thankful for the instruction in fieldcraft he had received back in England.

He could memorise routes to a given destination. A few minutes later as he approached the quarry he heard the muffled gun shots on target practice. Learning to shoot in darkness was a crucial part of training, especially since some acts of sabotage would be at night. His eyes scanned as best he could for Olaf's lofty shape in the dark. Geoffrey flashed his torch twice in signal as instructed earlier by Anders. Olaf came out of the shadows. 'What's up?' he inquired.

'It's Hanns. He's disappeared.'

'Heavens. Have you any idea where? Which direction?'

'No.'

'There's no time to lose. I'll inform the network. We have to find him and hope he still has enough sense not to jeopardise the whole operation.'

'I must get back to Anders,' said Geoffrey. They shook hands. Geoffrey turned and ran off into the woods towards Anders' lodge. With Geoffrey gone, Olaf walked over to the three young men standing by the heavy machinery used during the day to quarry stones. 'Stefan,' he hissed. 'Come, I need you to do something for me.' He took him aside.

'Yes?'

Olaf reached into his pocket. It was now 6 a.m. 'Please take this sealed pouch to HQ in Copenhagen. They will know what to do. I'm sending for Tom. He's one of the few in the military police the Nazis still trust and haven't incarcerated in a concentration camp. Now off you go!' He nudged Stefan's shoulder then turned to the other two. 'I'd like both of you to set the chain of communication in motion right away. You can leave me to clear up here.'

The two youths ran into the woods, leaving Olaf to clear up and contemplate possible locations where Hanns might be hiding. It wasn't only Hanns' personal safety he worried about. There was only a limited time slot in which Geoffrey could deliver Hanns to the border and then board the U-boat to retrieve the military documents. Also there was a limit to how many times they could get one of their men on board without arousing suspicion. The Kriegsmarine was still upbeat that it could win the war for Germany in spite of German losses from Allied torpedoing of U-boats in the Atlantic and around their bases. Adolf Hitler had sanctioned 'special treatment' for U-boat crews and, fortunately for Olaf and the Resistance, the Käpitans were complacent about checking seamen's identities. Olaf turned back to the rifle range to pick up cartridges. Having removed all trace of that night's training, he returned to the lodge in the grounds of Vallø Castle. To his surprise, Anders and Geoffrey had gone out, but not before Anders had lit the fire. He settled into a chair by the fireplace, warmed his hands and waited for their return.

Meanwhile, the cattle truck carrying Jonathan and nearly 400 Jews stopped at an isolated, unmarked station. In the darkness all sense of time had been lost to the inmates crammed inside. The sliding doors suddenly flung open, announcing another day had dawned. Cold air hit the stench of unwashed bodies of the Jews rounded up from the ghettos of Germany. SS officers swarmed the place.

'*Herraus*! Get out!'

During the journey Jonathan had kept his concentration focused on his feet, not daring to take in all around him. Now he glanced cautiously, surveying the scene outside on the tiny provincial platform, the atmosphere filled with unutterable terror. Ahead of him the prisoners were being formed into orderly lines, the guards eyeing them up and down before separating them into two distinct areas. 'You that way!' the senior SS officer pointed to the left. It was at this point that Jonathan realised the other carriages held children too. To take innocent lives beggared belief.

'You! That way!' came the next order, motioning and shoving a woman and eight-year-old boy towards the right. There seemed to be no logic to the way the people were being separated. Then it was Jonathan's turn.

'You! To the right!'

It was only a few minutes later and Jonathan's long line of some 200 souls was ordered to move. Flanked by SS and Gestapo, their every movement was clocked.

'March! *Schnell!*'

The elderly man next to Jonathan faltered. There was no mercy. The butt of the rifle hit him across the back of the head, knocking him to the ground. There was nothing that could be done to help him. Jonathan focused ahead. The scenario was familiar. His body, which usually felt no emotion any more, released an involuntary shiver down his spine. Teeth gritted to prevent any further reaction, Jonathan kept walking. One step at a time, however difficult, was the only way he could get through this. Not thinking about what may lie ahead. Fear of the future would paralyse him and make him ineffective. He knew the truth. He was on another Nazi death march. No food or water was distributed en route.

Two hours later they arrived at the gates of a camp, exhausted and with blisters on their feet. Fenced with barbed wire, the camp was little different from Dachau except it hadn't a moat around it. By now the long line of people was shorter; at least fifty having collapsed on the way. Their suffering was over. With fellow inmates,

Jonathan passed under the arched gateway. *Arbeit Macht Frei*. How he hated those words. Inside the camp, the distinct smell of rotting flesh hung in the air, turning his stomach. A handful of skeletal men in striped pyjamas scurried across the camp, the hated prisoners' uniform a symbol of death and human degradation. Jonathan had seen it all before. These men, barely alive, would be collecting the meagre dried-out black rye bread for breakfast for their hut. Camp survivors began shuffling out of the row upon row of huts for the early morning roll-call. No more than flesh and deformed bones, their haunting black-ringed eyes peered out of emaciated faces. He felt their pain. Horror that he hadn't even witnessed in Dachau now confronted him, eating at the core of his being. He began to feel nauseous. Not so much from lack of food, though he hadn't eaten for nearly twenty-four hours, but from the sight and stench around him. The next group, huddled together to his left, were ordered to strip naked. '*Schnell!* It's only a shower. We can't have filthy wretches in the camp. *Schnell!*' He never saw them again.

A guard shoved Jonathan hard in the back. 'This way!'

In obedience Jonathan walked, starring straight ahead.

'There's work for you,' added the young guard. Across the parade ground Jonathan became aware of someone staring intently, surreptitiously trying to catch his attention. Without moving his head, Jonathan averted his eyes to the left. There stood a pathetic wizened figure barely recognisable as his cousin's husband from Vienna. Mr Hermann Herz was a shadow of his former self. Their eyes momentarily locked. Jonathan's thoughts flashed back to the Sabbath meal he had had with him and his wife and son Günter in Vienna in 1938. Jonathan contained his reaction. The guards saw nothing. He continued walking. The camp commandant's office loomed ahead; the two guards goose-marched him in. Inside they clipped their heels and saluted '*Heil Hitler.*'

The room felt surprisingly warm and welcoming, not at all austere as Jonathan had expected. The 6-foot uniformed commandant was standing beside his desk, chatting and laughing with a young female of typical Aryan features. Her slim feminine body was tightly encased in a Nazi uniform. When she turned, her face had a cold, steely hardness that, for all his experience, Jonathan hadn't seen in a woman before.

'Irma,' the Commandant smirked, raising his eyebrows in flirtation. 'I see they've brought a new one for you.'

'Thank you Herr Commandant.' Her voice husky, she barely raised a smile in return. She turned to Jonathan, 'You! Follow me!'

Fatigued, bruised and aching, Jonathan could barely put one foot in front of another. Teeth still gritted, he was determined not to show any sign of weakness. He followed her, focusing his eye on the line of stitching on the back collar of her uniform. Survival was second nature to him now. It was revenge he craved. The thoughts pounded in his head.

Revenge … Kill the bitch. She must die. His breathing became rapid and shallow.

'Where are we?' he spluttered.

'Belsen,' she replied, turning around to look him full in the face. 'Co-operate and you'll survive.'

'I'm not who you think I am,' he tried. 'They've got it all wrong.'

He couldn't appeal to her compassion. She had none. 'All I know is you tried to kill an officer. That's punishable by death.' She smirked, revealing a gap in her blacked teeth.

By God she's rough, he thought. 'But the Commandant has decided to spare you. You've got muscles enough and we need a work force.' The gawping teeth with gaps smiled at him. He wished he could wipe the smirk off her face. He held it all in, mustn't buck now. If he did, he'd be taken out instantly by the guards pacing the perimeter fence. Bide his time. Temporary satisfaction couldn't jeopardise his chance for the big kill.

❧

In the couple of weeks since Lilian had been dropped near Kiel, daily broadcasts were successfully transmitted to a German nation hungry for information. She was proud of her work, a necessary part of the Allied propaganda machine. That night waiting until Helga was asleep, she sneaked out in her SS uniform into the nearby woods. She had to make contact with her counterpart at a designated radio station in North Devon. Crouching by a tree stump, shielded by the overgrowth, she reached into her kitbag. The radio transmitter was quick to assemble and she wasted no time to send the first message. She waited, scanning the darkness and listening for anyone around. The transmitter crackled, then the reply came through: 'Two at Böklund, north of Schleswig.'

Lilian re-packed her equipment, slung the kitbag over her shoulder and headed for the destination of her first mission. It had to be completed before Helga woke in about five or six hours. It afforded her little time. Lilian turned her thoughts to the pilots she was due to rescue. Their safety was paramount. A safe passage had been worked out for them by Captain Henderson as head of SIS. Lilian reached into the lining of her jacket, pulled out a silk handkerchief with a map of the region printed on it. Deciding it was safer to follow the minor roads, she walked half a mile to the first rendezvous – a gamekeeper's hut about a hundred yards from a crossroads. The vehicle was already there waiting to take her to the final meeting point. Her driver, an officer of lower SS rank, nodded in acknowledgement as she stepped into the car. He said nothing. In silence they drove on minor roads inland, following the coastline through Eckernförde, then north-west, skirting Schleswig on to Böklund. On the outskirts of Böklund the driver swung the vehicle through a dilapidated gate down a rough track towards a lone farmhouse. The faint sound of dogs barking could be heard in the distance. Lilian stared ahead, the headlights of the vehicle illuminating the hedgerow on either side. It had begun to rain; the single wiper barely cleared the windscreen. The driver pulled up outside a barn. He gestured to Lilian to get out, then pointed saying the only words of the entire journey. 'They're in there.' It was then that she realised from the tone of his voice that he was deaf. She smiled, mouthed her thanks and got out. He reversed the car around the back of the barn and waited for her return.

Lilian crept up to the barn door, listened, then pushed it open. Inside, various types of farm machinery cluttered the lofty space. At the far end a single stable with horse was cornered off. She flashed her torch three times and waited. The silence seemed endless. Maybe they weren't here, she thought.

Then out of the shadows two young men walked, both still in RAF uniform, one with bandaged arm in a sling. They were the fortunate ones, rescued by some kind farmer after being shot down over enemy territory. They must have got away before the SS search could find them. Ironically, now they were being protected by her SS uniform.

'Hello, gentlemen,' she said. 'Do you have papers?'

'Yes,' they answered in unison.

'Good. Let's go. Remember, if we are stopped, let me do all the talking.'

'Yes ma'am.' In spite of being obviously weary and their uniforms grimy from baling out, their smiling faces displayed a relief at her presence. Bemused but grateful for their guardian angel, their ordeal hadn't dampened their panache.

'If anything un-toward happens,' she added, 'make for Flensburg on the Danish border. Wait and the next link will take you on. Come let's go.' The silhouette of three figures ran around the side of the barn to the car. The farmer who had loaned his outhouses remained inside, turning a blind eye to the night-time activities. Lilian sat in the front of the vehicle, the two pilots in the back seat. Much of the journey was taken in silence. Just before Flensburg, Lilian handed the men over to their escort to be taken over the border. Her mission successfully completed, Lilian got back in the car to be driven back to her farmhouse lodgings. Two hours later she was back in bed; the SS uniform discarded over the dressing table chair. She hoped the pilots were on their way across the Sound to Sweden. From neutral Sweden they would be taken to England. Lilian's head hit the pillow. Exhausted, she slept solidly until Helga brought her a cup of coffee in the morning.

A thousand miles away as the crow flies, at Church Lane in Knowle, back in England, it had been a long night for Katharine. She yawned, sat at the monitoring equipment staring at the recent messages. Transmissions to her unnamed female source near Kiel had taken longer than expected to accomplish due to interference on the wavelength. In between Katharine had monitored and intercepted some intermittent enemy transmissions. Now her husband's distinct footsteps could be heard on the stone floor in the hallway. She called to him, 'George!' He came into the library, bent over her shoulder and kissed her cheek. 'Don't you ever get any sleep?' he teased.

'So you're missing my warm body next to yours?'

'Of course, but we both know there are sacrifices to be made.'

'I picked up an important transmission early this morning,' she said, suppressing another yawn. She reached into the top drawer of the desk and took out a cigarette, throwing the packet back in.

'Isn't it a bit early for that? It's only quarter to eight.'

'I need it, George.' She lit the end, took a drag, then a deep breath. She couldn't tell him she was still in shock over discovering Jonathan's death on the U-boat. She found herself wondering again if he knew about it. There wasn't much that escaped him. If he had been told it would have come from Hugo. She trusted Sir Charles not to reveal anything.

She continued, 'The signal I picked up early this morning came from Frederikshavn. You asked me to track her and I have been successful. The U-boat is ready to leave its base tomorrow.'

'Thank you,' was all he said. In his line of business he never revealed any more than that. And Katharine knew better than to ask him. 'Come, let's have some breakfast. Fraser said he was brewing a pot of tea five minutes ago.'

Katharine reflected how George was as regimentally reserved and exact as the day she first met him. The passing of time had deepened her love for him and his for her. His strength and protection was something she could rely on. She took his arm. Together they walked into the breakfast room where Fraser was pouring the boiled water into a china teapot. 'Good morning, ma'am. Good morning, sir.'

Captain Henderson gave a single nod, 'Good day Fraser.'

Fraser placed the pot on a mat on the table, turned to stoke the fire, then reached for a telegram perched behind the wooden clock. 'This was delivered a few minutes ago, sir.'

'Thank you Fraser. I thought I heard something just now.' Captain Henderson reached for a knife from the table, slit cleanly across the envelope and pulled out the telegram. Three simple typed words read: 'All stations go.' It signalled to him that their agent would now be given the order to move. Katharine stared intently, watching for the slightest reaction to the message. He looked up. 'Don't fret, my love. Everything is fine. If you will excuse me, I need to make a couple of phone calls.'

'Of course George.'

He moved towards her, placed his arm around her shoulder and kissed the top of her head. She looked into his eyes. 'And when I've done the calls ...' he said.

'We have a couple of hours to relax,' she interrupted. 'You can read to me while I lie in your arms. I love you reading to me, George. We haven't touched *David Copperfield* for days. I want to know what happens. There has to be hope somewhere in Dickens' plot.'

Captain Henderson walked towards the door. She called after him. 'When I've finished breakfast I'll be in the morning room. I am getting too lax with the violin. I need to practice. The war has changed everything.' She sighed, 'My best days are over.'

He turned, straightened his back. 'Never! You worry so, my darling. Your music is divine. You haven't lost your ability to touch people's souls.' Katharine looked at him with tenderness. How she loved his unquestioning support of her. She laughed, her mirth echoing around the kitchen. Captain Henderson disappeared into the hallway.

❧

Geoffrey and Anders returned to the lodge in the grounds of Vallø Castle just as the kitchen clock struck seven thirty a.m. Anders' wife had already laid out breakfast for their return. All attempts to locate Hanns had failed. The meeting with local resistance leaders had been brief. They had no information. Josephy got up from the fireplace and joined them at the table. Anders said nothing, just slipped him a piece of paper. Josephy glanced down. It was from Tom, recently promoted to head of Military Police in Copenhagen. He scanned the coded words: *the birds are nesting*. He looked up and nodded to Anders.

'It's all stations go, Geoffrey,' said Anders, pouring some coffee into the cups on the table. 'You board late this afternoon. You need to leave soon. Come. Josephy will drive you to a rendezvous outside Frederikshavn. Tom is accompanying you as well. He'll be here shortly – you remember I mentioned him to you. A lovely lad, was training part-time in college in Copenhagen and working on his father's farm until he was called up to the Military Police. '

'Is there any news of Jonathan … our Hanns?' asked Geoffrey.

'The trail went as far …' Before Josephy could finish, a commotion broke out in the hallway. 'Where's Anders?' came the breathless male voice.

'He's in the kitchen,' replied Anders' wife. Tom rushed into the kitchen, eyes scanning the three men before finally resting on Anders. Anders nodded approval for him to speak.

'There's news of Hanns,' he panted, holding his cap firmly in his hands. 'It's not good.'

'Come and sit down, Tom.' Anders drew up another wooden chair and poured him a coffee. 'Tell us what's happened.'

Tom took a sip, then a deep breath. 'An elderly lady outside Herlufmagle witnessed everything. So he'd got quite a distance already. Anyway … she heard a hullabaloo in the early hours of the morning. She's a bit of a busy-body. She peered out of the bedroom curtains. The Nazis didn't see her, but she saw a man being beaten up and carted off. His description matches that of Hanns.'

'Go on,' said Anders, leaning forward.

'She began the chain of communication. From the first link until it reached me in Copenhagen took less than half an hour. I went straight to our Police HQ to check the transportation lists filed in our office. Hanns' name was on it. Then I came here to tell you. He's in Belsen.'

A silence of disbelief pervaded the room. Josephy fidgeted in his chair. Tom continued, 'As I said, I came straight here knowing that you need me to escort him to Frederikshavn.' He glanced in Geoffrey's direction. 'He's going to need protection. Patrols are everywhere. I suggest Josephy doesn't risk it by coming too.'

'Very well. Thank you Tom.' Anders stood up. 'There isn't much we can do for Hanns at the moment. We have to get on with the task in hand.'

Geoffrey got up. 'I'll get my things.'

'Yes,' replied Tom before the other two could. 'We leave in five minutes.'

Geoffrey dashed up to his room and retrieved his haversack. In that moment, he thought again of Lilian as he had every night before he went to sleep. In his mind he often imagined their passionate reunion. Only hope would carry him through. He rummaged in the bedside cabinet, pulled out a small, red, leather-bound New Testament. Inside he had slipped a photograph of Lilian. Her sparkling eyes danced off the page, smiling directly at him. He brought the photo to his lips, kissed her face and whispered 'Till we meet again, my sweet.' He replaced it into the New Testament, closed the drawer and rushed back downstairs. Adrenalin now supplanted his melancholy. He was ready for what lay ahead. His adopted country needed him. He would not let England down – not now, not ever.

Later that same afternoon, Geoffrey arrived with Tom at Frederikshavn. Two streets away from the harbour, Tom stopped at one of the premises to collect Geoffrey's Kriegsmarine uniform from a known safe-house. Geoffrey had tried two on before he found one that fitted. Outside the building Tom bade him farewell. 'You're all ready with your kit, lad. Oh, here. I nearly forgot. Take these gloves. You'll need them. It gets damn cold in the U-boat. Now off you go!'

'Thanks.' They shook hands.

'You're one of them now. Good luck.'

Geoffrey turned. Without a backward glance, he walked towards the harbour. The background noise of shipping, engines and shouts of men loading supplies could be heard. As he approached, the hub and bustle of activity intensified. Men passed boxes down the orderly lines across the dockyard and onto the U-boat. Preparations were also being made with other shipping anchored in the harbour. Geoffrey stood still, momentarily surveying the scene. He glanced down at the emblem of the Smiling Shark on the cap in his hands. What terror it concealed. Allied shipping was still being knocked out, jeopardising supplies to Britain and the survival of a nation already struggling on rations. Geoffrey knew he must succeed. He put on his cap and walked with confidence through the harbour gates. The two guards saluted.

'*Guten Morgen. Heil Hitler.*'

'*Guten Tag,*' he replied, walking on. He focused straight ahead. The crew took no notice of him; too busy loading the U-boat with tons of supplies. As he approached them, the Captain finished giving his orders. He turned on hearing the footsteps behind him. Geoffrey saluted.

'Papers!' the Captain crowed.

'Here, Herr Ka-leu.' Geoffrey reached into his pocket and passed him the slim passbook.

The Captain flicked through before handing it back to him. 'Very good. Prepare for boarding. You're overseeing supplies during the journey.'

'*Jahwohl* Herr Ka-leu.'

'The little beauty is full to the brim,' the Captain smirked. Much as it pained him, Geoffrey saluted and walked towards the crew. The smell of stale beer hung in the air as he drew close to them. Behind them the order sounded: 'All boarding!'

Geoffrey joined the procession scrambling along the metal ladder up the side of the U-boat. A flag with 'the Smiling Shark' and swastika hung from the conning tower. The crew manned ship was ready for the salute to sail out of the harbour. The engines started up. The U-boat slipped graciously out to sea. A few minutes later the crew hurried down below in preparation for the dive. Inside, the men ignored the cramped conditions, engrossed in their tasks. Laughter filled the narrow chambers. They seemed happy enough, thought Geoffrey. He surveyed the scene, taking in every detail, making a note of who did what. A slap on the back, he turned. The clean-shaven youth with hair to a parting smiled. 'Hey mate, we're in supplies. Let's go. The crew will need supper soon enough.'

'*Jahwohl.*'

'You got the menus?'

'Yes,' Geoffrey replied quick-thinking. In his mind, he pondered how he could conjure up a menu little knowing what supplies were on board. 'I'll go check out the rations. Rumour has it a box or two didn't arrive. Overheard the Captain talking earlier.' He lied. His companion poked around in the makeshift galley, looking for pots and pans. A single plate stove, sink and cupboard constituted the fittings in the primitive kitchen area. How they were supposed to serve up eighty meals three times a day was beyond him. He was thankful that cooking the meals was down to the chef, not him. Geoffrey left his companion pulling a charred pan from under the sink. A few paces along the narrow corridor, he wiped the sweat from his brow. Pipes hissed and gurgled, the smell of the diesel engine permeated the boat. He couldn't complain. The temperature would drop soon enough. Passing the open toilet area, diesel mingled with the stench of sewage. The whole crew, with the exception of the Captain and his immediate staff, had to share this single toilet. Geoffrey contained an urge to retch. He craved fresh air. He pulled a handkerchief from his jacket pocket and held it over his nostrils, then hurried towards the supply room. Through the sleeping area the lights were dim. He carried on, all sense of their location and direction at sea lost.

Geoffrey entered the supply room, scanned the stacks of boxes to ascertain what was on board. Plenty of tins of meat, pickled vegetables and bars of chocolate. Suddenly the Captain's voice echoed through the U-boat. 'Dive, dive, dive! Enemy destroyer approaching overhead. Dive, then engines off!'

The U-boat took a sudden dive to the clattering of bells and chaos. For a split second, the lights flickered and went out. The engines went quiet. In the stillness they could avoid detection. It waited submerged at 10 fathoms. The destroyer proceeded to empty its load. The clunk of its depth charge speeding towards the U-boat echoed through its structure. Geoffrey clung to a pipe running the length of the wall of the supply room. It missed this time, but the aftershock tossed the U-boat like a cork. The lights flickered once again, then back on. Geoffrey looked around the confines of the compartment, boxes splayed open on the floor, their contents everywhere. He bent down and started replacing them as best he could. The U-boat, with engines still switched off, was cloaked in silence and eerie apprehension. Having stowed most of the boxes as best he could, Geoffrey returned towards the galley. In his mind he had the weekly menu worked out enough to satisfy any suspicious member of the crew. He also began to realise that this would be no quick mission. He would be cooped up in this goddamn U-boat for several days before he could attempt to retrieve any military documents and get off.

In the galley his fellow crewman stood washing a stack of dirty bowls in the tiny basin of the sink. He turned, throwing Geoffrey a stained tea-towel. 'Here, grab this and help me.' He carried on with the washing-up, muttering: 'We'll get that bloody destroyer before she takes us out, mark my words.'

In that moment Geoffrey didn't need reminding that his life might end at any point. Did he have God on his side? Would fate be kind to him and spare his life? Success was not assured however young and immortal he felt, however naïve his ideals about fighting a just war were. At least philosophising passed the time of day. He had only been on the U-boat a few hours, but it felt like days. He realised there would be plenty of time to get bored if he allowed it. In quiet moments the crew either rested or played cards. Playing cards substituted boredom. His mind worked over-time, taking in every detail, planning his next move. Without arousing suspicion he had to try and ascertain where they were heading and where he could disembark.

❧

Captain Henderson picked up the telephone receiver and dialled the operator. 'Would you get me Admiralty 307, please?'

'Certainly sir. '

He had chosen that moment to make the important call whilst Katharine was collecting a fresh supply of eggs from the local farm. She would be at least half an hour by the time she tramped over the field and back. It was the only free slot that morning off the radio equipment. Captain Henderson had offered to send Fraser, but she had wanted the fresh air.

A few seconds later Sir Charles answered on the line. 'Hello.'

'Sir Charles, it's me.'

Sir Charles recognised Henderson's voice immediately. 'Yes, hello. Everything alright?'

'I have some news. The destroyer nearly knocked out our man half an hour ago. Please tell her to back off if you would. And the others off the coast of Norway. That U-boat needs protection.'

'Why me, George? Haven't you got someone else?'

Captain Henderson disliked his insolence, which was inappropriate for a man of his position and age. 'Are you disobeying an order from me?'

'No, of course not George.'

'You know the procedure. I don't have to remind you. The orders cannot come from me as head of special operations. I have complete anonymity in the chain of command.'

Sir Charles coughed down the line, cleared his throat, '... so what do I tell them?'

'Operation Lighthouse.'

'I understand. All stations go then?'

'Yes.' Captain Henderson regained his patience.

Sir Charles persisted. 'Why didn't you inform me as soon as the agent boarded? How can I run things with such little information?'

'You are always informed at the appropriate time. In this instance the telegram was sent immediately.'

'Oh yes. The telegram.'

'Look,' Captain Henderson's voice was firm. 'You and I both know that I wasn't the one who authorised your coming out of retirement. The PM had his reasons. I didn't approve of you back on the job but now that you are, we have to make the best of it. And I would thank you to mind your position. You aren't M and haven't been for several years – difficult as you may find that.'

Sir Charles knew he could get his just deserts on Henderson if he wished. All he had to do was tell him that Katharine suspected Jonathan was still alive until the

U-boat went down. But this wasn't the moment. He held back, playing his cards the way he wanted. 'Come, come George. Let's be friends. We go back quite a way. And, if you remember, you still haven't repaid me for releasing you the information that Jonathan wasn't Katharine's legal husband. Without me you couldn't have married that wife of yours, darned obstinate forthright woman that she is.' He chuckled. Captain Henderson decided not to respond to the latter comment, but instead to release information from the latest intelligence. 'There's news of Jonathan.'

In the silence between them Sir Charles's heavy breathing came down the line. Captain Henderson carried on, 'He's been re-captured by the Nazis.'

'Ah … and?'

'He's in Belsen.'

'By God, Henderson.' After a pause he added, 'What now?'

'Well he stays there until we can think of a way to get him out … if he survives that is. This time it's doubtful, although my source tells me he's been put in a labour unit. If he's physically strong enough he might survive again. Who knows.'

'Not the Russian front?'

'No. He's still in the camp.'

'You should have taken him out ages ago, George. His survival is a risk to King and country. Remember your duty, George.'

'Don't talk to me about duty. If I sanctioned his death warrant and Katharine ever found out, our relationship would be a sham. It's duty which keeps Jonathan in the field and ensures he keeps breathing.'

'Yes, duty to your wife, George. Not to the King. I wonder what Counsel would say about that if they knew.'

'Are you threatening me? There are powers at work that even you don't know about.'

'Calm down George. You forget yourself. Emotions mustn't cloud the work. I understand your position. No one is more loyal to England than you.' He cleared his throat again, 'What about Jonathan – what if he is interrogated? This time he may not hold up.'

'My source tells me he hasn't been questioned this time. He was sent straight to the labour unit under that dreadful woman Irma Grese, the one the Americans suspect of atrocities.'

'Yes, I saw the memo last month. Jonathan's survival means we can call on him as a witness after the war.'

'It's a bit soon to be thinking of the end of the war. It will come, but I think we're at least a year away from victory. In the meantime, he has to stay put. We don't have the means to get him out. All efforts have to be concentrated on the agent now deep under the Atlantic in a moving time bomb. We need those documents. Anyway, that's all for now Sir Charles. Katharine is due back soon and I must get on. I will call later if there is any further news. Good day Sir Charles.'

'Goodbye George.'

Click of the receiver and conversation finished, Captain Henderson made his way to the kitchen for lunch.

Jonathan's arms ached with the stress of digging the frozen earth. The camp at Belsen was filling up every day with thousands more inmates. Many didn't last more than a few hours, dying soon after their arrival. Jonathan thrust the spade once again into the ground. Weak and gaunt from lack of food, his body was covered in open sores. The sharp cold sapped his strength as the wind whisked aside the thin striped uniform in torn threads over his body. His bare feet were immune to the rough rocks underfoot. He should have been covered in perspiration from the effort of digging, but starvation had stolen his sweat. Seconded to the burial gang, he spent from sunrise to sunset digging large pits, only to be filled later with hundreds of white skeletal bodies wasted away by brutality. The sight made him feel physically sick.

Nazi bastards. The day of reckoning was nearer.

Several times a day he waited behind the rear doors of the prison hut with the others in his team. His mind automatically blocked out the screams. The gentle sobbing of mothers clutching their children as they queued at the front to go in haunted his every waking hour and disturbed his sleep. Over and over again he heard their false reassurances: '*Ssh my darling. It's OK. It's just a shower.*' Those same bodies he had to drag out later, examining them for gold teeth, cutting off their hair. He tried not to think or feel, but cursed the Almighty for failing to intervene.

As he pitched his spade again and piled earth along a ridge line, he dug rhythmically. One of the inmates huddled in a group nearby asked for the latrine. Jonathan wanted to yell, 'No!' But it was too late. The guards overpowered the man, knocking him to the ground. One jackboot headed for his forehead. Another picked up a discarded spade as the others held him down. Jonathan turned away, hearing the bones in the man's face splinter under the force of the spade. The gurgled gasps lasted but a few seconds before the poor Jew choked on his own blood. The guards laughed. 'Any one else for the toilet?'

Jonathan stared ahead. He would take them out in a single blow. His teeth had become worn down from constant grinding. Biting his revenge, he saved his plan for maximum impact.

Chapter 8

1 March 1944

Lilian glanced at her watch. It was 2.10 a.m. Her contact was late. The moonlit night cast shadows across the bushes, shrouding the fields in an eerie spookiness. She pulled up the collar of her long, grey overcoat against the chill air and her cap down further over her forehead. The spring days were getting warmer, but at night the temperature still dropped to a few degrees above freezing. This was Lilian's fourth mission to rescue RAF pilots from enemy territory. Tonight was different. The message from England had indicated that she was to take them over the Danish border at Flensburg again, the same place as her first rescue mission. A double owl hoot – she turned. Nothing. Waiting, crouched against the hedge, her legs felt cramped. The double hoot sounded for a second time. She turned again. A slender shape ran towards her.

'Dawn will break soon enough,' he whispered.

'Not as bright as the moon in the night sky,' she responded.

Her identity established he motioned, 'Quick, come! There's no time to lose. There are three of them to get over.' Keeping within the shadows of the hedgerows, they skirted two fields before coming to a dirt track. Clouds had temporarily obscured the moon. At the end they saw an isolated barn and movement ahead. A man was getting into the driver's seat of a parked car.

'This is where I leave you,' Lilian's escort told her. Lilian got into the car. The engine started up. In the back sat three men who had already discarded their RAF uniforms. She didn't speak to them; neither did they to her. The car bumped along the rough track for about a kilometre before coming to a main road. An hour later they came to Flensburg. They travelled the final stretch of the long deserted highway towards the frontier post; a solitary house at the border the only sign of human habitation. The car pulled up sharp at the barrier. Lilian wound down the window. The guard leaned in, his face just inches from hers. She could smell traces of stale beer on his breath. His weapon pointed menacingly close. '*Heil Hitler!*'

'*Heil Hitler,*' she replied.

'Where are you going?'

'Frederikshavn.'

'This isn't a very direct route.'

'Orders. I just obey.'

'The men?' He glanced in the back.

'They're assigned to load supplies in the morning for the Kriegsmarine.' Lilian wound up the window and got out of the car. She closed the door out of earshot of her passengers. She continued, 'Then I'm escorting them south of Copenhagen. The Gestapo are using them for hard labour in a quarry there.'

'Papers madam, please.'

'Here.'

He flicked through each in turn, peering periodically into the car to confirm identity of the men from their photographs.

'Very good madam. You may pass.' He shot her another glance, raising his eyes up and down her feminine form. 'When you have some free time, madam … maybe I could take you out.'

She smiled. He took a scrap of paper and pencil from his pocket and scribbled down his number. '*Danke*,' she said, giving him another smile. He raised the barrier across the border. She got back into the car, stared straight ahead as the driver drove on. The headlights of the vehicle illuminated the deserted road, no signs of human life anywhere. A few minutes later the driver spoke his first words of the journey. 'Another kilometre and we hand them over.'

'Isn't it still too close?'

'It's fine. Everything has been sorted.' Ten minutes later he veered off the road onto a grass verge. He nodded to Lilian. Lilian got out of the car and stood leaning against the door. She lit a cigarette and took the first puffs. Moments later Josephy came out of the shadows. He motioned for the three men to alight. As the pilots got out and stretched their legs, Josephy chatted quietly with Lilian. Lilian passed him their papers.

'We can't thank you enough,' piped up the pilot. He was about twenty-five, Lilian reckoned. His wavy brown hair and mischievous smile could charm anyone.

'My pleasure gentlemen. I take my hat off to you bomber crews. Now you must go. You're in safe hands.'

Josephy led the men into the woodland where, half a mile on, Tom was waiting to take them to a safe house north of Copenhagen. There they would be hidden until they could be taken across the Sound to Sweden. Lilian turned and got back into the car. The driver seemed to second-guess her concern from the look on her face. 'Don't worry,' he said. 'The shift on the border changed half an hour ago. By the time we cross, it will be another patrol on duty.'

She relaxed back in the seat and closed her eyes. The remainder of the short journey passed without incident and they re-crossed the border with no difficulty. Before long Lilian was back where she had originally been picked up. This time the last part of the trek would be alone, back across the fields to Helga's farmhouse. She reached into her bag for water, took a sip, then walked on, keeping close to the hedges. On the eastern horizon the first sign of dawn was breaking.

The farmhouse came within view. The sound of dogs barking broke the quiet of the dawn. Something was wrong. She approached, peered cautiously over the hedge. Three vehicles were parked across the yard. SS officers swarmed over the place; two of them dragging Helga towards one of the waiting trucks. Lilian turned and edged herself low along the hedge towards the far gate. Once safely over in the next field she ran for her life. She had to get out of Germany. They were on her trail. She headed again for the Danish border crossing. There she could get help. In the meantime, with no proper kit or provisions, she would have to eke out an existence as best she could.

❧

After three weeks at sea, the U-boat carrying Geoffrey and its crew prepared to surface in a fjord on the Norwegian coast. During those long weeks the U-boat hadn't surfaced long enough at any one location to allow the crew off. Morale plummeted. Unshaven faces and unwashed bodies now took their toll. Within the last twenty-four hours some of the men had to be de-loused. The Captain had received orders from Admiral Doenitz not to continue to the Aran Islands.

'Prepare to dock!' The words through the U-boat's system seemed to be uttered from heaven. The men huddled in the corridors managed a unanimous cheer.

Geoffrey climbed out of the narrow bunk, having snatched a couple of hours sleep. He looked around the confines of the sleeping area. The clean shirt the Captain had issued to all of them ready for disembarkation had been removed by someone. He stood up.

The man lying stretched out in the bunk above guessed what he was looking for. 'Here.' He threw down a shirt.

'Thanks Fritz,' said Geoffrey. 'But can you spare it?'

'Yeah. You just need to know where to get them. I keep a small supply.' The whites of his eyes twinkled with mischief through his grimy blackened face.

'Where's that then?'

'Now that would be telling. Come, we best get moving. Let's not waste any time. I'm dying to go ashore.'

'Oh, I almost forgot. The Captain has asked me for a schedule from the supply room. I'll join you soon.' Geoffrey changed into the clean shirt and headed down the corridor beyond the Control Room. The crew broke into folk songs, their spirits soaring like kites on the wind; all eager to get off the U-boat for fresh air and beer. Geoffrey walked on. The bow of the U-boat was deserted. He turned the handle on the only door at the end. Across the door were the words: 'Admittance to authorised personnel only'. Walking through the torpedo compartment, he continued towards the far end, eyes scanning for any sign of a safe. The stifling hot air made it difficult to breathe. Everything smelt of oil and grease. His pristine shirt wouldn't last long in this atmosphere. Glancing to his left, he spotted a small inconspicuous safe. He crouched on one knee, pulling a long slim hairbrush from his trouser pocket. Hidden inside was all the kit needed to pick locks. He set to work. Five minutes later he succeeded in opening the safe door. In the dim lighting of the room he could see the safe contained only a single file. He reached in and pulled it out. The words 'top secret' were scrawled across it in fine ink; in the left hand corner the stamp of the double-headed eagle. Flicking through it, he ascertained immediately that the file came from the Ministry of Armaments. It had been signed by Albert Speer, a high-ranking Nazi in the ministry. This was it.

Geoffrey removed his right shoe, turned it over and used one of the picks to lever off the sole. Inside lay hidden a miniature camera. Smuggling out the whole file would be too risky, but photograph it he could. He photographed the first seven pages, then turned over the eighth and final page. There were several signatures underneath each other:

Albert Speer
Martin Bormann
Dr Joseph Goebbels
Heinrich Himmler
Adolf Hitler

Well, well, thought Geoffrey. The final signature was the Führer himself. *This goes all the way to the top*. He flicked through the file. It consisted of plans and technical explanations for a V3 rocket. Then he tore out the final page, realising that the plan could not be implemented without the signatures. He ripped it into tiny shreds and stuffed it behind a large maintenance pipe in the room. He replaced the camera carefully back in the sole of his shoe and left the room.

Moments later, standing on deck, Geoffrey looked in quiet dismay. Whilst he had been below examining the military documents he had not registered the U-boat releasing one of its torpedoes. It had hit its target. A British destroyer lay on its side like a stranded whale. Discarded lifeboats and jackets floated on the water around. Geoffrey turned to the crewman standing next to him. 'When did this happen?'

'About half hour ago. It takes a while to sink completely. Make 'em suffer.'

'Was it us?'

'No, unfortunately. Another in our fleet let off the bugger that hit it. Great pity, though. Would love to have been the one.'

The rest of the U-boat crew scrambled to the starboard side to watch. They jeered in exultation. British sailors continued to jump one after the other into the icy sea in a desperate attempt to douse their burning bodies. Now they faced drowning. Screams for help and waving of arms were to no avail. Geoffrey swallowed hard, trying to suppress a lump in his throat. These were His Majesty's forces, just like him. There was nothing he could do. The screams intensified with appeals to the U-boat crew for help. The crewmen laughed, taking bets on who was next to drown. The men struggling in the waters faced either death by drowning or shooting if they tried to land on the Norwegian coast. Either way their lives were over. Geoffrey turned away, unable to take their suffering. He climbed back down inside the U-boat. In the control room the Captain prepared to steer it the final few miles towards the port so they could disembark.

The Captain turned to his deputy. 'After a brief stop-over here, we head straight back to Frederikshavn. Orders from Grand Admiral Doenitz. The fleet is suffering some minor losses in the Atlantic. We are to re-group for the next major campaign.' He lied, deliberately understating the seriousness of the situation. The Kriegsmarine had effectively lost the battle for the Atlantic, not that he could admit it to his men.

'*Jahwohl* Herr Ka-leu.' The seaman went back to his post in preparation for docking. Geoffrey carried on to the sleeping quarters where he lay in the bunk he shared in different shifts with other crewmen. He had no heart to go ashore immediately.

❦

Two days later, Lilian walked towards the isolated farm a couple kilometres south-east of Flensburg. Over the last twenty-four hours she'd looted scraps of food from farm outhouses, but it wasn't sufficient. Weary, hungry and in need of a wash, she walked towards the farm buildings. She still wore the Nazi uniform loaned to her by Helga and carried her false identity papers. As she approached she noticed an elderly lady bent over a basket of washing ready to peg it on the line. Lilian coughed. The lady looked up, concerned at the sight of an SS officer, rare in provincial parts. 'Good day. How can I help you ma'am?' she asked, trying to contain her nerves.

'Good day. It's not bad for the time of the year, surprisingly mild for March.'

The woman glanced down at her basket of washing. 'But the weather's far too cool really to dry the clothes, but still … at least they get a good airing.'

Lilian smiled, looking around. 'Are you alone? Men fighting for our Führer?'

'Yes, but I'm not totally alone. There's my daughter-in-law and the grandchildren.' At the sound of their voices, a woman in her mid-twenties appeared in the doorway of the farmhouse.

'Elsa my dear,' said the elderly lady. 'See if the officer would like a drink. Take her inside.' Elsa turned to Lilian. '*Heil Hitler*! Can I make you a drink?' Lilian wondered if the *Heil Hitler* was genuine or done out of duty to impress her that they were compliant supporters of the regime.

'Thank you, that would be wonderful,' Lilian replied. She resorted to a cover story: 'Can you possibly spare bread and some cheese? It's been a long night on duty. I'm out of my usual territory so haven't had chance to eat properly. The Reich comes first, doesn't it?'

'Of course. Come inside.' Elsa seemed a sweet natured girl. A baby cried in the next room. 'Please excuse me a moment. Do help yourself to food in the larder.'

Lilian walked into the tiny cupboard filled with a ready supply of jars of pickled fruit and vegetables. She reached for a jar of pears, then, on the shelf, some cheese and bread, which she took back to the table. She tucked in as Elsa walked back into the kitchen with baby in a pale blue outfit in her arms.

'He's gorgeous,' commented Lilian.

'He's a little monkey. Wants all the attention.' Lilian suddenly heard other children playing around the side of the house.

'How many children do you have?'

'Five.'

'That must keep you busy.' Lilian smiled again. 'Could I possibly trouble you for some warm water? I'm due to report at a big Gestapo meeting this morning and I don't have time to go home and freshen up. I can't go in looking like this.'

Elsa glanced at her with slight suspicion before the voice of the elderly lady now standing behind her answered, 'Sure you can. Boil some water for the officer would you, Elsa.' The elderly lady sat herself opposite Lilian. 'Gammy leg, you know. Can't stand too long,' she muttered. They chatted for a while about pleasantries. An hour later, Lilian had enjoyed a warm wash and freshened herself. She bade farewell to the occupants and set off. The elderly lady went back to pegging out her clothes.

Elsa walked back into the kitchen and over to the window ledge. She picked up the telephone receiver and dialled the operator. 'Local Gestapo headquarters please.'

Moments later her mother-in-law stood back in the doorway. 'Elsa, how could you? I heard that!'

'I didn't want a nasty scene whilst she was here. She's headed for the border, that's what. She was no Nazi. A bloody Jew – I could tell.'

'You should have minded your own business. It's no good making trouble where it's not wanted. It's a bad omen.'

As befitting a Nazi officer, Lilian marched confidently towards the border crossing at Flensburg. The same guard stood at the post as when she had crossed a few days earlier. Maybe her luck was in with him or perhaps it wasn't. She couldn't tell what his reaction to seeing her might be. He recognised her immediately and came towards her. 'Hello again. You just couldn't keep away then? No prisoners this time?'

'I'm actually returning to collect them.'

'On foot?' he said, not asking this time for her identity papers.

'The damn vehicle broke down. They've got another ready for me when I get to the labour camp.'

'Here, why don't you let me escort you?' He offered his arm, glancing to the left, 'Those other two guards will cover for me. We'll take that truck over there.'

Lilian looked uncertain. 'I have plenty of time.'

'If we are too early I'll take you for a drink.'

'That would be improper whilst on duty.' Was he trying to catch her out? Maybe it was just her imagination working overtime. 'That's a very kind offer, but I prefer to walk. Thank you.' She took a few steps towards the barrier. He grabbed her arm. 'I will escort you.' In her mind she tried to think how she could get out of it.

'I would thank you not to be so rough with me,' she retorted. 'Know your place. I outrank you.'

'You're coming with me!' He pushed her roughly towards the vehicle. 'Inside!' Lilian was shoved next to the driver's seat. He started the engine and drove off. She decided to try to pacify him with talk of a Nazi rally she had attended and found inspiring. He drove on, looking ahead, occasionally smiling. He said very little. A few kilometres later he suddenly jerked across the deserted road into the woods. At that moment she knew she had been betrayed. She remained calm as she knew she must to survive. The truck bumped uncomfortably along the pot-holed track. Lilian surreptitiously glanced around. Could she make a jump for it and run?

She hadn't realised that two other men waited in the wings, sitting quietly in the back of the canvas-covered truck. The driver slammed on the brakes and leapt out.

Lilian jumped, running through the woodland. A few seconds later the three Gestapo men overpowered her. The one who had greeted her at the border stood over her.

'Hold her down, lads!' She struggled beneath their grip, trying to bring her knee up to their groin. 'I love a woman with spirit.' He laughed, unbuttoning his trousers. He leant over her, ran his hand up her leg. Lilian tried to scream. No sound came. Fear paralysed her like never before.

One of the others grinned and intervened, 'Let's save her a little longer. Take her to the usual place!'

They dragged her further into the forest to an unoccupied woodman's hut. Shoving her inside, they laughed as they joked to each other. Lilian feared her fate. She couldn't possibly overpower three of them. Individually, yes. They pushed her onto a single chair in the middle of the room and tied her to it. The leader of the group unbuttoned her uniform jacket, running his hands over the shape of her breasts tucked tightly in her shirt. 'Enjoy her,' the others laughed. 'She will be a willing dog now.' He began to unbutton her shirt, exposing her plain white bra. Glancing to the floor, the dark red drops of dried blood chilled her to the core. In her mind she heard the screams of those who had suffered before her. Ahead she noticed a small wooden table, instruments neatly laid out. Fear churned in her stomach. She couldn't contain a retch. She vomited. Her thoughts turned to Geoffrey. Would she ever see him again? Her heart and soul cried out to him. He couldn't save her now. The laughter of her persecutors became distant in her ears. Her eyes blurred, head giddy, she blacked out.

Geoffrey longed to get off the U-boat. Mission completed, he carried the evidence he needed in a tiny camera concealed in the sole of his boot. By now he found it difficult to tolerate any more of the squalor; his dishevelled hair unkempt from weeks at sea with no proper washing facilities. His face itched from the mass of unshaven hair. The matted beard added twenty years to him. All the crew looked like dirty peas in a pod. Their morale lifted temporarily only because they believed it wouldn't be long before they would disembark at Frederikshavn. Geoffrey had no way of contacting his base in Denmark, but relaxed knowing they would be monitoring his progress from Y-stations back in England. The bell for the first lunchtime break had sounded a few minutes ago. He walked along the gangway to the primitive eating area. The stench of the crew was no longer noticeable, their shoulders touching each other as they tucked furiously into their watery soup and stale bread. Geoffrey sat himself on the end and reached for the black bread. It had sprouted white fungi and nicknamed 'Rabbits' by the men because of its white, fluffy appearance. No choice. Eat it or starve. He craved fresh food. Supplies on the U-boat had been luxurious in the first few days: plenty of German sausages, smoked meat, chicken, cheese, lots of potatoes and various vegetables, maize flour and all types of fruit. But the small fridges on board meant that the rest of the food spoilt quickly in the damp atmosphere.

Halfway through lunch the bells clambered to instructions loud over the system: 'All men to stations. Prepare to dock!' The U-boat nosed its way upwards. Geoffrey jostled along the boat towards the companionway, followed his group of men to the conning tower. They lifted the hatch and took in the first breath of heady salt air.

'Prepare to anchor!' his mate shouted across to him. The port of Frederikshavn loomed large on the portside; people stood on the dockside waving. In the crowd, Geoffrey caught a glimpse of Josephy. They made brief eye contact. Josephy turned, pushed his way to the back of the mass and disappeared from sight. The U-boat captain surfaced from the control room and waited a moment whilst the remaining crew lined the deck for inspection. A few minutes later he walked along the line to the accolade of raucous laughter and cheers from his crew who had a comradely respect for him.

'Good work men,' he bellowed, eyeing them straight in the face as he moved down. 'We prowled the waters and made the enemy fear our very presence. Now off you get, clean yourselves up and report back for embarkation in two days. *Heil Hitler!*'

'*Heil Hitler!*' they responded with accompanying salute. They threw their caps into the air and disembarked for their shore leave.

Lilian woke in a sub-conscious daze surrounded by four whitewashed walls. Her head ached, eyes felt swollen. She had no idea of time or location. She could only surmise it was daytime from the shaft of light coming through the single barred window at the top of the wall. Shouts outside, keys in the cell door clanked as they opened the lock. In the doorway stood a young SS officer in full Nazi uniform. 'Come with me!' his voice loud. He took a few steps towards her. Lilian struggled to get up. Her legs felt like jelly, her arms as though they didn't belong to her. Her shredded uniform still stunk of sweat soaked into the fabric from the struggle with her captors.

'What day is it?' she asked.

'Tuesday.'

She had tried to cross the border on Saturday. She had lost nearly three days. Everything else about that day was hazy. No recollection of events after getting into the truck.

'Where am I?'

'Enough questions. You're wanted by the chief.'

Upstairs Tom paced the confines of his office. As head of Military Police, it fell to him to deal with Nazi traitors. He hated it. The fact that it was a woman made it worse. He heard the steps down the corridor, the knock on the door. He stared out of the window. Spring flowers already erupted in the flowerbeds and around the trees. One of his officers marched in, closing the door behind him.

'What news?' Tom asked, turning just briefly before looking back out of the window.

'Sir, the prisoner is being brought up now. She was arrested trying to cross at the German side of the border. We had an anonymous phone call which alerted us to her. But we had quite a struggle with her. She attacked two of the guards. We managed to sedate her and get her by ferry to Copenhagen. She's been in the cell ever since. Interrogation room?'

'No. Bring her in.'

The officer walked back to the door and opened it. A fellow officer stood immediately outside with Lilian in handcuffs. 'He says "bring her in".' Flanking her, they led her into the room. The bright light hurt her swollen eyes. Her head still thumped.

Tom turned. Lilian gasped. Her legs gave way and she slumped to the floor. The officers rushed to pull her up.

'Gentlemen, let me deal with her,' Tom said with calmness. 'Leave me alone, if you would.'

'Yes sir.' They saluted and left.

Alone with her, Tom bent down and put his arm around Lilian's back. 'By God, what have they done to you?' He held her close to his chest, then helped her into a chair. 'Here, let me get some warm water for your face and some brandy.'

'Brandy?' she murmured.

'In my position it's still possible to get hold of it.'

'The pilots … what about the …'

'Ssh, don't distress yourself. They're safe. You have done as much as you can. We need to move you – somewhere out of harm's way to recover.' He left her for a few moments, locking the door behind him so she felt safe. He returned in a matter of minutes with warm water; then took a bottle of brandy from the corner cabinet, pouring a double measure into a tumbler. He passed it to her. The liquid slipped with ease down her throat, temporarily numbing her pain.

He knelt beside to her, turned her bruised face towards him and looked at her in adoration. He began to bathe her face with the water. Her facial muscles relaxed at each touch. 'Why, Lilian?' he whispered. 'Why did you come back? Risk your life? You of all people. We got you out once. If your original identity was discovered …'

She swallowed hard. 'I thought you would understand, Tom. I had to do my bit for my country.'

'Do you mean England or Denmark?'

'I have loyalties to both now.'

Tom saw how strained and tired she looked. Their conversation, albeit brief, had overtaxed her. 'Dear Lil, I don't want you to get any more exhausted. As I said, we need to move you somewhere safe. Are you fine to leave now?'

'Yes.' Her voice weak, she managed a smile. Deep down she hadn't lost her spirit in spite of her ordeal. He loved her for it and dared to hope she felt the same for him. He helped her out of the chair. 'Here, rest your arm on mine. I'll support you.'

'Thank you Tom.'

Tom picked up the telephone. 'Could you kindly call in security, please Olga.'

'Very good sir', she replied. Within minutes, five military police officers knocked and entered. Tom spoke briefly. 'The woman here needs urgent medical care. I have a special warrant for her custody but under particular laws she comes under my direct jurisdiction. Because of her position I'm going to have to escort her to hospital. I'll be gone a few hours. In my absence I'd like you to ensure the smooth running of the place.'

'Yes, sir,' they answered. Tom proceeded to take Lilian's arm and walked out of the office. He had plans to get her out of Copenhagen.

At the safe-house in Frederikshavn, just a stone's throw from the harbour, Geoffrey placed his Kriegsmarine uniform over the back of the chair and changed into his old clothes. A few minutes earlier a woman with child in arms had opened the door for him and Josephy. Josephy marched into the house as if it was his own. The woman's name was Hilda. Geoffrey gathered that she'd been a childhood sweetheart of Josephy. Whilst Geoffrey was on the U-boat, Hilda had washed his clothes and kept them safe for his return. Now she had prepared a bowl of warm water for him to freshen his hands and face. Five minutes passed, then Josephy knocked on the door.

'Come in!' Geoffrey replied. 'I've changed.'

Josephy entered with Hilda a few paces behind. He cleared the kitchen table, pulled out a chair and sat down. He gestured for Geoffrey and Hilda to sit also. Then he spread papers across the table, sorting them into three separate piles. 'There's been a message from England.' He glanced up. 'Only half the military documents were on the U-boat, I'm afraid.'

'And the other half?' asked Geoffrey.

'Ministry of Defence in Copenhagen. They were separated for security purposes. Captain Henderson has issued new orders. Hilda here will kit you out with an SS uniform. Your brief is …'

'Is to retrieve the other half of the papers.'

'Precisely.' Josephy grinned.

'I photographed the ones on the U-boat because it was too risky to take out the originals without arousing suspicion,' Geoffrey explained.

'I wondered as much. But that's fine. As long as we have a copy of them.' Josephy rested his chin on his fist, flicking through the third pile of papers with his free hand. 'However, the other papers in Copenhagen are a different matter. We need you to bring out the originals. No photographs this time.'

'And when do I go in?'

Josephy glanced at Hilda. 'We reckon you should lie low here for a couple of days. Hilda will take care of you. Then Friday evening you enter the building with a warrant to search the premises.'

'Won't I arouse suspicion?'

'No. The head of the Ministry will have left for Yalta that morning. His staff has a habit of being a little lax in his absence. A crate of champagne will mysteriously be delivered for him. He won't be there to accept it and I reckon the men'll have a good go at it. By the time you get there, there shouldn't be much champagne left or a sober man in the building.' Josephy stood up. 'I have to go now. You're in very capable hands. I have to get back to Vallø.'

'Any more news of Jonathan?'

'As far as we know,' he paused. 'Our sources tell us he's still in a concentration camp called Belsen.'

'Belsen? Good God.'

'Quite.' Josephy walked up to Geoffrey, extended his hand. 'Good luck for Friday, lad.' Geoffrey shook his hand and sat down again. Josephy turned and left.

A few streets later Josephy knocked on the front door of another safe-house. The network was spreading faster than anyone could have possibly hoped a few months earlier. The Danish people had courage. Resistance was now the name of the game. All over the country small groups were training ready to unleash acts of sabotage against the Nazis and Danish collaborators. The local resistance leader Kurt let Josephy in. They passed the parlour where half a dozen men sat in a circle discussing their next attack. Kurt led Josephy upstairs and into the first room out of earshot of anyone below.

'There's word from the Captain.'

'Yeah?'

'Lilian has been compromised. She's had a rough ride. We're pulling her out.'

Josephy looked concerned. 'Where is she now? Still in Kiel?'

'No. She was betrayed and taken to Military Police HQ in Copenhagen. Fortunately Tom picked her up and is escorting her to safety. She needs to recover. It's going to take time. She's been badly treated.'

'How bad?'

'Not fit enough to travel back to England before mid-April. But there's something else.'

'What?'

'Shortly after she first came to England she had a brief relationship with a soldier at Anderson Manor. Geoffrey Hart.'

'Now I understand.'

'He's in Denmark now is he not?'

Josephy nodded, then second-guessing his concern, replied. 'Don't worry. I'll make sure he doesn't know she is in the region.'

'That's what the Captain contacted me about earlier this morning. He doesn't want Geoffrey to have any inkling of her whereabouts. As far as Geoffrey is concerned, his sweetheart is safely in England. Tom is escorting her to Vallø. It's the safest place for her. The familiar ground will also mean she'll recover psychologically much quicker.' He patted Josephy on the back. 'Come. Let's go downstairs and join the others.'

Anders stood at the gates to Vallø Castle waiting to greet Lilian. The last time he had seen her was the night she'd gone into hiding with other Danish Jews and he had got them into fishing vessels to safety in Sweden. Tom's report about her condition left him apprehensive. The car carrying her swept slowly into the drive and began the final few hundred metres towards him. He stood erect, hands clasped behind his back. The car pulled up in front of him. Lilian's pale weary face saddened him. She turned her head slightly and managed a weak smile through the car window. It was then that he saw the purple bruise over an inflamed right eye. He opened the door and held out his hand. She took his. 'Lilian, my dear. Welcome back to Vallø.' Her hand felt cold in his as he helped her out. Tom came around to her side with a blanket, wrapping it around her shoulders.

'I've prepared a room for you in the castle itself,' said Anders. 'It's more comfortable in there and you're totally safe. The Nazis will never search the home of the nobility.' They walked slowly towards the entrance. Anders continued, 'My wife has sorted some new clothes for you. But first you need rest.'

Tom followed them up the grand central staircase to the first floor. Lilian took each step slowly, her body ached all over. Along the corridor Anders opened a door onto a large panelled room with double bed, the edge of the crisp white top sheet turned back slightly in welcome. The half drawn heavy tapestry curtains let in a stream of spring sunlight. A bowl of steaming water had been placed on a dresser by one of the maids.

'Here,' said Tom. 'You can wash and change into clean clothes.' He shot a look at Anders, 'And when she's done, I'd like a word with her in private if I may?'

'Yes sure,' Anders replied. They both left the bedroom.

Half an hour later Tom knocked on the door, gently pushed it open and peered in. Lilian was in bed propped up slightly, her head sunk restfully into the pillows. She smiled as he closed the door and approached. For Tom it was as if the eighteen months of separation since she'd left Denmark never happened. He still loved her. Walking towards her, his heart leapt out to her. Her anguish was his pain. He gently placed his arm behind her back and cradled her in his arms. Now he understood Hanns. In that moment Hanns' deep-seated desire for revenge on the Nazis made sense. As Tom held the woman he loved, breathed in her delicate scent, he vowed to be more like Hanns. The Nazis would pay for the brutality they were inflicting on innocent people. Until that moment it had been a sort of intellectual game for Tom. But the truth lay in his arms as he stared down at her broken body.

'Lilian, I am always here for you.'

'Thank you Tom. You are so very kind.' Was that all she felt for him. Nothing more? He couldn't overtax her. He released his hug and stood up. 'I'll let you rest now, Lilian. If you need anything, you only have to ask. You are in safe hands.'

'Thank you Tom.' She smiled the smile he loved.

'I have to return to Copenhagen tomorrow but I'll come and see you every few days. I want to look after you.'

'You are so kind Tom. Thank you.' Overcome by tiredness, she closed her eyes. With one final backward glance, Tom crept out of the room to leave her to rest. There was plenty of time to be with her later.

That night in a safe-house on the outskirts of Copenhagen, Geoffrey waited for Olaf to arrive from the Vallø Castle estate with his small team. Geoffrey had already been briefed by Josephy about the simultaneous mission. In the parlour he waited in Gestapo uniform. In long, black boots and grey coat he cut quite a dash. Voices down the corridor alerted him to Olaf's arrival. The Victory Group came into the parlour. Olaf addressed them without delay: 'Precision is essential. In and out as fast as we can. Off we go.'

He nodded in Geoffrey's direction and walked up to him. 'We'll be the distraction that enables you to get in. Good luck.' They shook hands.

'You too,' Geoffrey replied.

They went their separate ways.

Olaf took his team out of the safe-house, through the quiet back streets, towards the harbour. Four U-boats of the 9th Flotilla were in for minor repairs. Keeping within the doorways of the buildings, they waited as Olaf went ahead on reconnaissance. Prior intelligence indicated that only a skeleton staff manned the harbour that night. Olaf scanned the docks in front of him. Two guards stood on the far side against a lamppost smoking and chatting. Olaf beckoned to his team. Keeping close to the wall of the harbour compound, they edged in single file towards the dockside. Within minutes they spread in two directions. Olaf smiled at the sight of the U-boats lined up perfectly side by side. He gave another signal to his team. They slipped off their top clothes, pulled on their underwater breathing apparatus and went down the concrete steps into the freezing water. Each armed with four magnetic limpet mines, one by one they attached them to the bow and stern under the water line. They had about nine minutes to get out. Olaf bobbed out of the water first, waiting shivering in the shadows for the other three members of his team. The fourth was back near the harbour entrance as watch-post. A single owl hoot; Olaf froze. He waited, crouched down in the shadow of the U-boat. The two Nazi guards must be approaching them. A few seconds later a double owl hoot indicated the all-clear. Olaf waved to the dark silhouettes of his men. Now they had less than five minutes before the harbour would erupt into total chaos. They ran back along the edge of the wall towards the gates. Glancing around, the coast was clear. In a single line they made it through the gates. A few streets away they stopped to catch their breath. Olaf took them to a known safe-house a few metres away. There they changed from their wet clothes. Olaf was just pulling on his dry trousers when three massive explosions, each separated by a couple of seconds, shook the area. He dashed upstairs, flung open the nearest door and looked out of the shattered window. The night sky was a blaze of deep red and black smoke. A few moments later the fourth and final U-boat erupted under the force of the explosives. A billow of yellow flares followed by red flames burst into the sky. Bells of the local fire brigade charged towards the harbour. Olaf smiled to himself. *A job well done*, he thought. He hoped Geoffrey was making the most of his moment.

As soon as Geoffrey heard the fire engines and saw the smoke-filled sky, he came out of the shadows and walked up the steps of the Ministry of Defence. He flashed his warrant at the security officer on the door.

'What the hell's going on tonight?'

Geoffrey looked at him steadily, 'Some problem down at the harbour, I believe.'

'I'd say. That was a hell of an explosion.'

'I've just come from that way. It seems to be under control. The fire brigade is tackling it. Anyway, must get on. Good evening.'

The security officer sat back down at his desk. 'Ah, before you go up. Orders, we have to give you extra security clearance. Just a moment.' Geoffrey hid his irritation as the officer picked up the telephone. 'Hello operator, please get me Abwehr 106.'

'Just connecting you, sir.' In the silence Geoffrey heard the beeps on the line as the officer waited to be connected. The operator came back to him. 'I'm sorry, sir. I can't get through. There's no reply.'

'Very well, thank you for trying.' He replaced the receiver and looked up. 'Can I see your warrant again?'

Geoffrey reached into his jacket pocket, pulled out the pistol with silencer and pulled the trigger. The security officer slumped to the ground, blood pouring from a wound in his chest and soaking into his jacket. Geoffrey looked around. The porter's broom cupboard would suffice. He dragged the body towards it and heaved him inside. Reaching into the man's pocket, he pulled out his bunch of keys. One of them must fit the cupboard. He took a cloth from the shelf and returned to the desk. Having removed all the blood from the floor, he threw the cloth back into the cupboard and locked the door. He ran two steps at a time up to the second floor of the building. Along the empty corridor he made his way to the office of the Minister of Defence. Outside it he put his torch in his mouth as he pulled out his roll of lock-picking equipment. Picking the lock took no time. Inside the office he shone his torch around the tidy space. The safe was on the far wall. He closed the door behind him, moved quickly to clear the desk, careful to memorise what he moved. He crept over to the safe. In his pocket he had a tube of toothpaste packed with a small amount of plastic explosives. Behind his belt, a fuse wire. He set to work. It took two attempts to blast the lock open. Having succeeded, he turned the wheel handle full circle anti-clockwise twice. The door swung open. Inside, a pile of papers lined the safe from base to its roof. He removed the bundles and placed them on the desk behind him. One by one he glanced at the top page. Time was running out. He had to be in and out within fifteen minutes before the next change of shift. Two-thirds of the way through the pile he came across the one he needed. He put it on its own and lifted as many files as he could back into the safe. He pushed the door ajar.

'*Was ist das?*' The deep voice behind him took him unaware.

He swung around, snapped to attention to *Heil Hitler*. The SS officer had his gun pointed at him. In these days it was shoot first, think later. By which time Geoffrey would be dead.

'There appears to have been a raid in the governor's office this evening,' ventured Geoffrey. 'We think shortly after the explosion yonder.' He nodded in what he thought to be the direction of the harbour.

'We? What do you mean "we"? Did you catch them?' The officer eyed him suspiciously, not convinced by his response.

'Yes, SS officer Herr Altern has taken her into custody.'

'Her?'

'Believe it or not, it was a woman. Herr Altern will be back shortly. You can ask him yourself.'

'Good work. *Heil Hitler!*' He turned and left the room. Geoffrey knew he had but a few minutes to get out of the building before the officer discovered the security guard missing. Geoffrey heard his footsteps down the corridor, then walking rapidly closer, back to the office. Geoffrey crouched behind the desk. He slipped his finger through the trigger of his Luger, waited in the darkness. The officer stormed into the office clutching his pistol and switched the light on. Geoffrey eyed up his target, a single pull of the trigger, the bullet cut the air straight into the officer's arm. He heard him thud to the ground. Geoffrey edged out from behind the desk to see the officer clutching his right arm, trying to reach for his gun, which had been thrown across the floor when the bullet had hit him. Geoffrey lurched forward and kicked the gun to the other side of the room. In the ensuing struggle, Geoffrey's uniform was smeared in bright red blood. He took no chances. Inside the pocket of his trouser a knife lay flat. The polished steel glistened for a second in the bright lights of the office. In a single thrust, the knife plunged into the officer's chest. Geoffrey held him down in his last struggle as the life drained out of him.

Running along the corridor, clutching the precious file – the object of his mission – he made for the staircase. He tried to block out the screams coming from the interrogation rooms at the end of the passage. He ran on, down the back spiral stairs, pushed open the fire door and out into the night air. Behind him the sirens sounded through the building. He flung off his blood-stained jacket, discarded it in the gutter and ran on towards a safe-house on the edge of the city.

Chapter 9

The following day was Wednesday. After having breakfast in bed at 9.30 a.m., Lilian sat propped up against her pillows. She hoped Tom would come before midday. She stared dreamily ahead through the window into the far distance, focusing her gaze on the long, neat avenue of trees at the back of the castle. Her body still ached, her concentration was weak. Occasionally in these quiet moments her mind turned to Geoffrey. She wondered where he was. Was he safe? She decided she must write to him. Reaching into the drawer of the bedside cabinet she saw that someone had left plenty of notepaper and envelopes. Slowly, thoughtfully, she began to scribble a brief note to him. What would she say? Unknown to her, Geoffrey was in Denmark. Having completed his Copenhagen mission, he was living with Anders in the manager's house on the edge of the Vallø Castle estate. Anders knew their paths wouldn't cross because by day Geoffrey worked in the woods and in the evening he helped Olaf in the quarry training the local resistance movement.

Lilian glanced up at the sound of the door creaking open. 'Tom!' Her face lit up.

'I'm glad to see you've drawn the curtains right back. Allow some of the morning sunshine in. You're looking less pale today I'm pleased to say. Here, I've brought you this.' He placed a tray of tea and biscuits next to the bed. 'Milk?'

'Yes please. Thank you Tom. How thoughtful of you to bring me tea.'

He poured the tea into a cup and offered her the plate of biscuits. 'They're homemade,' he said. 'Anders' wife is marvellous like that. How she finds time with doing all the stuff here in the castle, I'll never know.' Tom looked at Lilian steadily, trying to ascertain whether she was ready for the news. 'Lily.'

She shot him a glance, 'Yes?'

'We know who betrayed you at the border.'

'Oh?' She seemed disinterested.

'Lily, you need only say the word – a woman of your rank and position – and they will be dealt with severely.'

Lilian stared beyond him out of the window again. 'No, Tom,' she replied, forming her words slowly and with care. 'Revenge is not mine to take. No. I can't do it.'

'Lily, you could have died out there.'

'But I didn't. It's no, Tom. The answer is no.'

He wasn't satisfied. 'Won't you at least think about it?' Lilian didn't hear his response. She was suddenly back re-living the ordeal. It was as if Tom wasn't there – wasn't sitting on the edge of the bed listening to her. The temporary amnesia gone, her disjointed monologue rambled out: 'First it was men. A group of them, all in SS uniform. They dragged me into the hut. I must have been there for several hours strapped to that chair. The rope cut into my wrists. The tall man tore open my shirt, my underwear for them all to see. But it wasn't that that scared me the most. It was the woman. She came in. Evil eyes.'

'Did you recognise her?' Tom interrupted, thinking it may have been the same woman who had betrayed her. Lilian didn't hear his question and continued speaking whilst letting out an involuntary shudder: 'I was terrified. She ripped my clothes then ran her hands over my partly naked body. I can still feel her touch, her smell.' Lilian shuddered again. 'She squeezed my breasts until I thought she would rip them off. She kept saying my body was too perfect; that I needed some scars to make me more interesting. She started with my toe nails, then finger nails, ripping them out one at a time. Above my screams her breathing got heavier and heavier. Then she sank her teeth into my breasts. I lost control, wet myself. She left me – at that moment she left but vowed to return. For days the pain was horrendous. The men took pity on me. They had seen too much. It was them that let me go. I could barely run, but I did it. Then I was picked up later by a SS patrol, taken by boat to South Zealand and brought to your office. I have never been so pleased to be back in Copenhagen, knowing, hoping you would save me. The police officers were kind to me. They took me to a parlour and fixed me with some new nails.'

Tom took her hand, held it tightly. 'Lily, it's alright. I am with you now. I will take care of you. For the rest of your life, I will protect you.'

'That's not possible – you know that. The Danish government would never allow me to marry a commoner. Please excuse the term. No offence intended.'

'You have to go where your heart is Lily.'

'Right now I can't think of anything. Here can you post this for me please?' She passed him the envelope.

'Lily, it's difficult for post to reach England with the war on. Denmark isn't officially on the Allied side.'

'What about the Red Cross?' she persisted. 'I really do want the letter to go. Please, Tom.'

He took pity on her. 'Very well. I'll do my best. I must be going now. Anders wants to discuss a few things with me. I'll come and see you later this afternoon – I don't need to be back in Copenhagen for a few days, so that's lucky for us.'

'Us?'

'Yes. I'll look after you Lily.'

Lilian didn't like to contradict him. At the moment her feelings were still confused. What did she feel for him? She postponed the thoughts for another time. Tom stood up, took her hand, kissed the back with tenderness and left. In the corridor outside he glanced down at the envelope. It was addressed to Geoffrey. Tom decided there and then, that it would not be going into the post box. He couldn't have Geoffrey on the scene complicating matters for him.

∽❦

Deep in the quarry with Olaf and the young resistance fighters, Geoffrey bent over the section of track clipping the train detectors over the rail. Derailing a train was an art that he had learnt during SOE training. For two months he had gradually taught them all he knew about explosives, mines and picking locks and safes. Their missions were being stepped up to more risky, highly important industrial targets. Geoffrey explained, 'These tiny detonators contain a small explosive charge and were originally designed to warn workers near the railway line about an approaching train. They are small enough not to damage the track when they go off. We are going to experiment with a larger amount of explosives.'

Olaf stepped forward, crouched down and fixed the detonator to the spare track. Trailing the wires to a safe distance, he covered them with dirt as camouflage. 'Use whatever there is to hand as camouflage,' he said, then connected the whole thing to the box.

'When do we get to do this?' asked the youngest in the group.

'Soon enough,' Olaf replied.

'By which time the war will be over,' the youth moaned. 'I've heard rumours the British have landed in France.'

Olaf glanced at Geoffrey. Geoffrey shrugged his shoulders.

'Nonsense. Your time will come,' Olaf tried to pacify his impatience. He turned back to Geoffrey. 'Come, I'd like you to help me lift some stuff out of the shed at the far side of the quarry.' He nodded in the direction of what looked more like a tiny 4ft high box with corrugated roof. As they walked, now out of earshot of the others, Olaf explained, 'We may have another recruit with us tomorrow evening. A young woman.'

'Really?'

'A right princess she is if you ask me. Lilian has done some of this kind of stuff before, but the Captain wants us to make sure she is still up to scratch.'

Geoffrey stopped. He knew only one Lilian. She was Danish, but then wasn't she back in England? 'How old is she?'

'Don't know. I've never met her. I only saw her briefly from a distance when Anders …'

Geoffrey stopped him dead, clutched his arm. 'You mean she's here on the estate.'

'Ssh, you weren't supposed to guess that.'

Could it be *his* Lilian? Geoffrey wasn't letting him off the hook. 'Where is she?'

'Look, my lips are sealed.' Olaf shifted from foot to foot.

'If I'm going to be training her,' replied Geoffrey, 'then I need to know something about her.' Olaf bought his argument. 'Very well, but what's in it for me?' Geoffrey eyed him for a moment, 'More explosives? I can get you more.'

'Agreed. Let's shake on it, but you must swear not to tell Anders. Feign ignorance.' Olaf held out his hand. Geoffrey took it: 'A deal.'

'Very well.' Olaf rubbed the sweat off his forehead. 'She's in the castle with the other women of noble birth. Anders thought it was more appropriate after all she's been through.'

'Been through?'

'Yeah, she's had a very rough ride at the hands of the Nazis.'

'By God. Is she alright?'

'Yes. She is now.'

Geoffrey longed to see for himself that she was safe. If he admitted it, there wasn't a night that went by when he hadn't thought of her. She penetrated his deepest subconscious dreams. He had longed for her warm body next to his; wished he could be transported back to the hut in the woods near Anderson Manor. 'I must go to her.'

'No!' Olaf's firm response shook Geoffrey. 'Wait. You'll see her soon enough.'

Later that night, back at the lodge, Geoffrey tossed and turned in his bed. Would she still feel the same about him? Tomorrow he would probably know the answer. The agony of waiting drove him to the edge of insanity.

The next day was a couple of weeks off the longest day of the year. Training in the quarry at Vallø had to start at dusk, now around 10 p.m. every evening. Geoffrey could barely wait for that evening's session. He kept glancing at his watch. Would Olaf bring Lilian? He hadn't stopped thinking about her all day.

'You're restless tonight,' noticed Anders as they ate a late supper together in the lodge. 'What's up?'

'Oh, just getting a little apprehensive about the factory job.'

'But it's a few nights away yet. You've no cause to worry. It's second nature to you now. Anyway, I've ordered some extra explosives to make sure it's done properly. No point in doing half a job.'

Geoffrey gulped the last mouthful of potatoes, putting his knife and fork on the plate. 'If you have no objection Anders, I'm off to the quarry. Olaf has arranged to meet me a little early to go over the schedule before the others arrive.'

'Fine. But make sure you relax before the next job.'

Geoffrey ran all the way to the quarry. He prided himself in being as fit as when he had completed his training back in England. Life in Denmark wasn't quite how he'd expected it to be. At times it was hard to imagine there was a war raging just a few hundred miles away. Anders kept him updated with the latest news. The Allies had successfully landed in Normandy and were heading for Caen. Anders had shown Geoffrey some photographs in the newspapers. Before the ground troops could enter Caen, the RAF had flattened the city which now resembled something out of the apocalypse.

As Geoffrey approached the quarry he heard voices. He crept closer, hiding behind the trees. *She was there*. It *was* her. His heart missed a beat. In the twilight her sweet face looked up urgently to the giant of Olaf. Her impassioned expression touched him. Geoffrey came out of the shadows. The distance of time and separation dissipated.

'Lilian!'

She turned, froze, stared straight at him as if she had seen a ghost. He walked, half ran towards her. She remained motionless. As he came within inches of her, she broke into a little smile. How he wanted to sweep her up in his arms. He held back. Olaf looked on bemused. 'You two know each other?' He asked, feigning ignorance in front of Lilian.

Geoffrey swung around to face Olaf, 'Would you give us a few moments alone please?'

'Sure. I'll go and find the others; they must be on their way by now.' He ran off into the woods.

The nerves set in; his stomach doing somersaults. Geoffrey didn't know whether to take her hand or hug her. Instead he waited for her to make the first move. Nothing happened. He ventured, 'It's been a long time Lilian.'

'Yes.'

'How are you Lilian after …?'

'Oh you heard about that?'

'I'm so sorry. I wish I had been there to protect you.' Did she feel anything for him? She was giving nothing away. Looking into her eyes he noticed she had lost her childhood innocence; the pupils a veil hiding deep pain. He could barely fathom what she must have been through.

'Tom has been very good to me.'

'Tom?'

'Yes, Tom. He's head of Military Police in Copenhagen. He's barely left my side. He's taken special leave to look after me.' Lilian wasn't ashamed to tell Geoffrey. After all, Geoffrey hadn't even attempted to reply to her last letter.

'Lilian I was hoping we might continue how we left off.' A pang of jealousy soured his expression.

'Too much has happened.'

'It hasn't been easy for either of us. I've had to do my bit for the war effort too.'

She flung her head back in the first display of passionate anger. 'You have no idea what I've been through. I thought you loved me. And all the while I was the object of some petty wager with your friend Ian.'

'Ian? What's he got to do with it?' He paused then continued. 'Oh, now I see. So that's it, is it? You think I wagered your love for a packet of cigarettes. Well you're wrong, Lilian. Please let me explain.'

Her emotional eruption wasn't over. 'It's too late. I hate you, Geoffrey Hart. Hate you! You are half the man Tom is.' She turned and ran.

'Lilian, please.' Calling after her, he stood paralysed by her outburst. He could outrun her, but instead he decided to let her go. He sank to the ground, buried his head in his hands and sobbed. He had lost the woman he truly loved.

❧

Geoffrey returned to the lodge with spirits low. He didn't sleep a wink that night thinking about Lilian. Everything seemed hopeless. He hated life without her. By 6.30 a.m. the following morning, sleep or no sleep, he decided to get up. Work had to be done for planning the final stages of the sabotage on the munitions factory in a suburb of Copenhagen. His team needed to be fully prepared. He ambled downstairs, surprised to see Anders already up and dressed.

'Good morning Anders.'

Anders looked up from his newspaper. 'Good morning Geoffrey. You're early.'

'There's lots to do. Besides I couldn't sleep last night. It was a full moon. It always affects me.'

Anders ruffled his newspaper closed. 'I'm actually glad you're up early. I had an urgent telegram in the night.'

'Oh?' Geoffrey pulled a chair up opposite him and sat down.

'There's bad news from London, I'm afraid. Sir Charles is recalling you. It's the Captain. He's in a bad way. You're needed.'

'Me?'

'I don't have much information except to say that poor Henderson has lost his wife. She died suddenly from a seizure in the night. Felt ill and within minutes was gone. He's totally devastated. He wasn't there when she died. Only the housekeeper was present.'

'My God. I liked her. Katharine was a kind of aunt-by-marriage.' Geoffrey buried his head in his hands, barely believing the news.

Anders continued, 'Apart from her husband, you are her only surviving next of kin. You've been asked to form part of the guard of honour. It's to be a military funeral. I've just had the details about getting you back to England. Josephy will take you in one of the fishing boats across the Sound. Then a Lancaster will fly you from Sweden to RAF Manston. I'm not sure how long you will be away and whether you'll come back to Denmark.' He looked at him with deep respect. 'We, the Danish people, can't thank you enough for what you've done for us.'

Anders walked into the communal parlour on the ground floor of the castle. 'Lilian, I've been looking for you everywhere.' As she turned around, he saw her distressed face. 'What's the matter my dear? You're looking terribly pale. Is everything alright?'

'Yes, I'm fine. I think I've overdone it today. I haven't quite got my strength back yet.'

'Come and sit, my dear.' She obeyed, then waited for him to speak.

'I found something behind the cushion of the sofa this morning.' He passed her the envelope, 'Here, I think this belongs to you.' She turned it over. Her own handwriting – addressed to Sgt G.O. Hart. She gasped. Anders slipped quietly out, leaving her to contemplate.

So Geoffrey had never had her letter. Tom hadn't posted it. She glanced at the clock ticking on the mantelpiece. Tom was due within the half hour. She wouldn't see him. She would hide somewhere. But then he was persistent. She rationalised further – she must face her future. Geoffrey had returned to England and she hadn't heard a word from him. She had been a fool. The time sped by. Soon enough Tom ambled into the castle and caught sight of Lilian through the open doorway.

'Hello Lilian.' He closed the door behind him; brushed back his windswept hair and walked towards her.

'Hello Tom.'

'Anders has been talking about your future. We think it would be best if you settled here in the castle permanently. Your identity is totally protected here.'

'And it wasn't before. What's changed?' she asked. 'I had to leave with the other Jews once. If the Nazis discover me, I'll suffer the same fate as the rest of Europe's Jews. I've heard the rumours about the camps.'

'Don't be naïve Lily. You can't believe all that you hear. It's partly American propaganda and exaggeration. We know Hitler isn't going to win this war. It's not a matter of *if*, but *when*. Denmark will be free again. You belong here.'

'There's nothing to hold me here any more.'

'There's me. I love you, Lily. I'll protect you. Nothing would make me happier than for you to be my wife. Will you Lily? We can grow old together.'

Lilian felt pity for him. He *would* take care of her, that much she knew, but she couldn't marry a man she didn't love. 'Oh, Tom. We can never be together. The truth is – I don't love you. Not as a woman loves a man. I love you as any sister might a brother.'

'It's Geoffrey isn't it? I knew it.'

'I have no further contact with Geoffrey. I won't be seeing him again. Tom, I hope you understand. You should marry someone who will make you happy. I'll never make you happy.'

'And that's your final answer?'

'Yes.'

'If you ever change your mind, you know I'm there for you.'

Lilian looked with tenderness. 'Thank you. That's very sweet of you. I am grateful Tom for all you've done for me. I shan't forget you in all my life.'

'What will you do Lily?'

'I haven't decided yet. But I think I know where my destiny lies.'

They parted good friends. Their paths didn't cross again.

Henderson stared out to sea. The day he dreaded had arrived. Standing in Ilfracombe's Marlborough Road cemetery high above the town, he knew he had to adjust. His brown eyes scanned the horizon, waiting, as if something would fall out of the grey-blotched coastal sky of distant South Wales. It was late afternoon, a strong wind blowing off the sea. The treetops bent in homage and rustled their song along with the winds. The sea rumbled its own thunderous song, crushing its mighty waves against the jagged red cliffs. Seagulls whirled overhead, battling the summer wind, screeching their mantra to one and all. He heard none of it as he stood to attention, a lonely grey-haired figure occasionally looking with darting glances out to sea. He watched for no one knew what. Tall and lean, with a hint of toned muscle under his uniform, developed from years of drill exercise, he bent his head in homage, as if waiting for divine inspiration. A tear slowly crept down his face. Across the Channel, Allied forces were successfully pushing their way through France. Hopes were raised that the war would soon be over. For him it would be a bitter-sweet peace; his own life shattered by *her* death.

'Good day, sir.' The familiar voice with slight Austrian accent penetrated Henderson's thoughts. 'Geoffrey?' Captain Henderson continued to stare out to sea.

'Yes, sir. It's me. Second Lieutenant Hart.'

'So they've promoted you, lad.'

'Yes, sir.' Geoffrey felt awkward about even mentioning Katharine to him. Captain Henderson tried to make it easier for him. 'She was fond of you, you know.'

'Yes,' was all Geoffrey could manage.

'Thank you for coming.' Geoffrey saluted and left Henderson to his thoughts. He walked over to the chapel of rest where the guard of honour was forming up.

Henderson was alone to his thoughts again. He heard a distant noise. The hum in his head became louder, drowning his thoughts. Unbidden, the dreaded memories returned. Even now, half a life time away, he wanted to run. The screen rolled unbidden, unwanted.

The screech of torn air as the bomb fell. His mind frantic with despair. Deep in the basement, he had not heard the warning siren; his ears covered with the tap, tap of Morse code through the heavy earphones. Too late. Screaming, distraught with fear, he rushed upstairs. The child's room was torn apart, open to the cold night air. Tears streamed down his face, his body shaking, anger and fear flooding his being. Sarah's tiny limp body lay motionless, her teddy torn apart. 'Take care of Sarah whilst I'm away,' Katharine had begged him that morning. He clutched her body to his breast. He screamed from the depths of his soul. 'Hitler. The Third Reich. Nazi Bastards.'

Now he had lost both of them. His wife and daughter.

'Sir, are you alright?' Fraser's familiar voice pierced his pain.

'What? Oh, yes, thank you Fraser.'

'The mourners are arriving sir.' Standing back to give Captain Henderson space and his dignity, Fraser gave a sad smile. Quietly they watched the mourners arrive one by one. There must have been around seventy people, mainly men in military uniforms, waiting for the hearse to arrive.

Henderson took a couple of steps forward: 'Time to go over and join them, Fraser. Here she comes.' The black cortege swept through the gates into the cemetery. A single spray of white lilies adorned the simple wooden coffin. Henderson stood motionless as the pall-bearers slid the coffin out. One of the pall-bearers was the Knowle village postmaster, Edmund Fry. He, more than most, knew the nature of her covert wartime work. He had witnessed her signature on her last will and testament. Geoffrey gave the quiet order. The military guard lined the path as the coffin made its last dignified journey towards the grave. Henderson followed behind the pall-bearers. Keeping control was harder and harder.

The wind caught the trees, shards of sunlight flashed off the handles of the coffin as it began its descent into the ground. Another death, another funeral for this war-scarred family.

'Ashes to ashes, dust to dust, in the sure and certain knowledge of …' Inside, something felt like it was going to snap. His throat tightened. He loved her. Burying her was the hardest thing he had done; except laying his daughter to rest. He wanted to yell, '*Look, here lies the soul of a true warrior. A woman who gave her all so that you might live your petty dreams. Have you not a care for her sacrifice?*' He didn't. Too many years of conditioning. Too many secrets, all bottled up in his chest.

'Are you sure you're all right, sir?' Fraser's voice brought him momentarily out of his grief.

'Yes. I'm fine,' he snapped, half under his breath. 'Thank you for your concern.' Captain Henderson turned as if seeing Fraser for the first time. His face distorted in grief. Life would be intolerably hard without his soul mate. Katharine was his life, his all.

Chapter 10

15 April 1945

Jonathan shuffled across the narrow wooden bunk he shared with three other inmates and climbed down the side. Rumours in the camp suggested that liberating forces were on their way. In the eleven months since D-Day, in spite of some setbacks, the Allies were winning the war. Victory was now inevitable. Germany had been crushed on every front. But Jonathan cared little for liberation. His concern was the guards who might get off free and never be brought to justice. He promised himself that wouldn't happen. Some guards had already made themselves scarce, thought to be hiding in disused huts on the perimeter. Blinking in his own dismal hut, Jonathan's deep sunken eyes rasped in their sockets from lack of moisture, constantly moving, yet dull as death. His sinuses were destroyed by the overpowering putrid smell of faeces. Bringing his filthy bony hands up, he scratched his emaciated face. His starved mind craved revenge, yet longed for death. He had survived longer than most.

He moved slowly towards the doorway, leaning against the wooden frame as if to summon the strength to take further steps. The ground beneath his feet shook like an earthquake. The rumbling of what could only be heavy armoured vehicles and tanks could be heard long before they came into view. *So it was true.* Liberating forces were on their way. Excitement surged through Jonathan's weary body. His moment had come. He limped back to his bed, climbed the ladder and fumbled in the straw covering the slats of the bed. The inmates stared blankly at him in silence. *They deserve justice*, he thought. He removed a single knife. It was all he really had, other than a small hoard of blunt implements stolen from the guards whenever he could. He stumbled out of the hut just as the camp gates were flung wide open. The British liberators entered. In disbelief the skeletal remnants of humanity stared at the healthy men in khaki now mingling with them, their faces ashen with shock. What confronted them were mounds of corpses piled high, a horrendous sight unseen by human eyes in history. The stench of death impregnated the clothes of the soldiers. It seemed they would never be able to get rid of the terrifying smell of death. This was no sweet liberation. Utter hopelessness and horror faced the British soldiers, typhoid rampant amongst the survivors, people collapsing and dying in front of them. As if given an order from their commanding officer, the soldiers reached into their pockets for handkerchiefs to mask their faces. Three of them ran to the perimeter fence and vomited.

Jonathan hobbled towards the derelict huts on the far side of the camp. Time was running out to trap the perpetrators. He reached the first hut, pushed the rickety door to let in the bright April sunlight. Two camp guards sat huddled in the corner, both had changed into striped pyjamas of the camp. He recognised one, the other unknown to him, but both were too healthy to be inmates. Jonathan spoke in German. 'I have been asked by the commandant to give you an urgent message. To save your lives you need a numbered tattoo. I've been asked to do it. There isn't much time. The enemy has entered the gates.' Jonathan walked lamely towards them. They believed he was their last hope of survival. Jonathan didn't care for his own safety. *It was him or them. They were defenceless.* One of the guards stood up. Jonathan grabbed him by the throat and spun him around. He brought up his right hand clenched around the handle of his knife. With a single action he slit his throat. The man thudded to the ground, blood spurting from below his Adam's apple. The blood-stained knife dropped to the floor. Jonathan hastily bent down to retrieve it. Glancing up, he saw the other guard making for the door.

There will be no escape for him. The bastard.

In a last attempt to muster all his strength, Jonathan lurched towards him. The guard hadn't reckoned on him being able to move so swiftly. Jonathan grabbed his clothing, locked his arm around his neck and brought him to the floor. The second guard suffered the same fate. Jonathan stood laughing over the last body, his mirth quickly turning into insane hysterics. *Two dead – this was swift, sweet, satisfying revenge. There would be no escape for the others in hiding.*

He moved on to the next hut. Scouring the confines he discovered it was empty. The third and final hut harboured only one guard still in his original uniform, crouched behind a disused cart. The guard hadn't noticed him. Jonathan eyed him up, crept along close to the wall. Coming within a few feet of him the guard suddenly spun around, fumbling for his gun. Jonathan threw himself at the guard, thrusting his knife into his chest. The guard doubled over and sank to his knees, clutching his chest and screaming in agony. *A painful death – this was his just deserts.* Jonathan stood over him, his legs weak and shaking. Revenge had drained him of any last remnant of energy. He bent down, lifted the guard's chin and slashed a single line across his throat. The life drained from his body. Jonathan came out of the hut, his eyes barely tolerating the sunlight. He scanned the utter horror and degradation ahead of him. Trucks marked with a red cross were now lining the central road of the camp.

Where were the other bastards hiding? They were his for the taking. He slunk off towards his hut, watching, waiting for his next catch.

Later that afternoon, in the weak sunshine, Jonathan shuffled past the lines of Allied soldiers ministering to the needs of the half-dead survivors of the camp. It took him several minutes to limp across the compound to one of the watch towers on the far side of the camp. The watch towers were no longer manned by anyone. Only the main gates of the camp had a soldier check-point. The other soldiers were too busy with the survivors to take any notice of him. He skirted around the perimeter fence to the base of a watch tower and sat down at the foot of the ladder. He began to pick the blades of green grass, the only sign of nature growing in the camp. He ate them one by one, chewed them as a cow would the cud. His begrimed fingernails held each blade before carefully putting it in his mouth. Rocking to and fro comforted him.

He had seen too much. The desire for total revenge ate at him. He rubbed his hands over and over, faster and faster, until the red sores on his raw skin bled. He hated life. Craved death.

He pulled out his blood-stained knife. Turning the blade over and over in the daylight he laughed manically as he had earlier in the day. Bringing the edge to his throat he diced with death. He lowered the blade, balancing it on his knee. His mind swirled with ugly thoughts; his head pounded. He glanced up. In the distance he saw the last pits that he had been forced to dig, filled with the stiff white remnants of horror. Standing on the edge of the mass grave a Jewish chaplain looked as if he was saying prayers over them.

That was the trigger. Jonathan could take no more horror. He couldn't rid his mind of the images. Slowly, he brought the blade nearer his throat. In a single swift action he sliced across. His life flashed before him. A different world. A career as a doctor – saving life, not taking it. Then the image of Katharine's sweet face, her youthful innocence betrayed by his misguided understanding of duty. Finally images of Dachau and Belsen merged with each other.

His head spun as it slumped to his chest. His limbs lifeless; death finally brought him peace.

A week later Geoffrey walked up the steps of the War Office in London. Rumours had it that he was to be posted back to Austria on war crimes investigations. In the previous twelve months since he had attended Katharine's funeral he had been assigned to the War Office in London translating documents seized by the Allies as they had advanced through Nazi-occupied countries. In quiet moments he often thought back to his time in Denmark. Now it seemed an eon away. Britain breathed a sigh of relief that the war was nearly over. Geoffrey made his way up to Room 307 on the first floor. Captain Henderson was already waiting for him. The clock struck ten o'clock as he entered. A huge oil painting of the Duke of Wellington on horseback hung over the fireplace.

Captain Henderson stood by the open window smoking a cigarette. 'Good afternoon Geoffrey.'

'Good day sir.'

'I trust you are keeping well.' He closed the sash window.

'Yes sir. I am.' After a momentary pause he ventured, 'I know it is nearly the anniversary of Katharine's death. I hope you are coping, sir.'

Captain Henderson's face clouded momentarily. 'Yes. I am as well as can be expected. Thank you for asking.' He shuffled some papers on his desk in distraction, then suddenly added: 'But I have not had the courage to visit her grave. Not *once* in that time. It's too much. It's why I came to live in London. In London I wouldn't have the time to go down there and see her grave.' Geoffrey stood silently, observing him.

'Do you understand Geoffrey? Is it so very wrong of me?'

'Who am I to say, sir.'

Captain Henderson muttered, 'So be it.' He seemed distant, then came out of his thoughts. 'Now to business. We aren't here to talk about her or pleasantries. Please take a seat.' Geoffrey obeyed.

Captain Henderson cleared his throat. 'At the end of the week you are to be posted to the Interpreters Pool, Brussels for a week. Not that anyone can teach you refugees anything about German. It's a formality, you understand.'

'Yes sir.'

'Then to Fallingbostel with 3 Counter-Intelligence Corps. Your duties under Captain Reid will be various. The camp was liberated by the 7th Armoured Brigade earlier this month. They freed several thousand British and American POWs. Fallingbostel is shortly to become a camp for German POWs and Nazi war criminals. Your fluency in German is vital for the work there. Hamburg is about to surrender any day now. The war is effectively over. The German army is surrendering in large numbers. Then the hunt begins to bring the perpetrators to justice. It's going to be a long, slow process but a necessary one.'

'I am not being sent to Austria then, sir? I was hoping I could look for my mother and father.'

'No, I'm afraid not. But I do have word that your mother is fine. She survived most of the war with relatives in the mountains after your father was … taken.' He paused to allow the information to sink in. 'I am sorry to say, it's bad news. Your father … he didn't survive, Geoffrey. He died in Belsen.'

Geoffrey stared numbly ahead, then blurted out: 'When?'

'Towards the end of last year. But I am sorry to say he was not the only one of your relatives to die in the camp.' Geoffrey raised his eyebrows.

'Jonathan too, your uncle by marriage. After all he went through, we weren't able to break him out as we did when he was in Dachau. He managed to survive until the liberation of the camp, but later that same day we think he committed suicide.'

It was too much to take in. Geoffrey paled, his stomach nauseous, head spinning. Captain Henderson wondered whether he should break the final piece of news. Before doing so he went over to the corner cabinet and poured them both a brandy. He put one tumbler of alcohol and one of water on the desk in front of Geoffrey. Geoffrey's hands shook as he took the water first. Captain Henderson took a sip from his own glass of brandy, then revealed the last news: 'Your mate Ian did not survive the war. I am afraid I cannot disclose exact details for security reasons, but he died somewhere in Yugoslavia. It is thought he was betrayed by partisans.'

Geoffrey stared blankly at the window behind Henderson; the morning mist still hadn't cleared, shrouding everything in an eerie cloak. Captain Henderson reached into the top drawer of his desk and pulled out the new passes for Geoffrey's work with 3 Counter-Intelligence Corps. In the silence between them he slipped them across the desk. Geoffrey took them and made as if to leave.

'Wait! Please. There is one more thing that has been on my mind,' said Captain Henderson. 'I should have done something about it months ago, but it was not possible.' Geoffrey sat down again.

'I hope you will not mind me broaching a sensitive subject. It is about the Danish woman, Lilian.' Geoffrey had never heard him mention her before.

'Look, I know about you and her.' He smiled. 'There isn't much that escapes me. I would not want you to live with regrets. I nearly lost the woman I loved on more than one occasion because I was not brave enough to tell her. At one point I thought it was too late. I had a second chance. You and Lilian ...'

'There is no me and Lilian, sir.'

'Be that as it may, I happen to know that she is deeply unhappy. But she's proud. Too proud to admit it. Danish women are all the same, incredibly beautiful, yes, and forthright but often too proud to disclose their feelings, especially after a painful episode.' He cleared his throat again. The story unfolded:

'She's not who you think she is. One day in the early 1920s a child was born to a royal couple. Out of wedlock. The King's surgeon, as the closest advisor, was asked to place this baby daughter with a suitable family where she would be raised in comfort and security. She was placed with a highly respectable Jewish family of good breeding whose roots went far back in Danish history. It was deemed an ideal situation. The girl would never know. And she didn't until recently. She thought she was Jewish. But then no one knew the madness of Hitler would take over and threaten her life. It was too late to say she wasn't Jewish. No one would believe it and the royal couple would be disgraced. It would cause an utter scandal. The lie had to continue. Being politically conscious and spirited, she decided to join the young resistance movement after Hitler occupied her country in 1940. She became highly trained. Two years later, when the Jews had to flee Denmark, she was naturally amongst them. She went into hiding and eventually made it to England. What could we give her to do? She was ideal agent material. And that's what happened. In due course she worked for us on the German/Danish border.'

'And then she was captured.'

'Yes, she was eventually taken to Vallø Castle to recover from her terrible ordeal. Which is where you finally met her again. After you left Denmark she travelled to Sweden where she headed the Danish Free Army. She remained in Sweden for ten months, then earlier this month the Danish Free Army headed back to Denmark to fill the void where the Germans had been defeated. Their work done, the regular Danish army has taken over and the freedom fighters have been disbanded. I offered her a post back here in England with the opportunity to start a new life. She is back at Anderson Manor finishing off some work for me. You might like to take a trip there before you head to Fallingbostel.'

Geoffrey suddenly felt embarrassed. He wasn't used to admitting his feelings with anyone, least of all the usually reserved Captain. Captain Henderson sensed his discomfort. 'Look, it is only a suggestion, but I know she is miserable. She loves you. Go to her. You have nothing to lose except your pride … and the woman you love. Don't make the same mistake that I did. I waited a lifetime. I was lucky – through circumstances I finally married Katharine. And now where am I? At the top of my career, but she is gone. I would do anything to have her back.'

Geoffrey's mind buzzed in turmoil. He felt giddy from hyperventilating with the suspense of listening to what Henderson had to say.

'Here, Geoffrey. I have taken the liberty of getting a train ticket for you.' The slim billet looked identical to the one given to him when he had first taken the train to Hampshire for SOE training. His eyes lit up: 'Thank you sir. I am very grateful to you.'

Captain Henderson smiled, then tutted, 'The youth of today. Now off you go before you miss that train.'

Geoffrey stood up, shook his hand and walked, almost skipped, out. A mixture of emotions flooded his body. Sadness at the loss of his father, Jonathan and his dear friend Ian. He would miss them all, especially his father, who had always been the perfect role-model. This was combined with a sense of elation that he might have a second chance with Lilian. Out of sight of Captain Henderson, he ran along the corridor, down the flight of stairs two steps at a time and headed out into the drizzle of London. Getting wet didn't bother him. Nothing further could dampen his spirits. He was off to see *her*.

The late April drizzle failed to dampen Geoffrey's spirits as he walked down the familiar drive of Anderson Manor. It felt good to be back. Lilian didn't know he was coming. During the journey he had spent the whole time rehearsing his lines. Now, as he reflected how much he had to be thankful for, he gave a fleeting thought for his mate Ignaz, or Ian as he became. Ian wouldn't see old age and didn't live to see the victory that everyone knew was coming. Ian had given the ultimate sacrifice for his adopted country. It touched Geoffrey with sadness. He missed his mate's realism and confidence. Carrying on down the drive, he thought back to the first day they arrived and had queued in front of Colonel Bennett to change their names. Hands in his pocket, Geoffrey whistled to himself. On his left the rhododendrons were just bursting into bloom, an array of different coloured bushes: deep red, pink, yellow, orange and white. This was what he loved about England's quintessential landscape. Geoffrey turned the handle on the large, oak front door. Inside the hallway was brightly lit. Memories came flooding back. In his mind he heard Colonel Bennett's sharp orders to his men. Bennett had been a fair man, much liked by the men.

'Good day, can I help you?' The female voice came from the desk. Geoffrey averted his eyes: 'Oh, good gracious, Betty. How are you?' It was Lilian's best friend and room mate from her days at Anderson Manor.

'I'm very well, thank you,' she fluttered her eyelashes. Nothing had changed about Betty, such a charming, sweet girl. All the continental soldiers at the training school had fallen for her. She'd had no shortage of dates. 'I'm married now,' she said, holding up her finger.

'I'm very pleased for you. Who's the lucky man?'

'Sebastian Waters. He was in the group that came after your lot.'

'Congratulations, Betty.'

'Thank you.' She blushed. 'And what can I do for you?'

'I've come to see Lilian.'

'Well you're in luck. She's about to come off shift for today.'

Geoffrey could barely contain his excitement, trying to stand still and keep his voice level. He felt like an impetuous child again. 'Good timing then. Where might I find her?'

'I suggest you wait in the billiard room. You remember – down there on the left.'

His parched mouth barely managed the response. 'Yes.'

'I'll make sure she knows you're there.'

'Thank you Betty.'

Geoffrey walked with a spring in his step towards the billiard room. This was the moment he had dreamt of for so long. Maybe he still had a chance with her.

He opened the door. The smell of stale cigars pervaded the empty room. A couple of glasses with traces of red wine had been left on the edge of the billiard table. The clock on the mantelpiece had stopped. Geoffrey walked over to the French windows which faced the east side of the estate. In the silence he heard the distinct sound of the cuckoo. The first sign that May was coming. The misty rain clouds had lifted by now; everything glistened with fresh raindrops. The door handle turned behind him. He swung round. Lilian stood in the doorway. They stared at each other in complete silence. She tossed her auburn curls, broke into a smile and walked towards him. Geoffrey's knees felt like jelly, his body more tense than when he'd jumped out of the Halifax bomber. He loved her to distraction. No one else could fulfill his dreams.

'Lilian.' The word choked out.

'Geoffrey.' She smiled again.

'I have missed you,' he said.

'And I you.' In spite of her ordeal in Germany, part of the innocence he had loved so much had returned in her dark brown eyes. 'Things have changed for me,' she said. Geoffrey dreaded her next words, wondering what she would say. 'I have decided to make England my home permanently, but I am not the woman you thought I was.'

'It's okay, Lilian. I know about that.' He placed his hand on her arm, desperate to scoop her up and feel her body pressed against his. He didn't dare.

'Do you?' she seemed relieved.

'Yes. A government official by the name of Captain Henderson thought it appropriate to tell me about your past.'

'I have decided not to go back to Denmark. I have an income from the royal purse, so that helps, but I have relinquished any rights to a royal life.'

'Your background need not be a barrier for us. I love you, Lilian. Always have. That rainy day in the woods when we became really close, when our bodies touched, I thought I'd orbited the universe and back. Later, when I was parachuted into Denmark, I thought of nothing but you. Falling through the sky I saw only your face, not the danger ahead. I hoped upon hope that I would survive to see you again. And I did survive, but you were in no fit state to receive me properly at Vallø. I thought then it was all over for us. I have tried to forget you, to convince myself that you are better off without me, but it hasn't worked. Something deep inside me ...'

She placed her delicate hand over his hand, still resting on her arm. 'I have done a lot of thinking in the last year Geoffrey.' Could he dare to hope that she felt the same way about him?

'Shall we take a walk?' he suggested.

'That's an excellent idea.' She slipped her arm through his. Together they headed into the gardens. The warmth of her body next to his as they tramped through the moist grass sent his feelings soaring.

'Oh, the sun is trying to come out. And I know a wonderful place for a picnic.'

She laughed. 'But you haven't got a picnic with you!'

'How very observant of you,' he teased. 'I'm sure we don't need it.'

A few minutes later they were walking through the familiar woods, hand in hand. Being with her felt so natural.

'There's a secluded hut,' he said, glancing at her. Her eyes now sparkled with life. The sun struggled to penetrate the canopy of leaves covering the treetops. In that moment they cared for nothing except being in each other's company.

Geoffrey pushed open the dilapidated wooden door of the hut, allowing Lilian to pass through first as any gentleman would. Inside, nothing had been disturbed or changed since their last visit two years earlier, except a few more cobwebs around the dirt-covered windows. The same rusty saucepan stood on the stove. The sofa and two chairs were in the same spot as if no one had been in the place since. Geoffrey closed the rickety door behind them as best he could, the rusty hinges making it more difficult. He strode over to Lilian.

It was now or never.

He swept her into his arms, tilted her chin and brought his lips onto hers. It was as if the separation between them had never happened. Her lips felt sweet. She responded to his firmness with passion, kissing him wildly. A thrill surged through her body.

'I love you,' she murmured. In no time they were making love again.

The hours passed. Evening came. They lay in each other's arms until dark. 'Do you know what day it is?' she asked him.

'Am I supposed to?' He smiled down at her and pecked the top of her head still resting against his chest.

'Denmark was liberated today. Come! I want to show you something.' They got dressed. Lilian couldn't suppress her laughter.

'What's the matter?' He looked at her enquiringly.

'You've got dust and cobwebs all over the back of your uniform.' She giggled and began brushing him down. 'You can't let your commanding officer see you like that. Where have you been, Lieutenant Hart!' Then she took his hand and dragged him outside. She found a clearing between the trees. Holding his hand tightly, she urged him to look up. The moon cast its celestial light down on the earth below. 'Isn't this just magical?' she said. 'There's a tradition handed down in my family that says it's a good omen for the moon to shine when a man proposes to the woman he loves.'

Geoffrey took that as his cue. He turned to face her and looked into her eyes. 'I still have to find a living when I'm demobbed from the army next year. And shortly I'm off to Germany for post-war work. We have a lifetime ahead of us, but what the heck. I love you and want you.' He squeezed her hand gently. 'Will you be my wife? We can marry on my next period of leave. What do you say?'

Lilian flung herself into his arms, her face turned urgently up to his. 'Yes … yes I will.' Then she drew back slightly, still clasping his hand, her eyes focused on him. 'I hope the moon is shining over Denmark tonight.'

Epilogue

26 June 1945

A year to the day since he had buried his wife, Captain Henderson finally summoned the courage to pay his respects at Katharine's graveside. The year had been a difficult one. Her death had crushed him – he who could do anything for his country; take anything except the loss of the one he loved to the core of his being. He returned to North Devon to face his grief, give her due respect and then move on. He had planned it all as a military tactician might. He glanced at the neat lines of graves to his left, then right. The headstones stood proud testament to lives lost; the deeply incised lettering of adoration memorialising the life of that person. He left the path to cross to the section where she was buried. His shoes squelched on the springy wet turf; this day was the only respite from two weeks of rain. He clutched the single white rose as if it was the last remnant of the most precious thing in the world. It was her favourite flower. 'Never red,' she had told him. 'White – for the purity of our love.'

'Katharine,' he whispered under his breath, glancing momentarily back at the cemetery gates. In his mind's eye he saw the watermarked ghostlike shadow of the cortège sweeping into the grounds. He blinked to erase the image and the pain. He had not been at home at the time of her death. The guilt ate at his sanity but he suppressed it as he did all feelings. Back regimentally upright, shoulders square, chest out and stomach in, he marched morbidly towards her resting place.

Section D, number 36.

He knew the co-ordinates by heart. He stopped at Section D. His eyes scanned the words incised in the first two headstones. He counted along the row, '33, 34, 35 ...' There was a gap at 36. He retraced his steps from the beginning of the row. No headstone at plot 36. But he had paid the bill for its erection at the local stonemason's just days after the funeral.

'Good morning sir.'

Captain Henderson turned; somewhat surprised there was someone around. The gravedigger tilted his cap in respect. 'Good morning,' Henderson replied distantly.

'You be looking a bit puzzled sir, if I might say so.' The gravedigger lent on his spade, one hand thrust deep in his jacket pocket.

Captain Henderson still couldn't get used to the Devonshire dialect. It grated on his nerves. 'Yes, I am,' he replied, looking him straight in the face. 'Last year I buried my wife, Katharine Simmons-Henderson. It was here, at this spot but I can not find her grave. It is the first time I have been able to get back to pay my respects. I have been stuck in London the past year.' He glanced down at the white rose still clutched in his right hand.

'I understand sir. Grief can do all kinds of things to folks. Let me help you. I can look her up in the burial register in yonder chapel.'

Captain Henderson shot him a glance. 'I remember precisely the spot. It is here – Section D, no 36. How could I forget?'

'I understand sir,' he repeated in reassurance. His spade sunk further into the ground as he lent harder on it. Captain Henderson took a few paces forwards. 'Look here,' he pointed. 'I buried her here. I am not a man to make misjudgments.'

'Yes, sir. I'm sure ye did. It maybe t'other stonemason overlooked his job. It can happen.' The gravedigger's face, rugged from years of work outdoors, betrayed a simple compassion. 'If you come over to the office at the back of the chapel, I be looking in the burial book for you. Cemeteries can look different when you return.' He glanced at the stiffness of Captain Henderson's face. He had said enough.

Silently, Captain Henderson followed him along the winding path to the chapel at the entrance to the grounds. Inside, the stone building smelt damp and fusty. A dilapidated desk squatted under a plain arched window which was covered in a layer of dust allowing only a little sunlight in. Dangling on a grimy cord, a single light bulb hung from the ceiling. The gravedigger pulled a large, leather-bound ledger from the drawer. 'What date?' he asked, already beginning to thumb the pages.

Captain Henderson cleared his throat and leant over the gravedigger's shoulder: 'Twenty-sixth June last year.'

'Ah, that might explain why I don't remember. That was on my annual holidays, sir. Always takes it same time every year.' He turned to the correct page in the burial book, his thin finger moving down the list of names. Henderson couldn't help but notice the traces of soil caked under his broken fingernails. The gravedigger looked up. 'There were two burials that day but there be none by the name of Katharine Simmons. Er, not her 'cause both burials were males in their late 60s. How odd.' His eyes instinctively

235

scanned the entries for the whole page, then the two pages either side.

Captain Henderson tried to remain level, his voice straining under the tension, 'That can't be. I was here exactly a year ago. I buried her. There is a gap in the row. She *was* there.'

The gravedigger coughed before answering, 'Yes sir, I quite understand your distress. It is a mystery. Here, look for yourself.'

Captain Henderson leaned directly over the ledger. He carefully turned the thick, cream-coloured pages, his eyes frantically scanning the black ink of any names for 26 June 1944. Suppressing an inner panic, he checked a full week either side. The scrawling, black, tight writing jarred, stabbing at his grief.

Her name was not there.

The gravedigger moved closer to him and touched his arm leaving a dusty mark on Captain Henderson's dark blue jacket. 'I don't know what to say, sir. But she ain't yer.'

Captain Henderson closed the ledger. 'Thank you for looking. If you do not mind, I would be grateful of some time to myself out there.'

'Certainly sir. I wouldn't dream of intruding.'

Captain Henderson walked through the arched doorway of the chapel back into the sunshine. He walked over to the boundary wall, stared out to sea just as he had the day of her funeral. The calm sea and still quiet in the air contrasted with his utter turmoil. He decided to go over to the spot of her grave one more time. He stared at the empty space between 35 and 37. His thoughts raced with a thousand theories, emotions swirling like a tornado, spinning him into an unknown abyss of lost love. He straightened his back, needing to re-focus. Doubts crept to the fore. Had he really known her? Even after their marriage she had retained a mysterious side. He hadn't wanted to pry, hadn't wanted to ask her. She had been a closed book.

Then it came to him in an instant. It was obvious – he of all people should have realised. Why hadn't he thought of it earlier? *What had she done such that they had faked her death, even from him?*

There was hope. At that moment, in the depths of his soul, he felt her consciousness as alive as the day he had last hugged her.

'I will find her … I will find her.' His whispered oath floated on the breeze to an unknown destination. He would hunt the ends of the earth for her and bring her home.

Printed in Great Britain
by Amazon